Sister *of* Mine

MARIE-CLAIRE AMUAH

MAGPIE
BOOKS

A Magpie Book

First published in the United Kingdom, Republic of Ireland and Australia
by Magpie, an imprint of Oneworld Publications Ltd, 2026

Copyright © Marie-Claire Amuah, 2026

The moral right of Marie-Claire Amuah to be identified
as the Author of this work has been asserted by her in accordance
with the Copyright, Designs and Patents Act 1988

All rights reserved
Copyright under Berne Convention
A CIP record for this title is available from the British Library

ISBN 978-1-83643-003-2
eISBN 978-1-83643-004-9

Printed and bound in Great Britain by Clays Ltd, Elcograf S.p.A

This book is a work of fiction. Names, characters, businesses,
organisations, places and events are either the product of the author's
imagination or are used fictitiously. Any resemblance to actual persons,
living or dead, events or locales is entirely coincidental.

No part of this publication may be reproduced, stored in a retrieval system,
or transmitted, in any form or by any means, electronic, mechanical, photocopying,
recording or otherwise, or used in any manner for the purpose of training artificial
intelligence technologies or systems, without the prior permission
of the publishers.

The authorised representative in the EEA is eucomply OÜ,
Pärnu mnt 139b–14, 11317 Tallinn, Estonia
(email: hello@eucompliancepartner.com / phone: +33757690241)

Oneworld Publications Ltd
10 Bloomsbury Street
London WC1B 3SR
England

Stay up to date with the latest books,
special offers, and exclusive content from
Oneworld with our newsletter

Sign up on our website
oneworld.co.uk

Praise for
One for Sorrow, Two for Joy

Winner of the Diverse Book Award 2023

'A triumphant ode to resilience, friendship and love. Marie-Claire's writing sparkles, reminiscent of Adichie's *Purple Hibiscus*.'
Bisi Adjapon, author of *The Teller of Secrets*

'A vivid, deeply felt exploration of intergenerational trauma… Stella is an utterly unique heroine who you'll find yourself rooting for from page one.'
Angela Chadwick, author of *XX*

'A bittersweet rites-of-passage novel… [Amuah's] interrogation of trauma is powerful… A heartfelt debut.'
Observer

'Extraordinary… Amuah's haunting story of the tragedy of violence is authentic, poignant and alive. This is an accomplished debut and I look forward to reading more from Marie-Claire.'
Cherie Jones, author of
How the One-Armed Sister Sweeps Her House

'An evocative and gorgeously narrated story that broke my heart and stitched it back together again even stronger by the end. I laughed and cried and hurt and healed in the course of reading Stella's deeply-felt story. I loved this book so much. Intense and beautiful and heartbreaking!'
Buki Papillon, author of *An Ordinary Wonder*

'Brilliant. I loved it! *One for Sorrow, Two for Joy* is a rollercoaster of emotions throughout… I got lost in it and couldn't put it down. Here's to resilience and friendship!'

Jamz Supernova, BBC Radio 6 DJ

'A dazzling debut… Brimming with compassion.'

***Damian Barr's Literary Salon* podcast, 'Book of the Week'**

'A beautiful, brave and deeply moving debut that explores the complexities of intergenerational trauma, belonging and love through a tender yet powerful voice… Stella, as well as her friends and family, will stay with me for a long time.'

Sussie Anie, author of *To Fill a Yellow House*

'This is a beautifully written account of domestic violence and intergenerational trauma, and the resilience and hope that can break its power.'

***Debut Digest*, Editor's Pick**

'There are so many words to describe this beautiful book, and on reflection, one of them is 'generous'. It's such a generous, sometimes painful portrayal of a beautiful soul. I really enjoyed it and Stella is definitely still with me.'

Jeffrey Boakye, author of *I Heard What You Said*

'Stella is caught between an abusive home life and a cold-hearted world. The story chronicles her struggle, growth, and fight for survival.'

***Brittle Paper*, '100 Notable African Books of 2022'**

PROLOGUE

THE MOSQUITO

Mosquitoes are easily maligned as nefarious parasites whose sole purpose is to spread disease and death. This view places us at the centre of their worlds, objects around which they orbit before a targeted and deadly strike. In a world that roots women at the heart of man's wrongdoing, it should come as no surprise to learn that it is the female mosquito who uses her proboscis to pierce the skin and draw blood. It is she who causes the stinging sensation, the raised bump and unbearable itch that establishes itself after her visit: the parasitic postcard to say that she has been. It is she who is cunning and stealth. It is she against whom we must beware.

In a world which forces women to bear responsibility for the male gaze, his action or inaction, his control or lack thereof, it should come as no surprise to learn that it is the female mosquito who must feast on blood in order to produce eggs while her male counterpart feeds on the sweet nectar of flowers. It is she who is the transmitter of diseases such as malaria, whose symptoms include fever, muscle pains, headache and fatigue. Malaria which, if not treated quickly, can cause death. It was Eve who ate the apple, after all.

To understand that malaria is a medical emergency can, at the very least, complicate a trip for a foreigner to a foreign land. It requires the visitor to think and plan ahead. To take antimalarials a few days or weeks in advance to develop the body's immunity to the foreign thing. To invest in mosquito repellents which contain high percentages of Deet, a chemical which can strip the polish from a perfectly manicured hand. To sleep under a mosquito net but only find sleep if that mosquito net has been treated with insecticide. And yet, despite these efforts, the foreigner is already at a disadvantage. They are more likely to be targeted as they emit heat and sweat, to which the mosquito is drawn, in this new climate to which they must adjust.

To know that malaria is a life-threatening disease which, if not diagnosed and treated quickly, can cause death, does a number of things to a cautious traveller. If underinformed or underprepared, it can promote alarm and fear of such dimensions that the mind fixates, obsesses even, for the thing to bite. If they listen, they can hear it approach. The high-pitched buzz that hovers over a body on the brink of sleep. The examination of skin for a sweet spot, exposed at the wrong place and at the wrong time, offering sustenance. Conversely, to be complacent or dismissive can cause effects so grave that the moment the skin is pierced and blood drawn can be the single worst thing to happen in a person's lifetime.

Let it be known that malaria is not a case of a thousand bites. Just one is needed. A single bite by an infected female can transmit the parasite. Ten to fifteen days later, the symptoms will appear.

GHANA

KOTOKA INTERNATIONAL AIRPORT

I see Dad's spirit at an altitude of ten thousand feet as we begin our descent to Ghana's Kotoka Airport. When the pilot switches on the fasten seat belt sign and standing passengers are asked to return to their seats. His silhouette in the sky. I trace his Adam's apple against the cloud formations. The breadth of his nose and square of his jaw. I do not need to look at the photograph to call his features to mind; I have spent my lifetime studying them. I hear his voice when the cabin lights dim and the pilot instructs the crew to take their seats. His honeyed tones, hoarse from tobacco, calling my name as the lights below come into sharp focus.

'Sika! Sika!'

Smile lines etched deep in his skin are exacerbated in effect by his dimples.

'Sika, you came!'

His eyes are narrowed by the appearance of crow's feet because his heart is full of joy. 'I'm so glad you came!'

Dad dries a tear from my eye when the wheels of the plane touch down on the hot tarmac in Accra and passengers on board the Boeing 737 begin to clap. Not only have we arrived but we have arrived safely. The occasion merits thanks to God. A wave of excitement spreads through the cabin as the plane slows to its final stop. It encourages people to ignore the instruction of the flight attendant to remain seated until the seat belt sign is switched off. Mobile data is switched on, lipstick reapplied and young children woken from sleep. The pilot thanks us for choosing to fly with British Airways as layers of clothing are shed, immigration cards collected and hand luggage brought down from overhead compartments. He welcomes returning passengers home and wishes those visiting a pleasant stay.

On the tarmac, the ground staff wear high-vis vests over short-sleeved shirts. One of their number has found entertainment dancing with his wand lights in a way that threatens to cause problems for air traffic control. The performance brings a smile to my face as I shake off the dregs of sleep. The ground temperature is twenty-eight degrees Celsius.

'Are they going to fly through the door?' Mum shifts her gaze from the passengers, impatient to disembark, to the window which frames a snapshot of the city. 'I am not going to race them.'

She waits until the remaining passengers on the plane consist of the elderly and mobility impaired before rising from her seat to join the short line of people spilling into business class to leave the aircraft. I walk in Mum's shadow but not in her footsteps, because I cannot imagine what it is to be in emotional exile for twenty-seven years, or how it must feel to return home. She walks slowly down the aircraft steps, gripping the handrail for support and concealing tears behind thick-rimmed glasses. Dad walks beside her, his hand supporting the small of her back as she navigates the way.

'My God!'

Like a newborn baby laying eyes on the world outside its mother's womb, she examines her surroundings in shock.

'This place has changed!'

'Akwaaba, you are welcome.'

A committee of airport staff greet us as we head inside the airport.

'Akwaaba, you are welcome.'

The words are offered through beaming smiles and spoken on a loop.

Ahead of us, two male officers are locked in a lingering handshake which ends with a click of their fingers. To our left, their colleague enjoys the benefit of the airport's uninterrupted Wi-Fi connection as he scrolls through his phone. He is undistracted by our arrival. We walk past adverts showcasing the premium banking services of Ghana International Bank. The mobile network provision of MTN Ghana. The refreshing taste of Star beer in the mouths of the airbrushed and beautiful. And the luxury apartments offering an unparalleled Western living experience in the heart of Accra. Under a ceiling of bright lights and the uniformed guard of airport officials, we walk in the direction of Arrivals.

Mum says that when she left in the eighties, Ghana Airways had not yet gone into administration and Kotoka Airport did not merit the prefix 'international'. The industrial fans that once cooled the inside of the airport have been replaced by an air conditioning system backed by a powerful generator should electricity fail. It suggests a coolness to the evening which is deceptive. To step outside the airport, and beyond the boundaries of its carefully controlled Wi-Fi network, is to be greeted by a distinct wave of warm air. We are met by a sea of faces bathed in the evening light and glowing from the day's rays. People waiting for relatives, friends and guests. That much has not changed. Signs bearing the names of the city's finest hotels dance like puppets for the attention of the newly arrived. To hesitate, retrace your steps or scan the waiting crowd too long is to invite offerings of assistance and solutions for travel from those exchanging services for a fee.

'Madam, let me help you with your bags!'

'Please, we are fine.'

Mum rebuffs the offer from a man whose small stature showcases impressive muscle tone and definition. He positions his hands to steer our luggage in a direction of his choosing. Sold by the power of his confidence, I relinquish it to his control.

'Is it by force?!'

Before he has left our sight, another determined man appears to try and take the reins from Mum's grip. This causes her to speak in a more forceful tone; it lands with no impact. The man shouts something to someone standing somewhere in the crowd to our left and walks towards them without a glance back in our direction. To our right, the man who asked the air hostess to take landscape and portrait photographs of him in business class reclining at a forty-five-degree angle, champagne in hand, is talking loudly on his mobile. The woman whose suitcase ripped at the zip and sent frozen fish circling round the conveyor belt at baggage reclaim is questioning the driver who has pulled up to the kerb: 'Is this Uber Lux? I ordered Uber Lux!'

The driver of the Nissan saloon confirms his identity as the Uber Lux driver. He is not supposed to park where he has. He will be fined. There are quick movements, followed by a hasty departure. I turn around to see a young couple locked in the embrace of lovers reunited. The small man reappears pushing another trolley. He balances, with skill, large shapes wrapped in white plastic and secured with brown industrial tape. The packages almost exceed his height. His clothes are wet from the humidity of the night and the sweat of the industrious.

'Taxi? Taxi?'
'Taxi? Where are you going, please?'
'Taxi?'

'This is Ghana, Sika! Welcome!'

Dad is laughing now. A hearty laugh. His face, illuminated by the happiness that has taken hold of him. It is a contagious happiness that has infected me too. I smell cedarwood, cardamom and cocoa; I smell my dad. He holds my face in the palms of his hands, the tributaries that map them pressed softly against my cheeks. They speak of the roads he travelled when he lived and walked and breathed. Those are the journeys I want to trace.

I have imagined this moment a thousand times over, but never in scenes so vibrant or colours as bright.

SISTERS

A little girl emerges from the crowd, zigzagging between the legs of waiting adults with hands on hips and phones to ears. She wears colourful beads at the ends of her braids which bounce against her skin as she moves. Like a bright feather, she floats through the crowd, offering glimpses of her small frame. Her words are drowned by the hum of the conversations she darts between and across, around and through. As she approaches, anticipation charges the space between us. And when I see the small gap in her milk teeth that mirrors Mum's, I know she is my cousin. It is into outstretched arms that Lololi folds when we meet for the first time. Her arms wrap themselves around my neck like a scarf, and her sweetness envelops me.

'Lololi!' Mum coos.

Lololi detaches her left arm from my neck and wraps it around Mum's, placing us in a headlock secured by the strength of a five-year-old. She smells of talcum powder and cocoa butter.

'Atuuuuuuu!' Auntie Edem gives voice to her embrace. 'You are welcome! Atu! Atu! Atu!' She alternates between embracing Mum in Loli's headlock and hugging the back of Lololi hugging me. 'Selom! My sister! Sika! Is it really you?' She examines us from head to toe, blinking between takes to satisfy herself that she has not dreamed us into being. 'My sister!'

'Edem, wow!'

'How long has it been?'

Mum's eyes widen in disbelief as she digests the scene in front of her. Her older sister and the niece she has never met.

'It's been a long time, Edem. Twenty-seven years.'

'A whole twenty-seven years?! It even feels longer than that! Welcome home, my sister! Welcome home!'

Released from Lololi's headlock, I work to put Mum into the context of being Auntie Edem's younger sister. Shoulder to shoulder, I can see they share the same almond-shaped eyes, high cheekbones and unmistakable smile. Auntie Edem looks the older of the two by more than the four years that separate them.

'"My auntie and cousin are coming from London!" That is all I have heard for the past how many weeks! Loli, are you happy now?' Auntie Edem asks.

Loli is quiet with delight.

'Heh, I like your T-shirt,' Mum says. 'Can I wear it? Will you share it with your auntie?'

'It won't f-f-fit you!' Loli replies, the smile on her face morphing every word into a sweet lullaby.

'Oh, are you sure?'

'No! You are too big! It's not f-f-for adults, just f-f-for children.'

Loli swings her body from left to right to mirror the movement of her head. In her giggle, the extent of her genetic union with Mum is revealed: the gap between their teeth that neither me nor Auntie Edem share. Grandma had it too.

'Okay, I've heard.'

'Loli, tell your cousin how you fasted and prayed for her and auntie Selom to come home after all these years. To see her face again. And meet your niece. That you wondered if the day would ever come—'

A wave of emotion catches Auntie Edem and sweeps us up in its tide. We hold each other close in a brief moment of stillness before she pulls back to examine us once more.

'Heh Selom! You've put on weight!'

'Are you sure? It is you who has rather lost weight!'

Mum's accent changed as soon as we stepped into the queue for Ghanaian and ECOWAS passport holders as if shedding a layer of London from her person. Auntie Edem is the leaner of the two. Her skin the dark coffee brown I imagine Mum's would be if she lived under the constant glare of the sub-Saharan sun.

'So Larjey and Papa had to celebrate twenty-five years of marriage before you could come to Ghana to see us?'

'Haven't I invited you to London?'

'You want me to come to that cold country of yours?' Auntie Edem raises her eyebrows in a questioning manner which suggests that many things would have to happen in order for her to brave the British weather, and that those things are both unlikely and unimaginable.

'Your phone is f-f-flashing.' Loli points her finger at the flashing screen just visible inside my bag. Its vibration is absorbed by the activity around me and I cannot feel it ringing. I make a mental note to move my passport to the zipped compartment and fumble past lip balm and hand sanitiser to reach the phone. The call ends before I can swipe right to answer. I note six missed calls before it rings again. *Caitlyn, CEO, Melon Marketing,* illuminates the screen.

'Caitlyn? Hello?' I plug my left ear with my finger and press the phone tight against my right, straining to hear what is being said. 'Hello? Caitlyn? Hello? Can you hear me? Sorry? The what? Hello? Sorry, I can't hear you very— I just landed— Hello?'

Mum has shifted her focus from Auntie Edem and Loli to my furrowed brow. 'What does she want?'

I press my finger against my lips to shush Mum. She is unmoved by the gesture and ignores it.

'The samples?'

'I thought you said you've taken two weeks' leave?'

I turn my back to shield Caitlyn from Mum's comments, which include the suggestion of blocking her for the duration of our trip so we can have some peace. My bulging eyes lock squarely with Mum's but fail to persuade her to lower her voice. She is too close to drown out.

'The reception isn't very— A different supplier— We changed suppliers. Su-ppli-ers! New samples! Yes—'

I realise I am shouting when I remove my finger from my ear to take Loli's hand and hear my voice. Loli's palm is open and waiting.

'I'll email you! Yes! Email! As soon as I get—'

'Was that your f-f-friend?' Loli asks when the reception cuts. Or when Caitlyn hangs up; it's difficult to know which.

'It was my boss.'

'Your boss?' she repeats, turning the idea over in her mind.

Mum does not know why Caitlyn thinks it's okay to call me when I am on holiday on the other side of the world. Or how she would cope if we didn't have the internet in Africa and she was unable to reach me. She suggests I tell her just that; that there is no internet or electricity in Ghana so I will be incommunicado for the next two weeks.

Mum does not know when she became so intolerant of heat. She retrieves a folded piece of paper from her bag and uses it to fan herself, the effort-to-relief ratio entirely disproportionate. With her left hand she uses a handkerchief to dab at the perspiration forming a translucent necklace at the base of her neck.

Auntie Edem insists on pushing the trolley holding our luggage. She navigates the route with determination and responds to my offer of help with reference to food: 'I hope you are hungry?'

It is a rhetorical question to which she does not seek an answer. Instead she begins to list the meals she has prepared for us, those she intends to prepare, and the selection of mineral drinks chilling in the fridge and awaiting our arrival.

'Eiii. My sister!' she says again, smiling at Mum.

Mum makes utterances which suggest she is listening, but I can tell she is not. She is lost in the sights and sounds of Accra, unrecognisable to her after so many years away.

'The prodigal daughter returns!' Auntie Edem announces as we approach the car, a smile of restitution beaming across her face.

Her words have the effect of a seat belt locking on sudden impact. A retraction system, stopping Mum's body in the middle of the car park amidst parking and departing cars, their headlights and their horns. She stands still, her neck snapping in Auntie Edem's direction with such force it is vulnerable to whiplash.

'What did you say?'

The smile on Auntie Edem's face evaporates like hot water and leaves something parched in its place.

'The prodigal what?'

The intensity of Mum's stare causes a change in the direction of travel and alters the wind velocity. Her pupils beam like a laser into and through Auntie Edem.

'Who?'

Auntie Edem's attempt to swallow is made difficult by the dry state of her mouth.

'Me?'

'Oh, Selom…' She hesitates.

'What sin have I committed?!'

'We are just…celebrating your return…' Auntie Edem's voice drops by some decibels. She does not raise her eyes to meet Mum's, but busies herself instead with the task of loading our suitcases into the boot. This time she accepts my offer of help.

Inside the car, Auntie Edem attempts a song she does not know the words to beyond the first line of the first few verses: 'You are Alpha and Omega…' In place of the remaining lyrics, she hums at high pitch.

Mum has shifted her gaze to the changing frames of the passenger window on her right. She consumes the landscape in silence.

'Sika, will you sleep in my room? Do you like pink? Can you run f-f-fast?'

Loli reminds me of me at the age of five: an only child with a singular focus on companionship. In the back seat, she fingers the bracelets on my wrist and turns the rings on my fingers.

It is only when we arrive at Auntie Edem's house that Mum speaks again. Between the unloading of the car and the opening of the front door. To herself and to an audience of one.

'Prodigal daughter indeed!'

She speaks in a low voice that is too loud to go unheard.

'Am I the one who should ask for forgiveness?'

THE COLOUR BLACK

I follow Auntie Edem to the Church of Incredible Miracles to give Mum some space to sit on the veranda and look at the stars. To hear the chirping of the crickets and the croaking of the frogs. To see fireflies dance in the evening sky. And the wings of bats cast shadows against the full moon. Space to settle the nerves that preceded our trip. The anxiety that showed in the packing and repacking of her suitcase. The three calls in as many days to check I had scheduled my typhoid and yellow fever vaccinations. The frown lines on her forehead following calls with Auntie Edem and Auntie Larjey to decide when we would stay, where and with who. I follow Auntie Edem to the Church of Incredible Miracles to give Mum time to acclimatise and to settle into the place she used to call home. In any event, she does not want to come with us.

Auntie Edem scans me closely with an enquiring smile when I present myself in my first choice of a scoop-neck bodysuit and denim skirt. 'Erm…do you have something else?'

I follow her gaze down to my strappy sandals and the neon orange painted on my toes. Against the peach of the living room walls, the wooden furnishings and the cream of the lace curtains, the neon looks bright and loud. Loli wears a blue-and-white batik dress, and on her feet, the frilly white socks and black patent shoes of little girls everywhere. She has attached herself to me with devotion and convinced me of the beauty in siblings. I search my mind for an alternative outfit. One that will find harmony with the simplicity of Auntie Edem's brown dress: no frills, no fuss. She has covered her hair with a patterned headtie. If I hadn't seen her wrap it as she walked from her bedroom to the living room, I would have sworn she had sat in front of the mirror, bottom lip bitten in concentration, and arranged each fold just so. In a way I cannot imagine she intended, Auntie Edem's headtie channels India Arie. And I briefly think of her as boldly anti-establishment. But those vibes do not match her energy, which is agitated by the fact that we are running too late to be early. She rewraps the headtie into another style, notable for its simplicity, and suggests that it would be better if my chest was covered.

In the bedroom, I ask Mum for help as I rifle through her suitcase for something else to wear. I feel cold and exposed, like I have unwittingly flashed Auntie Edem and shown her the extent of my bikini wax.

'Sika! Why are you messing up my things?'
'I need to change!'
'Those are linen trousers! Don't throw them on the floor like that!'
'Can you help me, please?'
'Help you with what?'
'Auntie Edem says I need to change for church!'
'What's wrong with what you are wearing?'
'I don't know! But she said we're running late—'
'Running late for what?'
'Mum! Please, what should I wear?'
'There is nothing wrong with what you are wearing, Sika.'

I interrogate Mum's clothes with urgency as wetness starts to dampen my creases. She is not as moved by my panic as she is by the rearrangement of her clothes.

'What about this one?' I hold a patterned maxi dress against my body.

'Sika, that dress is very expensive and it is silk. Put it down.' She looks at me above oversized frames lowered down to her nose until I return the dress to its hanger.

'What about this top?'

She doesn't take time to deny my request. Or to remove an unworn ruffle-sleeved blouse, still attached to its label, from my hands. I settle on the linen trousers and a plain T-shirt.

'Is it the Mormon church you people are going to?'

If she had taken me to church for more than four weddings and a funeral in my lifetime, I might have half a clue.

'Mum, you're not helping!'

I present myself in the door frame of the living room for a second time, my damp hands smoothing the folds of the linen trousers into submission.

'Eh heh, this one covers your shoulders nicely!'

Auntie Edem receives the ensemble with greater enthusiasm than my earlier choice.

'This is much better.'

She rubs the cotton down the curve of my shoulders to satisfy herself they cannot be exposed by the accidental brush of a hand. I am surprised by the way her approval calms me. But it is withdrawn almost as quickly as it is offered when her gaze lands on my ears and the gold hoops and studs that decorate them. Loli is transfixed by the sight.

'Eiii! Is this the fashion?'

Auntie Edem's eyebrows are raised against flawless skin,

causing deep lines to wrinkle her forehead. I hold my ears in the place her hands have just been to check whether they are responsible for the heat spreading through my body. I understand her horror at my piercings and imagine the task of removing a dozen earrings from my ears.

'Come on, let's go! We don't want to be late!'

When she announces that it is time to leave, I am relieved that I will not have to do so. Church is close enough to walk.

We walk with more purpose and pace than I have seen anyone walk since we arrived in Ghana, where no one is in too much of a hurry and no task too urgent. The heat does not allow for that. Loli's legs move at impressive speed to keep up with her mum's; I can tell she is used to this pace. We pass a group of men engaged in an animated discussion of politics; the subject elicits loud voices and big gestures. A barber cutting hair by evening light suspends his clippers mid-air while his client shares news that causes his mouth and eyes to open wide in disbelief, half-shaved head shining under the glare of a single light bulb. A man broadcasts the sale of bath nets and salted peanuts with impressive marketing skills. Another does his best to woo a woman engaged in the business of selling coconuts. On the street corner, a group of teenage boys snacking on roasted plantain showcase dance moves and body-popping skills to Afrobeat. A woman in her twenties wearing a pink Lycra dress and poorly attached wig commands the attention and comments of passers-by:

'Brazilian virgin hair.'

'These days that's what the women want.'

The manoeuvring of cars around potholes and the honking of horns provides a soundtrack to our walk. There are few street lamps but we do not walk in darkness, not when the path is lit by the headlights of cars, bulbs from the insides of shops and a full moon. I realise that animation and urgency are not to be confused with each other. Loli holds my hand with a tight grip and, when space allows, skips beside me.

Auntie Edem has been in a place of spiritual preparation for the ten minutes we have been walking. She suspends it abruptly when she catches sight of an older woman running in her direction, poorly supported breasts flapping against skin dusted with talcum powder. A bag containing balls of kenkey knocks against her right thigh as she advances. Auntie Edem follows the gaze of the panicked woman to identify the son of her friend. Her walk turns into something quicker, and soon she is also running. Loli and I are behind Auntie Edem. Before we realise it, we have picked up pace and started to run too.

'Kofi?'

We do not know why, but Loli and I repeat his name after Auntie Edem: 'Kofi?'

'Kofi, what is it?' Auntie Edem cries as she runs towards him.

I feel a wetness to the grip I have on Loli's hand and I am sure my expression of worry is mirrored by hers.

'What has happened?'

'Kofi?!'

'Who is dead?'

'Kofi?! Kofi?!'

Auntie Edem and the woman run from opposite directions of the path, firing questions at Kofi, who turns his head from left to right, following their voices like a tennis ball travelling back and forth across a net.

'What is it, Kofi?! Who is dead?!'

The voices of Auntie Edem and the running woman overlap, the urgency and fear in their words adding heat to the night.

'Auntie, good evening.'

'Good evening, Auntie Edem. How is it?'

Kofi's surprise at seeing his mother's friends quickly turns to alarm as he hears their questions repeated with increased volume.

'Kofi, who is dead?!'

'Oh! Auntie, what is it?'

'What has happened?!'

'Nothing has happened, please.'

'Who is dead?!'

'Nobody is dead, please.'

'What do you mean?'

'What is it?'

'Why are you wearing black like that?'

It is only then that I notice Kofi is dressed entirely in black. He looks down at his T-shirt and jeans as if he has forgotten what he wore to leave his house. 'Oh, this?' he asks, pulling at his T-shirt with a limp right hand. 'Oh, please, I'm not wearing anything. This is just a T-shirt and jeans, Auntie.'

'Kofi! Black is not a colour to be wearing head to toe like that!' Auntie Edem says. 'Please, go home and change!' The panic does not leave her voice immediately.

'Ahhh! What is that?!' The kenkey woman kisses her teeth.

By now a small crowd has circled the Man in Black. They gaze at him intently; we all do. The kenkey woman is out of breath and clearly frustrated by her unnecessary expenditure of energy. She wipes away a bead of sweat from her forehead with the back of her hand.

'Is your mother still in hospital?' she asks, switching from reprimand to neighbourly concern.

'No, please. She has come home.'

'We thank God. Give her my greetings,' she calls as she leaves in search of garden eggs. Relief slows her pace as she walks away.

'Yes, please.'

Loli and I follow Auntie Edem back in the direction we ran from, walking briefly in single file to allow a hen and her chicks to pass us. When we turn off the main road and around the corner, I see in large blue writing on a white board the words THE CHURCH OF INCREDIBLE MIRACLES. We have arrived.

Before we go inside, Auntie Edem wants to tell me and Loli something important. We should take note.

'Black is not a colour like other colours,' she says. 'It is not a colour to be worn recklessly.'

THE CHURCH OF INCREDIBLE MIRACLES

'Anybody here who is praying for success should come forward!'

The Prophet says he can see someone in the congregation who has been praying for something for a very long time. The Lord has heard their prayer and wants to grant that person's wish. They should come forward and lay their troubles at the foot of the cross.

A movement of bodies draws my attention to the back of the hall, where people are creating space for their neighbours to make way to the stage. From their lips they offer feverish prayers. The barren woman whose endometriosis is yet to be diagnosed stumbles forward, clinging desperately to the miracle of Sarah. The lazy farmer who seeks the riches of Solomon walks with novel and uncharacteristic urgency. The mother who fears that her son's delayed speech is a sign of spiritual warfare is ushered in the direction of the call. They line up side by side, the people who have been praying for success, their eyes shut, their bodies swaying.

'If you are hearing me, your money is coming to you!'

The sound system crackles as the Prophet shouts into the microphone. It adds to the sensory chaos of the space. A collection of fans stationed at various corners of the room whirr with enthusiasm but little power. With the movement of people the temperature soars.

'If you are hearing me, I am talking to you!'

The Prophet invites the person who has been praying for something for a very long time to come forward with a pointed finger. The force which moves him causes his voice to quiver and his body to quake. The pointed finger is at once accusatory and inviting. He holds it like a wand in my direction. I look at the woman behind me. She is poised to catch showers of blessings, her arms outstretched in readiness.

'Sika! Prophet is inviting you to the stage!' Auntie Edem speaks in a loud whisper, her eyes widening as she hovers at the border of favour.

'Me?' My index finger points automatically inwards as I look at the woman to the left of Auntie Edem and the man to my immediate right. The Prophet is not pointing behind but at me. 'Oh! Oh, it's okay. I'm fine, thank you.'

'Sika! Prophet is inviting you!'

A rising urgency threatens the whisper of Auntie Edem's voice. And I understand from the exaggerated movement of her mouth and the sight of her tonsils that my delay is disturbing the status quo. There is no RSVP option to the Prophet's invitation. My feet adopt a robotic shuffle as Auntie Edem ushers me out of my seat. In my ribs, her fingers convey a strength from which I read haste. I feel the heat of a single spotlight as eyes behind, in front and to either side of me follow my journey to the stage. Loli releases my hand to enable the process. 'Go to Prophet,' she encourages.

'But. But I'm not sure…'

I swallow my words as I am ushered towards the stage by two Prayer Warriors. Their hands grip my elbows, one on either side, like a vice.

'You have been praying for something for a long time, eh?'

I don't know if it is prayer, the thing I have been doing. The longing to come to Ghana to feel and be closer to

Dad. To see the place he grew up and know the streets he walked. The hope that Mum might remember one more thing about him by virtue of being here. That I might know him that much more in turn. I don't know if prayer is what it is called, but I do know that my need to know Dad is more than Mum's pain in losing him will allow her to share. I don't know how the Prophet knows that I am searching for the missing part of me. And that when I find it I can set the wondering part free.

'If I bless you today, you are blessed!'

'Thank you,' I manage, my voice reduced to a shy whisper.

He holds the microphone to his mouth like a child about to eat an ice cream: vanilla with strawberry syrup and a chocolate flake. It is too close. The vibration in his voice matches the movement of his hands: manic. His other hand rests on top of my head.

'I deliver you from the chains of bondage!'

'Sorry, the chains of—?'

With each syllable he increases the pressure.

'I re-lease the blood of Je-sus! The blood of Christ!'

'Sorry, can you mind my—'

His fingers move across my head without regard for my hair. I attempt a *Matrix*-style move to dodge his touch, but my thoracic spine disagrees with the effort. At the same time the congregation stirs, the volume of mutterings rising. If I am blinking quickly, it is because he is digging his fingers into my scalp. Everyone knows you don't touch a black girl's hair! With the rapid movement of my eyes, an audible fever spreads amongst those gathered.

'Release!'

He digs.

'Release!'

His fingers, like pincers.

'Release!'

I think he has broken skin. Drawn blood.

'Release!'

He elongates the first syllable and lands abruptly at the word's end. In shiny black patent shoes branded *LV*, the Prophet catches my sandal-strapped baby toe with a hard sole. I wince at the pain. It travels from the tip of my toes to the top of my head. To ease the discomfort, I shift my weight from my right foot to my left. My movement causes any member of the congregation who remained seated to rise to their feet.

The Prayer Warriors on either side of me steady themselves as if preparing for something familiar. They wear the serious expression of people experienced in the art of combat. I can only imagine my dishevelled state: the topknot in which I styled my braids to follow Auntie Edem to church unpicked to the messy tangle of a scarecrow.

The Prophet squeezes his eyes so tightly shut that his features disappear.

'The Holy Spirit is moving! Moving in this place!'

His voice is shrill. It echoes through the room where we are gathered, bouncing and reverberating off the walls. The room is brightly lit. I can see Auntie Edem clearly. Her eyes are closed. I want her to open them so she can see what is happening; what he is doing to me.

'Whoever conspires against you shall be banished from the arena of your life!'

Her hands are raised towards the ceiling.

'I condemn your enemies before they plan their first strike!'

Her lips, in constant movement.

'To any friend harbouring the will of Satan, the vengeance of the Lord is promised!'

She sways left and right at her hips around which she has tied a wrapper.

The Prophet's words are punctuated with murmurs of 'Amen' and other words I am unable to decipher.

'Every head shall bow! Every mouth confess!'

I look at Loli. Her sweet face is knotted in an expression of wonder. It merits a T-shirt that says I'M WITH HER. It confirms that she is used to the spectacle I am experiencing for the first time. He prays into existence my health, wealth and prosperity.

'And the Lord said to Moses, "Let my people go!"'

That's when he applies so much pressure to my temples that it causes the light around me to dim and the room to fall silent. I stumble backwards, but he continues. To inch towards me. Closing the gap between us. Invading my personal space. He is like a titanium-clad superhero whose exterior repels bullets as quickly as they strike. It is stifling here in the Church of Incredible Miracles. And suffocating. I am struggling to breathe. I stumble. Forwards. Backwards. Backwards. Blood surges from my heart to my head. Before a black curtain descends.

I come to slumped on a chair stage left and surrounded by people in varying states of consciousness. Across the stage, the Prophet celebrates his spiritual victory in the form of a shuffle, his black patent shoes clicking at the heel and converging at the toes. He has exorcised the demons from us. And the congregation has borne witness to it.

They celebrate in tongues.

TAXI

The day is hot. It is a sun partially masked by the movement of clouds and the pollution of a bustling city. Mum is competing with the sound of Accra in the early afternoon. It is not a task for the timid. The traffic carries its own cacophony: engines running, horns beeping, hawkers selling. The sounds clash and harmonise in full surround sound. She questions the roadworthiness of various cars with reference to the colour of the smoke billowing from their exhausts while waving her hand to flag down a taxi. My eyes dart between hers and the motorbikes swerving around cars manoeuvring past tro tros in front of us.

A red car, sporting yellow panels on the sides of its bonnet and rear, is swerving between moving vehicles – and people – towards us. Mum's efforts have paid off. To make sure, she rounds her tongue and blows air through her lips to get his attention:

'Ssssss ssssss!'

She is lighter outside the walls of Auntie Edem's house. Her energy, effervescent and familiar once more. There is a fluidity to her words that Auntie Edem's conversation fractures, a seamlessness to her movements that her sister's presence disrupts. The driver has heard. He has crossed two lanes of traffic and narrowly avoided a collision. I wonder if his indicator is broken. What other reason could he have for not using it? The surrounding chaos allows me to cushion the question that's been weighing on my mind: 'Mum, what's the deal with Auntie Edem?'

Neither of them would make good decorators, Auntie Edem or Mum. There is a crack somewhere between them that they have papered over but not repaired. It exists in their conversations about Grandma and Grandpa. Their childhood home. The fit of Loli's clothes gifted from London. The colour of the sky. It highlights their difference like the fracture along a fault line.

'Auntie Edem?' Mum's lips move in the direction of disdain as she speaks her sister's name. 'Edem?'

'You seemed so angry with her at the airport—'

'Do you know, if I trace a circle with my hand like this, the driver will take us to Circle?' Mum draws a circle in the air, her index finger pointing downwards.

'What is Circle?'

'Kwame Nkrumah Circle. It's a busy intersection for people travelling through Accra. You will find people there selling clothes, shoes, electrics, music, all sorts of things. We'll find time to go there so you can take a look around.'

Today Mum wants to visit an old friend, someone she hasn't seen or spoken to in years.

'Before we got in the car—'

'My sister Edem?' She turns her name around in her mouth and mind. 'Don't let her trouble you, okay?' And like an irritating mosquito, she swats the subject away.

Cars surrounding the taxi driver beep like a swarm of angry bees. This does not deter him. He crosses the third lane and stops a metre away from the kerb where we are stood, screeching to a stop.

The driver is beaming when he motions for us to get inside. I assume a combination of adrenaline, triumph, pride and sweat. From outside the car, I hear him pull the handbrake and wonder if it will ever work again. A chiropractic adjustment to the anatomy of the vehicle that appears to cause him no alarm.

There is another passenger in the front seat. I am waiting for him to get out when Mum takes her seat behind the driver.

'He's not getting down, Sika.'

'Oh?!'

'That is what they do,' she says without attempting discretion. 'He will drop him off on the way.'

'Circle?' the taxi driver asks.

'Pokuase,' Mum clarifies. She asks if he knows where the fantasy coffins are made. That is where we are going. She speaks to him in Twi. The taxi driver confirms that he knows Pokuase well. He has the most mischievous smile. When he flashes it, my arm reaches for the seat belt.

'Mum, where is it?'

'Ask again! Mine is broken!'

On the rear windscreen of the car, in adhesive white letters, are the words HOPE AND PRAY.

The journey reminds me of a funfair ride for thrill seekers. I am shunted in the back seat from left to right at an adrenaline-inducing speed that causes my stomach to somersault. I cannot speak for fear that breakfast will escape my mouth instead of words. Mum asks the driver to slow down. His smile indicates that he has no intention of doing so. My head ricochets back and forth with every application of the car's brakes. I reach for the handle on the inside of the door to steady myself. It is broken.

'Mum, I'm scared!'

Mum asks if the driver's indicator is also broken.

'The traffigator? Sometimes it works. Sometimes it doesn't work!'

He is smiling at me in the rear-view mirror. A white rosary hangs around it, along with a green air freshener tree whose scent I cannot detect. I try to return his smile, but fear is distracting. The driver and the other passenger speak Ga over the radio, which blasts distorted and patchy sounds through the car's speakers. They argue with the radio host, callers to the station and each other. It is irrelevant that neither the radio host nor the callers can hear them. The fact they can't serves instead to deepen the conviction of their arguments. They shout louder to convey their points. In the next breath they are laughing.

Mum reads my mind: 'That's just the Ga language – it sounds like they are fighting.'

'Can you speak the Ghanaian language?' The taxi driver locks eyes with me in the mirror. I open my mouth ready to answer him when a caller refers to the need to 'immobilise' against political corruption.

'He is talking rubbish,' Mum says. Her no-nonsense commentary makes the taxi driver and his passenger vociferous in agreement.

We are navigating potholes with alarming speed when a car cuts in front of us, leaving little room to brake. The windows of the taxi are lowered as far as they will go to compensate for the broken fan system, for which the taxi driver apologises without a hint of regret in his voice. The car blasts black-grey smoke through its exhaust and in our direction. The fumes reach us through the windows of the car, prompting a simulated asthma attack from Mum. She struggles with the window handle that turns without traction on the glass it is supposed to draw up.

'Sika, roll up your window!'

'Oh, Auntie, don't worry. We will soon pass!'

The car's lack of safety does not stop its driver from making a Formula 1-style pit stop exit when the traffic lights turn green. I wonder if he can see clearly, and if so, how.

The taxi driver is as cool as the day is hot. 'You are from London, eh?' he turns around to ask me.

'Please, driver, watch the road. We want to get to Pokuase in one piece!' Mum says.

'Auntie, please, don't worry. I will take you.'

He tells us that his name is Yaw.

'Yes, yes. London,' I say. I hope in vain that a prompt answer will focus his attention on the road, but the panic in my voice makes both men laugh.

'Are you afraid? Can you drive in Ghana?'

I assume both are rhetorical questions. But when I see that he is looking at me in the mirror, I understand that he is waiting for an answer.

'Yes. No.'

'You can drive here?'

'No, no! I can't.'

I don't understand the rules. Are there any? I am so scared that I am smiling. From ear to ear, my teeth on full display. My answer prompts more laughter from the front of the car before we brake abruptly. I grab Mum's forearm with one hand and grip the seat with the other.

Suddenly, Yaw sticks his head out of his window. 'W'agyimi anaa?? Kwasia!' His foot is on the accelerator before the driver of the offending car can provide an answer to the state of his stupidity. 'Look at his face! His head like goat!' The taxi driver offers this observation to the inside of the car. There is a double standard in the quality of driving that I want to reconcile. But before I can try, Mum and I are pushed back in our seats by what I can only assume is G-force.

'Yaw, I don't like this kind of driving!'

Yaw appears to take Mum's pleas for him to slow down as a challenge to do the opposite. She chews her gum intently as I add more to the tasteless piece in my mouth. When I attempt to release the tightness in my jaw, a shriek escapes involuntarily. The driver and his passenger are enjoying the entertainment. Yaw says he will give us his number. We can call him anytime, day or night, and he will take us wherever we need to go. Mum locks eyes with him in the mirror. Hers are wide in their sockets; his are glistening with something like glee.

POKUASE

We defy all sorts of odds to arrive at Pokuase alive. Yaw mounts the kerb to park before getting down to open the door for Mum. He is smiling like a Grand Prix champion who has secured pole position. Mum's flame-red, half-up, half-down sister locks have dislodged along the journey to hang loosely around her face. From her purse, she gives him a handful of cedis and asks a question to which there is no answer: 'Yaw, what kind of driving was that?' Rewarded for the task, he thanks Mum for her generosity.

I don't move immediately. I can't. I rest my head against the back of the torn leather seat and practise stillness. Mum appears with a coconut bought from a vendor metres away. It is large and smooth and yellow-green. She guides the open part to my mouth.

'Drink that, you'll feel better.'

Yaw instructs us to take our time. He is going somewhere but will be back. I sip the coconut water slowly and fix my eyes on a palm tree in the distance, a ballerina 'spotting' to prevent dizziness while pirouetting in the stationary car. It is the same palm tree Yaw faces, his back towards me, as his urine patterns its trunk.

He walks back at a slow pace, effortlessly at home in his surroundings. The back doors of the car are open. The air that circulates through them is warm.

'Are you feeling fine?'

'The coconut water is helping, thank you.' I open my mouth carefully at its hinges to speak.

'It's your first time in Ghana, eh?'

I look at him before taking another sip. My fragility must show; he smiles but does not press for an answer.

'I have a cousin in Milton Keynes.'

I smile at the fact shared. Spot and breathe. Smile, spot, breathe. Smile, spot and breathe, until Pokuase stops spinning.

Mum is standing outside the taxi, presenting her empty coconut to the seller to cut. With an expert hand, she uses a machete to split it in half. Mum uses the top of the coconut, its lid, to scoop out the fleshy goodness and eat it. She surprises me when we say goodbye to Yaw and she takes his mobile number, 'just in case'. We watch as he drives off, manoeuvring carefully around potholes before disappearing around the corner with two beeps of his horn.

'Eiii, so he knows how to drive slowly?'

It is only when Yaw is out of sight and I have stopped wondering at the irony of him driving carefully, as if in charge of some precious cargo, that I look around to see where he has dropped us off.

'Sika, this is Pokuase.'

I follow Mum along a path of red earth which coats my feet in fine dust and ages my chale wote in a vintage way. We pass a mechanic deep in thought as he examines the intestines of a car, his right hand at the head of the bonnet, a rag in his left. A woman balances bagged water in a basket on top of her head, while another supports a basket of bagged nuts beside her. In an impressive showcase of talent, small children play football in Crocs and sliders. Some play barefoot, unperturbed by the uneven earth, unrivalled in their display of skill.

'Ice water! Ice water!'

I wonder how the water stays cool under the heat of the early-afternoon sun. At the perfection of her posture. Her ability to take cash from a customer and retrieve change from her bra while keeping the basket perfectly still on her head. Her ability to bend down. Her ability to labour under the glare of the sun for hours and hours like that. She wears chale wote with socks. To protect her feet from the dust, I guess. I wonder how much money she can make in a day and how many mouths she has to feed with it. An unintentional moment of eye contact forces me to look away and down. A visceral reaction; the discomfort of guilt and shame.

The ground is hard underfoot, baked by the relentless heat of the sun. It is the kind of colour that points to the wonder of nature; it is almost like rust. We walk past a stall on which a pyramid of yellow-green oranges is built. The seller sits on a stool beside it with her head tied and an infant asleep on her back.

'That is how I used to carry you when you were a baby,' Mum says. A patterned cloth tied above her chest and at her waist, securing me like a baby koala, my cheek resting against her back, my legs poking out on either side. 'The way you resisted sleep, heh! I think you had YOLO, or whatever they call it.' She smiles at the memory now she has lived through it.

'Do you mean FOMO? Fear Of Missing Out? YOLO is "You Only Live Once"! And there's no need for you to use words like that, Mum!'

'Yes, FOMO! You would be fast asleep on me and as soon as I put you down, see Sika!'

I laugh at the image of which I have no memory.

'It's the only way I could soothe you some days or get you to sleep at all on others.'

I loved the rhythm of her movement. The warmth of her body. The sound of her heartbeat. The way it synced with mine through the wall of her back. It freed her hands. It allowed her to cook and clean and just do things. It enabled her to function as a solo parent.

'For a single or busy mum, that thing is a godsend.'

The sound of her voice, shhh, shhh, like mobile white noise.

'Or a single dad?'

'Hmmm?'

'Helpful for a single mum or dad.'

'No.' She responds without hesitation. 'Look carefully. See how the cloth is secured above her chest? It is her breasts which keep it in place like that. It depends on the very shape of her body. A man cannot back a baby.'

I would have sat on Dad's shoulders instead. And seen the world from his height of five foot eleven inches. I imagine how it would have been to rest my hands on his head of thick hair and drape my infant legs over his broad shoulders.

'Was he a good driver, Mum?'

'Who?'

'Who?! Dad!'

It happens like that sometimes. When I realise there is a thing about him I don't know. A question I have not asked. A detail about his life that Mum has not shared. That is when my longing becomes a physical thing.

'Yes, he was.'

Something squeezes my heart and causes pain to radiate through my body. It is more than a dull ache or even a sharp stab. It is the pain of never having known him. Despite the fact that I am half of him. Because of it. It can turn the taste in my mouth bitter regardless of what I've eaten. It is worse than quinine and the taste it leaves if you let an antimalarial tablet sit on your tongue before you swallow it. That feeling can make you retch.

'He was a very good driver. And he knew the streets of Accra like the back of his hand.'

It can linger. The pain.
It can keep me awake at night.
Full of longing and empty with loss.

AGAPE

'Agape? Agape Mensah?'

The Boss Man replaces the handset of a cordless phone on its stand as Mum hovers at the entrance to the workshop and sends her voice in his direction.

'Agape, is that you?' she asks hopefully but cautiously.

'Hello, can I help you?'

The glare of the midday sun, hot against our backs, casts us as shadows before him in the shade of his workshop. His dust-free hands and checked shirt distinguish him from the men on the workshop floor. Two silhouettes: one who speaks, one who doesn't. A powerful fan rotates beside him. I want to walk inside and towards its breeze.

'Agape, is that you? It's me, Selom.'

The Boss Man uses his hand to shield his eyes, like a visor, and walks towards us with the gait of a silver fox. When he is close enough for me to see the closeness of his shave and the grey in his beard, he removes his hand. Without the distraction of the sun that cast Mum and I into anonymous shadows, he is able to process the person before him. In the reduced space between them, there is a questioning pause.

'Selom?' His furrowed brows add wrinkles to the plane of his forehead and his narrowed eyes suggest doubt, even disbelief. 'Selom? Selom Akollor?'

He is still but for the movement of his mouth. It opens so wide that were he a little boy standing there with his tonsils on display, his mother would say, 'Close your mouth before you catch flies!' He covers the scene with his hand. When it falls slack to his side, his mouth is left ajar.

'Agape?'

'Selom?'

He takes tentative steps towards her until his six-foot-one frame stands over her five-foot-eight one. I am a silent observer of the repetition of names which characterises their exchange. They examine each other as if for the first time, familiar strangers.

'Mum, I think I've been bitten!'

The sound of my voice draws them out of their reverie and they turn their gaze from each other to me.

'Sorry, sorry. Please. Come. Come inside!'

The Boss Man ushers us inside the workshop and issues instructions that result in the production of bottled water and a repellent coil, which he lights and places beside me.

'There shouldn't be mosquitoes around at this time of day,' Mum says, examining the spot on my ankle where I swear an itchiness has set in. She hands me repellent cream to reapply just in case.

The Boss Man invites me to sit down and increases the power of the fan beside me. It is only when I have settled, taken a sip of water and stopped scratching that they return their focus to each other. It is only then that I wish I was watching from a distance.

Mum widens the space between her arms and waits for her embrace to be filled. They stand for a moment like that, mismatched puzzle pieces, not sure which way to fit. A bottle of Fanta appears on a wooden tray, a bottle of Coke beside it. The Fanta is a neon shade of orange which I fear would interfere with my kidney function should I drink it. The Boss Man steps slowly into Mum's arms. She closes her eyes when he is there. And clasps her hands around his torso to secure him. There is a strangeness to the intimacy. Her frame shifts as she exhales, and from her shoulders something lifts.

'Selom?' He pulls himself away from Mum to look at her before she pulls him towards her again.

'Agape, I can't believe it's you!' Her voice is louder than a whisper but quietened by a choking tear.

'Selom?' He has big hands and doesn't know what to do with them. Whether he should pat her back or rub it.

'Wow. You haven't changed a bit!'

'Are you sure?' His uncertainty is endearing. It makes him look younger than the grey in his beard suggests.

'Well, I don't remember you having red hair!'

Mum raises her hand to her locks to touch the thing that has changed between then and now.

'Agape, you look exactly the same!'

He sends his gaze southwards, an attempt to see what she does.

'Sika, this is Uncle Agape!'

I am startled to hear my name when Mum steps outside her old life to join real time.

'Agape, this is my daughter, Sika.' Mum takes me by the hand and presents me, her prized possession.

'Your daughter?' He turns to me with wide eyes. 'You have – a daughter?'

'I do.'

He is slow to blink. And quite possibly stunned.

'Sika?'

'Nice to meet you.'

Slow processing precedes his warm welcome. And he exhales deeply as he takes my right hand in both of his.

'Sika. That's a beautiful name.'

I wonder if Mum should have called ahead to give notice of her visit instead of turning up unannounced at Uncle Agape's workshop, a blast from the past. He seems both surprised and overwhelmed.

'Sika, do you remember I told you that there was a very naughty boy in my class who lived around the corner from Auntie Larjey and me when we were younger?'

'The one who nearly drowned?'

'Eh heh—'

'Heh, Selom, you told your daughter that story?'

'Of course! Well, this is the boy who convinced me and Larjey to follow him to the beach and time him as he swam to the buoy and back. So we started counting. One, two, three...by the time we got to nine, he had started to struggle. His hands flailing in the air as the waves swallowed him.' Mum moves her hands wildly to recreate his desperate movements.

'If your mother hadn't sounded the alarm that day, I don't know that I would be standing here today.'

'The way we panicked!'

'The way my parents scolded me!' He laughs at the memory of punishment after his parents' relief had passed.

'Did it put you off swimming?'

'I could never swim. Can you imagine? I had seen the older children doing it, so I studied their moves. The way they used their hands and kicked their legs.' He gestures by flicking his hands up and down at the wrist. 'It didn't look too difficult until I tried to impress your mum!'

Silence takes hold of Mum and Agape when their laughter subsides. It causes them to examine the ground on which they stand. I wonder if I should excuse myself for a few minutes. Longer, perhaps.

'Selom. I'm…I'm lost for words.'

'It's been a long time, I know.'

'What…what are you doing here?'

'I came for Larjey and Papa's anniversary.'

'But what are you doing here, in Pokuase?'

'Oh! I wanted to surprise you.'

'To surprise me? Selom – it's been – at least – twenty-five years?'

'Twenty-seven!'

'Twenty-seven years? Wow.'

'It's been a long time, I know.'

They struggle to hold each other's gaze, oscillating between fleeting eye contact and the scattering of wood shavings on the floor. In silence, they travel between memories of the past and emotions of the present.

'So you've been coming to Ghana over the years and—'

'No! No! This is my first time back!'

'What?! You haven't visited Ghana in all this time? How?!'

'I know. I left it so long, Agape. Too long. Life eh?!'

'Life?' he asks, trying to reconcile its relevance with Mum's quarter-century absence. 'Life?'

'I couldn't miss Larjey and Papa's wedding anniversary, not after missing the wedding itself.'

'Oh. Oh, I see.'

Silence takes hold once more and adds weight to the air around them. This time, when she embraces him, Mum draws me into their fold. Her left hand lingers in his when they pull apart. I feel surplus to requirements.

'Forgive me, I just…I didn't expect…' He wrings his hands before looking at us both, gentle eyes matching a gentle smile. He blinks twice before speaking again. 'You look so much like your mum,' he says.

That's what everyone says. That I am Selom 2.0, her mini-me. That the apple did not fall far from the tree, if it fell at all. A tearful pride shines through Mum's eyes while Uncle Agape wears a smile that resurrects each time it settles.

'It's so good to see you, Agape.'

He searches her features for something to say. Her well-shaped eyebrows and the deep, dark brown of her irises. The bump on the bridge of her nose and the unmistakable prominence of her cheekbones. He examines her full lips painted in matt mahogany, and the delicate gap between her front teeth that is visible with her smile. He examines her face in microscopic detail before he finds his words, and speaks them quietly.

'Sorry, you've caught me off guard. I just…I did not imagine…I didn't think I would ever see you again.'

DANCING PALLBEARERS

In Uncle Agape's workshop is a giant fish. Perhaps three feet wide and ten feet long from its mouth to its tail. It is supported by a steel frame, and in height reaches the chests of the two men who stand on either side of it. One is in a white vest and khaki trousers. The other wears a yellow T-shirt with the words No Woman No Cry on its front. In their hands, they hold small pots of paint. The giant fish is made of wood which has been carved and shaped and sanded to smoothness. Fins have been carved for its side, back and tail to add to its anatomy. Its gills, eyes and nose are all identifiable. The body of the fish has been painted a salmon pink. Its black pupils are set in yellow irises and it looks straight ahead. It wears a neutral expression which errs on the side of a smile. One of the men paints the fins grey to add texture. The other paints scales along the length of its body. Uncle Agape notes my intrigue and encourages me to take a closer look.

'What do you think?'

I step across a bed of sawdust to examine the oversized fish. 'What is it?'

'It's a fantasy coffin.'

'A coffin?'

'Yes. The deceased was a fisherman. Before he died, he asked to be buried in a fish. So that is what his family is doing to celebrate his life.'

My eyes work hard to marry the object in front of me with its purpose. 'It's amazing!' I look around the workshop at the other wooden creations: a giant chicken, a pack of FanIce ice cream, an aeroplane bearing the Ghana Airways logo. I imagine the professions, lives and dreams of the deceased whose families have commissioned them. A bottle of Club beer, green with white writing, is open at its hinges. Inside, it is lined with white material. Somebody's satin resting place. Functional.

Mum's phone rings.

'It's Auntie Larjey!'

'Eiii Larjey!' Uncle Agape says.

They exchange a smile before she steps outside and away from the sound of the workshop to take the call. The workshop is a place where the sound of machinery and tools competes with exchanges in Ga. It is a lot to take in, and yet I try. I step out of the path of a chicken walking rhythmically in my direction. She pecks the floor of the workshop for snacks of sawdust. I am an obstacle in her way.

Uncle Agape manages my intrigue alongside multiple conversations with different workers who present questions and seek answers. 'You know, we Ghanaians, we like to celebrate death,' he says. 'We celebrate death even more than life. Did you know that?'

I did not. There has never been cause to celebrate Dad leaving Mum a widow and me without a father. It is not an event about which we can find peace let alone joy. It is a story which, once told, is difficult to revisit. It is not one Mum wants to tell over and over again. We do not visit Dad's grave because a Ghanaian cemetery, Mum explains, is not a place where one goes after they have laid their loved one to rest. It is not like Nunhead cemetery in south-east London, where people walk among monuments commemorating the lives of those who have been. They do not visit out of choice, or go there for walks with dogs on leads. There are no tours or open days where an expert guides a curious group around headstones and answers their questions about the people buried there and the monuments that mark their graves. There is no committee created with the purpose of conservation or planting. Visiting is not a social event.

'Fantasy coffins are a way for a family to celebrate the life of their loved one. And Ga people believe the deceased will continue their job in the afterlife, so the fantasy coffin is a reminder of that.'

'I've never seen anything like it.'

Uncle Agape smiles at me in a way that suggests he knows what he has done. He has lit a match of thought which he knows will continue to burn long after we have parted ways. I am not the first visitor who has come to his workshop to look at fantasy coffins and left questioning what her own would be. 'People travel from far and wide to see them,' he says. 'We even get international requests.'

My hand hovers over a tiger. It is polished in a way that suggests it is finished and ready to house somebody.

'Go ahead. You can touch it.'

I hesitate before running my hand along its back. Its mane and tail and paws are finished with intricate detail. It is smooth and shiny and carefully carved.

'How long does it take to build?'

'Oh, it can take up to three or four weeks depending on what it is.'

I look from my fingernails to the hands of the men in the workshop. Next to the tiger, two are sanding wood in the shape of a pen. Their hands are covered by dust and specks of paint. I imagine their palms to be rough and covered in calluses. It is hard not to be in awe of their skill.

'Where did you learn to do this?'

'My father was a furniture designer. His mother came from the village and had never been abroad. She told him that when she died, she wanted to be buried in an aeroplane. So he built one for her.'

Uncle Agape tells of the dancing pallbearers who carried the coffin of his grandmother on their shoulders from her home in Teshie to her final resting place, a plot of land owned by the family where their relatives were buried. The dancing pallbearers danced to the music of a band: trumpets, drums keh ni bii – and such things. A choreographed dance to joyful music. One minute the coffin was balanced on their shoulders and they were shuffling on their feet, the next they were on the floor, shaking their legs in the air like jesters, before crawling on the ground while balancing the weight of the coffin on their shoulders. What else? They balanced it on their backs to do kneeling press-ups. And again on their shoulders, standing to showcase James Brown dance moves.

They are dressed in tailcoats and top hats with shiny, shiny black-and-white shoes. Their pinstriped black trousers are coated in dust; so too are the gloves on their hands. With the free hand, the one that does not support the coffin, they wave their white handkerchiefs in the air between dance moves. They have enviable upper-body strength that explains the definition of their hidden muscles. And an ability to do that which others would not dare. They are fearless and skilled, talented and brave.

The lead pallbearer circles the coffin to make sure everything is as it should be. That each man has a firm grip on the coffin. That he has good balance and that the corpse is not at risk. He has a bird's-eye view of the performance. He is the conductor of the show. The MC provides a commentary to the spectacle: 'Look at these pallbearers! Wow! Wow! Wow!'

The praise of the crowd gets louder with the complexity of the choreography: 'This is serious! I like it! I like it! I like it!' The dancers are saluted for their agility, strength and skill by mourners waving handkerchiefs. With the same handkerchiefs, the mourners also bid farewell to the departed.

'I learned from watching my father before I started to work with him.'

A family business.

'How much do they cost these days?' Mum asks when she rejoins us. I read happiness on her face after speaking to Auntie Larjey, her oldest and best friend.

'It depends on the design and the level of detail the person wants. Is it for a local burial or for international display? That is the kind of thing that will affect the price. For something local we can charge...' He does some mental arithmetic to arrive at an average price of £300 for a local coffin and up to £10,000 for an international export.

'Leh leh?' Mum expresses her surprise.

'But Ga people believe that our ancestors wield great power, so honouring them with a fantasy coffin is a good way to curry favour with them.'

'Funerals in Ghana are no small thing,' Mum says.

'They must be really expensive too.'

'They are. But guests give donations to help with the costs.'

I understand that by continuing his father's trade, Uncle Agape will always have food to eat and clothes on his back.

'Agape, you will never go out of business!'

'Well, death is a constant. It is certain for us all.'

'Is it true that at one time people wanted a three-day weekend so they could attend more funerals?' Mum asks.

'Yes! People were asking for that.'

There are many things I would do with a three-day weekend, but going to funerals would not be one of them, I think.

'Really?'

'Yes, they are big social events.'

'And this weekend?' Mum asks hesitantly. 'Will we see you at the party of the year?'

'Larjey and Papa?'

'Who else?! You are coming, aren't you?'

'Oh, I, ummm…I had planned to but…I…I have another engagement…I don't know…'

I am surprised to feel my stomach sink at the thought that Uncle Agape might not make it. He needs to be there. For Mum. She wants to be in his orbit. I want him to be in hers.

'Oh! Does Larjey know?'

Mum adopts a policy of persistence to mask a disappointment which is tangible.

'Agape, you know Larjey will not allow that. Have you told her? Do you know what she will do to you?' It does not allow room for Uncle Agape to manoeuvre.

'Lady Justice?' He smiles at the moniker. 'No. I haven't mentioned—'

'You know this is not the party to miss.'

'Hmmm.'

'Can you imagine, the four of us together again? It will be like old times.'

Uncle Agape looks at the freshly glossed gills of the giant fish and back at Mum. There is a gentle raise to her eyebrows, an upwards draw to her smile.

'I came from London, Agape. Please.'

It is pleading masked as wishfulness, longing masked as hope.

'Okay,' he says finally. 'I'll be there.'

AUNTIE LARJEY

Auntie Larjey shrieks so loudly when she lays eyes on Mum that it makes her housegirl run from the kitchen with a knife in one hand, half a chopped onion in the other and a look of panic on her face.

'Ma?'

The high-pitched sound triggers the bark of a white Bichon Frise who runs laps around Auntie Larjey's ankles. The dog's movements are as frantic as Auntie Larjey's gestures. The air is chopped with words of Ga which she delivers rapidly. Mum returns powerful prose heavy with emotion before their voices reach fever pitch. The dog gives an unrelenting monologue alongside them. When the housegirl understands that the screams from the unravelling scene are celebratory in nature, she returns in the direction from which she came. Confusion causes the Bichon Frise to bark at inanimate objects and dart from one set of pot plants to the other.

Auntie Larjey's garden offers a contrasting calm to the chaos of the moment. Hibiscus, lilies, bougainvillea and other floral companions border the courtyard where we are gathered. A bird box sits underneath a mango tree. On the other side of the garden, a coconut tree provides shade. The grass is a vibrant green and perfectly manicured. Large terracotta pots provide homes for aloe vera, orchids and other plants whose names I do not know. There is an outdoor bar, barbeque and extended seating area. A rock pool from which a fountain flows. In front of the door is a wind chime whose silence confirms the stillness of the heat. A canopy protects a fleet of cars from the direct glare of the sun.

On the central footpath, Auntie Larjey runs her hands through Mum's locks and consumes her with hungry eyes. She runs her hands along the lengths of Mum's arms, examines her palms, her eyebrows, touches her face. She hugs her, squeezes her, kisses her. Over and over again. And Mum does the same. They repeat each other's names as if learning them for the first time.

'Selom.'

'Larjey.'

'Selom.'

'Larjey.'

Mum's right hand oscillates between her mouth and her close-to-bursting heart. They separate briefly to behold each other after so many years, too many years, apart. I film the moment on my phone because it is so special.

The Bichon Frise has settled and follows the housegirl towards the outdoor kitchen. The smell of food excites the air.

'Selom Akollor bi neh?'

Auntie Larjey's voice begins its ascent.

'SELOM AKOLLOR BI NEH?!'

Her gaze is now on me. Her tone is disbelief. Her questioning impatient as she waits for someone, me, or Mum, God – anyone – to answer the question.

'IS THIS SELOM AKOLLOR'S CHILD?'

'Larjey, didn't we FaceTime just last week?'

Mum is laughing her kikikiki laugh. The phone's lens does not do justice to Auntie Larjey. It does not adequately capture the size of her personality, the warmth or her smile or the heart on her sleeve. Despite meeting her for the first time, I feel like I have known her forever.

'Yes, it's me, Auntie Larjey!'

'Sikaaaaa!' Auntie Larjey shrieks before winding me with the embrace of an auntie who has never had the pleasure of meeting her beloved niece. Her breasts cushion the blow. When her excitement settles – and this takes some time – she leads us from the courtyard towards soft and shiny furnishings indoors.

On the walls and table surfaces are framed pieces of art and portraits of Auntie Larjey in all her glamour and glory. Auntie Larjey with a proud-looking Uncle Papa; Auntie Larjey, Uncle Papa and their sons; Auntie Larjey and the Bichon Frise; Auntie Larjey and more Auntie Larjey. She holds one of our hands in each of hers as we walk inside and sits between us on the sofa despite the ample space.

'The air con is on, is it too cold?'

She has told the girls to spray the place so there are no mosquitoes. What will I drink? Am I hungry? I must be hungry. Can I eat peppeh? Okay, good. They have prepared banku and okro stew for us. It has just a little peppeh but not too much. So, how is Ghana? Do I like it? Is it too hot for me? Who is my boyfriend? Does he have a kind heart? Because that is the most important thing. Does he make me laugh? Will he make me happy? Should she buy a hat?

Auntie Larjey holds multiple conversations at once. With Mum, she chops and changes between Ga and English. She discusses meal preparations with Esi, the housegirl, in Twi, takes a call from Uncle Papa in Fante, and interrogates me in English.

'Uncle Papa is on his way home now now now.'

She wants to take a proper look at my face and guides my chin with her hand to the light.

'The spitting image of your mum at your age, enu shi shi?' She looks to Mum for agreement.

Mum is beaming. 'She is more beautiful than I was.'

She always says that.

'Permission to remove?' Auntie Larjey asks.

'Permission granted.'

At Mum's response, Auntie Larjey whips off her wig in a swift hand movement designed to disarm. The wig, black and shoulder-length with a gentle wave, takes on a lifeless form as it lies in a shapeless heap on the side table. Underneath, her hair is in neat cornrows. She has, in addition to flawless skin, a beauty spot just above the cupid's bow of her mouth. It may, or may not, be drawn on.

'We are at home, aren't we? Feel free!' Esi presents an array of soft drinks from which I choose a bottle of water. It is chilled and leaves a cool imprint on my hand. I leave the glass on the tray and take a sip from the bottle.

'Esi, do you have Carnation milk?' Mum asks.

'Yes, please.'

'Please, can you make me tea?'

'Yes, please. Will you take sugar?'

'Eiii Esi! Carnation milk and sugar? You want my teeth to fall out eh?'

Esi laughs the sweetest, shyest, most deferential laugh. 'No, please, auntie.'

I don't know how I'm going to go back to drinking coffee with oat milk. Not now I've enjoyed the alternative of sweet evaporated milk in Ghana.

'Can I have a cup of tea as well, please?'

Auntie Larjey looks me in the eye and drops her hand from mine.

'Sika. Is that why you have come to Ghana? To drink tea? Tea that you can drink in England? Not in my house! Esi, please bring the white wine. And some large glasses. Or will you take Muscatella?' She takes up my hand again before hitching her boubou at the knee with her left hand and issuing rapid instructions to the air conditioning remote to cool the room further with her right. 'Eiii this menopause…' she says, before expanding on a topic that elicits knowing utterances from Mum.

'Hmmm.'

This word travels back and forth between them. Hmmm. The meaning it carries depending on the way it is pronounced, the number of syllables spoken, where the emphasis is placed and the context in which it is used.

'We will eat soon, hmmm.'

Anyway, when will I come back to Ghana? I don't need to wait for my mum to come, I can come by myself. The boys will be home from the States at Christmas. I can plan with them. They will take me out to all the cool places. Or she can even take me. Do I think she doesn't know where the cool places are? She knows how to have fun, I should ask my mum. Next time I come to Ghana, I will stay with her. She will fight Auntie Edem for me.

'Will I come to Ghana again and stay with Edem?' Mum asks.

It is a rhetorical question to which Auntie Larjey responds with one syllable, long, laboured and lamentable.

'Hmmm.'

KRIFEH

When I tell Mum and Auntie Larjey about the Prophet and the Church of Incredible Miracles, I worry that their rage will set fire to some flammable thing. The cowhide rug on which Mum shakes her feet at the ankles. The cloud-soft sofa on which Auntie Larjey adjusts and readjusts herself with each new detail of my experience at his hands.

'Praying for something like what?'

'Who told him he could put his hands on your head?!'

'In her hair even! How dare he?'

'And then what happened?'

'He started speaking in a different language. Hashabolasetehteh! Rashabalobahbahlahba!'

'Heh! Tongues?!'

'What did Edem do?'

'Nothing...Well, she was praying, I think.'

Auntie Larjey questions the mental faculty of the 'self-styled Prophet'. And wonders what those men paid to earn the title of 'Prayer Warrior'.

'I challenge that man to touch you in my presence! To touch a hair on your head! I defy him!'

Mum is simmering.

'And Edem sat there and watched?'

She crosses and uncrosses her feet at the ankles, where they shake like maracas.

*

The Prophet started to sing Whitney Houston's 'I Will Always Love You', the church band accompanying him with such perfect timing that it was clear the song had either been recently rehearsed or was regularly performed. Frustration rose through my chest at the sound of his voice. Auntie Edem had not mentioned that church would go on for more than three hours. In any event, I had been too quick to say yes. He performed a one-legged dance, toe-tapping to the clash of the cymbals and the beat of the drum, spinning on the spot as the music reached its crescendo.

'Prophet is going to dance past us!' Loli pointed excitedly along the length of the centre aisle and my agitation quietened. I understood through her loud whisper that the performance was coming to an end – but not before a finale of bum shuffling across the stage. My need to leave became acute.

'Do you like what I'm doing or not?'

The Prophet's question was met with cheers and clapping from the congregation. It found rhythm with the music and amplified the celebratory atmosphere in which I found myself lost.

After the singing and dancing and clapping and cheering, we joined a procession of energised people to exit the church. It was a slow shuffle that took us to the church shop next door, such was the number of people and the restriction of space. They were satiated in the way that those who have tasted salvation can attest to, buzzing as if emerging from a Beyoncé concert and in search of merchandise. I had lost track of time in the way that is possible when you are having too much or too little fun. It turned out that we had not simply gone to the church shop but the church after-party. The hotel lobby. Minus Belvedere or Cris. Instead, emblazoned on the bottles of soap, powder and shea butter that Auntie Edem took to the counter, was the face of the Prophet, his smile exposing strong teeth, sparkling white – unnaturally so – through a wide smile. Too wide. His forehead highlighted by the flash of the camera. Above it, the words *The Church of Incredible Miracles* in cursive font. Underneath the Prophet's chin was the price of each item written in blue biro. After mathematical gymnastics to convert cedis to sterling, I grappled with the amount Auntie Edem was spending on the three items, all of which she could buy from the market for a tenth of the price.

It wasn't until she started telling me how and when to use the soap, powder and shea butter that I realised Auntie Edem had bought them for me. I wanted to tell her that she shouldn't have, that she should have saved her money or that she should keep them for herself, but instead I said thank you. She told the sales assistant and others that I was her niece from London. In her voice, I heard joy. As we left the shop, Auntie Edem told me that the shop assistant was the wife of the Prayer Warrior. The man who had gripped me at the elbow with the lock of a pit bull's jaw. The man who dragged me off the stage when I fainted.

'You see how God works?'

I didn't tell Auntie Edem I had returned to my seat feeling violated that a man I don't know and had never met had thought it was okay to touch me like that, to apply pressure to different parts of my body. To make me stumble. I didn't tell her I had felt embarrassed that he had shone a spotlight on my head and made everyone look at me. Or that he had stood on my baby toe. I didn't say that it was not a nice feeling to be surrounded by two burly men, one on each side, restricting my movement and rooting me to a single spot. That it had felt intimidating and uncomfortable. I didn't tell her anything because in her eyes I saw and understood the breadth of her pride.

'Eiii, when it comes to God, no one can beat Edem!'
 'Hmmm.'
'Edem never used to be like that.'
'At all!'
Auntie Larjey says Auntie Edem is too krifeh. She cannot understand what happened to the Edem she used to know. If Mum knows, she doesn't say. They begin a journey down memory lane in which they struggle to reconcile the old and the new. The leaves that have fallen from the tree that remains. The newly gravelled pathway that covers the old potholes. The Edem that is and the Edem that was. They are unrecognisable from each other.

'Edem was happy-go-lucky, fashion and fun.'
'She used to use my mum's sewing machine to make her clothes, do you remember?'
'Some stylish designs!'
'Always ready for the catwalk!'
'She was the envy of so many girls.'
'Do you remember when she straightened her hair?'
'The way it bounced when she walked?'
'And we would wrap towels on our heads to do the same!'
'Eiii Edem!'
'She liked to party!'
'Who would have guessed Edem would become krifeh like that?'

The idea of Auntie Edem occupying any dance floor for the purpose of entertainment and fun is one that does not match the auntie I have met.

'She had dreams of setting up her own business as a dressmaker.'

'She would have done well. She had the talent.'

Mum looks ruefully into the distance. 'I've heard that she works in the church, is it true?'

'That's what she says, "administrative" work.'

'As for that church of hers—'

'Hmmm.'

Auntie Larjey cannot understand how 'that man who calls himself a Prophet' can live in one of the most expensive areas in Accra while many of his congregants are struggling to buy bread to feed their children.

'Selom, if you see his house, and the cars parked in front of it! Show me which road in Ghana you can use to drive a Ferrari? A yellow one at that!'

'Will it fly over the potholes?'

'Hmmm.'

'So Edem is using her tithe to buy sports cars for her Prophet?'

'That's if they pay her at all.'

Auntie Larjey's prayer is that she does not cross paths with that man, because she cannot be held responsible for the words that will come out of her mouth if she does. And she is doubtful that his bodyguards or whatever they call themselves, in their ill-fitting suits and shiny shoes, will have the strength to restrain her.

TOGBEH

We sit down at the table, where Auntie Larjey thanks God for delivering Mum and me safely to her before she removes cling film, wet with condensation, from the balls of steaming cassava it protects.

'Mmm, banku. My favourite!'
'What else would I make for you?'
'Thank you!'
'Is this size okay, Sika?' Auntie Larjey asks as she places it in my bowl.
'It's a bit big, actually.'
'Don't worry, you will manage.' She takes the lid off a pan of steaming okro soup and mixes it with a large spoon. My mouth waters at the sight of the sliced okro, garden eggs and lightly wilted spinach. At the slimy texture of the green goodness I am sure only a trained palette can appreciate.
'Oh, Auntie Larjey...' I hesitate. 'I'm a pescatarian!'
'A pescatarian? What is the meaning of that? Don't worry, it's chicken!'
She laughs on seeing polite alarm on my face.
'Esi, please bring the other stew! Don't worry, your mum told me. We have prepared for you.

I feel a wave of relief that I am not an unmanageable inconvenience, and that I don't have to forego the delicious food in front of me.

'Sorry, ma,' Esi offers as she brings a smaller bowl of okro soup with mackerel, crab and prawns to the table.

Auntie Larjey takes a separate spoon from Esi which she uses to fill my bowl until the banku is swimming in a pool of stew.

'I'm not going to give you a spoon to eat, so you better use your hands.'

'It tastes better when you eat it with your hands anyway,' Mum says.

Auntie Larjey agrees as she pushes a bowl of soapy water in front of me to wash my hands and a dishcloth to dry them. Even though there is a spoon next to my bowl, I leave it untouched and scoop small morsels of banku and stew to my mouth with my fingers and thumb. Auntie Larjey tells me Esi has prepared a lot, so I will have some more when I have finished what is in my bowl. It is not as much a question as a statement of fact. Feeding: an expression of her love.

'Oh, Selom. Papa has a funeral in Kumasi this weekend, the in-laws of his cousin. Will you come? There will be eligible men there. You think I'm joking?'

'Larjey, are you okay?! Did I tell you that I am looking?'

'There is no harm in looking, Selom!'

Mum looks at Auntie Larjey like she is her favourite crazy person in the world, and Auntie Larjey smiles like she knows it. She says she has told the boys that when they are ready to settle down, 'as in seriously ready', they should tell her. She will take them to these funerals and they will meet some good prospects. She has heard that dating is not easy for young people these days. And having two black sons in the States...

'Selom, sometimes I don't even want them to leave the university campus!'

'The way black men are suffering in that country, eh?'

Mum tells Auntie Larjey that she is brave to let them pursue their education in America, because it is something every mother of every black boy in that country must worry about.

'To carry a child for nine months only to lose them in a matter of seconds to gun violence or police brutality?'

'Hmmm.'

It is a fear Auntie Larjey cannot allow to germinate in her mind. She takes our memories back to the workshop.

'So, how was Pokuase?'

'It was amazing! I had no idea funerals are such big business in Ghana.'

'Oh, they are!'

'We saw so many different types of coffins, didn't we? And the woodworkers are so talented.'

Auntie Larjey's smile conveys her pride that I am seeing my country and a small selection of its offerings. She takes a sip of water before turning her attention to Mum. 'Selom, how was it?'

Mum is savouring food that her hands for once have not prepared. 'Oh, it was nice.'

Auntie Larjey looks at her hungrily, her eating paused. 'And Agape? Did you see him?'

'Yes, he was there.'

'And? How was he?'

'He is well. He looks well. He is just as I remember him.'

They hold each other's gaze, hands covered with banku and okro stew, eyes unblinking.

'Heh! Larjey, do you remember Mrs Akufo-Addo? Vida's grandmother?'

'The waakye woman's daughter?'

'Eh heh!'

Auntie Larjey's eyes remain fixed on Mum as Mum turns hers towards me.

'Sika, we had a friend called Vida whose family said they wanted to give her grandmother a dancing trip to her maker. But her mother nearly cancelled the funeral at the last minute!'

Vida's mother had become obsessed with a fear that the dancing pallbearers would drop the coffin carrying the corpse of her late mother, who had died at the age of ninety-two. Not a deliberate act so much as an unfortunate misstep, an unannounced pothole, an inaccurately timed dance move, a stray dog.

Auntie Larjey takes over narration of the story to finish what Mum has started.

'What if they dropped it between the foundations of a new building and the abandoned structure of an old one, the coffin on the ground swinging open on its hinges?'

'Eiii Larjey!!! You don't want us to sleep tonight, eh?'

'With "Sweet Mother" playing through the sound system and the MC accompanying with his commentary, "Ago! Ago!"'

'What type of risk is that? I mean, how would you recover after such a thing?'

I succumb to her comedy because it is irresistible. By the time my laughter has quietened, Auntie Larjey has returned her focus to Mum.

'Okay, so?'

'So, what?' Mum is distracted by the task of chewing a bone that has long lost its meat. Sucking the marrow in a way I could never.

'Ah, Selom! Agape? Is that all?'

'He is coming to the party.'

'Eh heh?'

'Larjey…'

I know I am on the periphery then. When they look each other squarely in the eyes and communicate without words. On the outside of some unspoken thing, between friends. A part of Mum's life before I was in it. I want to journey with her back in time. I want to know.

'So, Sika, what is his name?' Auntie Larjey pivots so smoothly and expertly that she can leave the listener in the wake of her footsteps.

'Who?'

'Your boyfriend. Do you have one? What is his name?' She allows no time for the recovery of breath. 'Oh, are you shy?'

The questions land on me at pace.

'Is it time to plan the knocking ceremony? Are his people bringing kola nuts? Can they pay the bride price?'

'Auntie Larjey!' I am struggling to chew and conceal the food in my mouth. 'I don't have a boyfriend!'

'Oh! How?!'

'This Sika who is always working!'

'Oh! Is that so?'

'Day and night. Ask her if she sleeps.'

'I've been working long hours recently, but it won't always be like that.'

'And weekends. She works weekends too.'

'Oh Sika, what kind of life is that?'

For this bit, Mum feels the need to move to Ga. 'Have you seen that film, what is it called?' She snaps her fingers in quick succession as if the act will help her to recall the title.

I won't help her. I won't give her the weapon for the assault.

'*The Devil Wears Prada*.'

Auntie Larjey says she has seen it. And even though she hasn't, I know the insult will land.

'That is her boss. Caitlyn McSomebody.'

'Leh leh?'

'But no Prada! Enu shi shi?'

'Mum, that's harsh!'

Through utterances of disdain, disgust and everything in between, Auntie Larjey confirms that she knows exactly the type of character Mum is describing. That she has no tolerance of, or patience for, them. And that if she found herself alone in a boardroom with this Caitlyn McSomebody, she would give her a real piece of her mind. Oh, she would give it to her! And tell her where she can go to find some real Gucci to wear, or Prada, or whatever it is! She looks to me for embellishment.

'Mum, you're exaggerating! She's not that bad. She just has high standards.'

They are riding high on the waves of injustice on my behalf, but not at my request. I don't think they can even hear me.

'Marketing Executive, Melon Marketing,' Mum says to conclude her closing speech.

'Permission to advise?'

'Permission granted.'

Auntie Larjey is delighted that I have learned the response to the call and that I am putting it to effective use.

'Always make time for love, okay?'

'Eiii, Lady Justice or Cupid's messenger?'

'Don't mind your mum. I will aim my arrow at her next!'

'Larjey, leave me alone!'

'Make time for love and the people you love, okay?'

'Okay, Auntie. I will.'

She moves again, same leg, different direction.

'Anyway, there is fresh bofrot waiting for you.'
'Oh, I love bofrot!'
'The togbeh type. Do you know the meaning of togbeh?'
I do not.
'Goats' balls,' they answer in unison. 'You can have that with the tea you wanted to drink when you got here.'

ESPRESSO MARTINIS

Mum insists I tell Auntie Larjey what Caitlyn did to ruin my plans for her birthday last year. Auntie Larjey sits forward in her seat, ready to listen. Outrage already at the front of her mind and dissent on the tip of her tongue.

Sika, Vignette want to bring their launch date forward by two weeks. We've got a shit ton of work to do. Can you come over so we can work out the strategy? I want to give them an update tomorrow.

'Hi Caitlyn, I'm outside, but it looks like there's no one here.'

'You're outside?'

'Yes, but the door is locked and the lights are off. I don't have my key—'

'I can't see you— Oh my God! Did you go to the office, Sika? I meant come over to mine, silly! Do you think you can make it in the next half-hour?'

The sense of triumph I felt at answering Caitlyn's call at 7.36 a.m. on a Sunday, and leaving the house in record time, quickly vanishes. 'Oh, I didn't realise you meant…I don't have your…Can I grab your address, please?' There had been nothing in Caitlyn's message to suggest that 'come over' meant to her house and not the office.

Weekend engineering works conspire against me and I find myself on a rail replacement bus service with a driver who does not understand the relationship between speed, distance and time. I retrace my steps at a snail's pace. It is not a good start to the day. I don't want Caitlyn to think I am like those people who don't know how to keep time. The ones you have to tell to arrive at 11 a.m. if you want them to come for 1 p.m. Or those who bring uninvited guests to an event that is 'invitation only'. I know there is no place for Tupperware at an event described as 'silver service'.

'I'm not going to a function to wait for three hours before it starts,' Mum would say whenever she was asked.

Turning down invitations to attend birthday parties of old friends from Ghana, who, like her, have made London their home. Missing her twenty-five-year secondary school reunion, an event she claimed was as hotly anticipated by some as it would be anticlimactic. She does not need to dress up to eat baked beans and sardines in a salad of any kind. And she does not even know if she would describe those people as her real friends, not like Larjey.

I am in a liminal space somewhere between the adrenaline that working with a force like Caitlyn induces and the state of fatigue that comes with learning what it is to create showstopping marketing campaigns. To propel small businesses from obscurity to international recognition. To send sales skyrocketing as a result.

I hesitate at the front door between the knocker and video doorbell to announce my arrival an hour and twenty minutes later. Sweat gathers in the pits of my arms. I can't remember if I have worn deodorant. I lower my head to my right armpit as the sound of footsteps nears the door. I think I'm okay.

Caitlyn appears before the bell has finished its melody and reveals a smile so glorious it betrays the urgency of her early-morning phone call.

'Sika, hi! I wasn't sure if you were still coming!'

I didn't know I had a choice. Behind the front door is a hallway of black-and-white diamond-shaped floor tiles. They are large in size and imposing in effect. Her smile and the effect of the checked pattern is enticing, hypnotising even. She protests when I bend down to take off my sandals in the hall.

'Oh gosh, don't worry! There's no need!'

Her gold bracelets jangle against an expensive-looking watch. It is the protestation of a house owner unburdened with the responsibility of house cleaning. It isn't as much a luxury as it is a necessity. She is too busy and her house too big for her to add that burden to her load. And why should she? She can afford a cleaner.

I am not comfortable with the idea of wearing shoes inside. That is not Mum's vibe. She does not want the soles of shoes that have stepped on streets littered with rubbish and saliva and God Knows What Else stepping inside her home, no thank you. I catch my reflection in a gold-framed mirror above the hallway table and rearrange my sleeve to cover my bra strap. I follow her inside, my sandals padding softly against the polished tiles. The hallway is immaculate.

I am flustered by the mix-up of the morning. It shows in the curve of my shoulders and the arch of my back. I am tired and sleep-deprived. I am not the best version of myself. Caitlyn looks as she does every day: perfectly put-together. She makes her way across the hallway in black, fur-lined mules. Gucci, I think. If they are her house slippers, who needs outdoor shoes? The house is silent but for the sound of leather softly slapping against the soles of her feet. It provides a gentle percussion to her walk.

The hallway leads to large reception rooms on the left and right. I spy dark wall colours, gold accents and neon-coloured artwork. I can see, from her exposed heels, that the bottom of Caitlyn's feet are as soft as a baby's. I imagine her toenails to be painted a devilish red.

In the kitchen, there is a dark-grey island the size of Tortola topped with marble and a fruit bowl dedicated to lemons. Three brass nests cocooning bulbs of light are suspended from the ceiling. To the right, there is a stove which thinks itself capable of heating food without the use of a naked flame. It does not look like it is often used. Floor-to-ceiling doors open out onto a large garden with the type of patio and rattan garden set you see in interior design magazines. There is a swimming pool surrounded by trees of vibrant green and colourful plants. The trees look newly planted, befitting the modern home they adorn. I want to stand barefoot on the grass; to feel the blades between my toes. To relax.

I try my best to maintain eye contact with Caitlyn. She moves around the kitchen in an elegant frenzy: from the island to the cupboard, the fridge to the fruit bowl, and back again. In her moments of stillness – which are brief – she looks at me with the intensity of a puppy. Her eyes are big and beautiful; they make me want to dream. Her hands move around the island and kitchen counter at pace. But nothing is ever disturbed. Nothing is moved. Nothing is out of place.

I try to absorb the details of her home. It is a showcase of what a house looks like when its occupant's dreams come true. It houses things that may be wanted but are not needed, a mixture of extravagance and excess. I look and look but no matter how hard I try, I cannot see any kind of kettle to make the cup of coffee I so desperately need to be holding in my hand. The hit that will help focus my mind and eyes on the task at hand. The adrenaline that carried me from my bed to Caitlyn's front door at unnatural speed is wearing off, and my body aches for caffeine. I scan the kitchen for a stainless steel, copper or cast-iron contraption capable of boiling water. Nothing. Caitlyn offers me gin and tonic, prosecco and access to her wine fridge.

'I'd love a coffee, if that's okay?'

'A coffee? Sika, you can do better than that!'

I settle for an espresso martini on principle and in hope. We cheers to Melon Marketing and the 'dream team' we are.

'Should I grab my laptop so we can make a start?'

'Sure! Let's finish our drinks and have some lunch before we get stuck in though, shall we?'

'Okay…'

Caitlyn is making a lamb tagine with ras el hanout. I don't know what that is or how long it will take to cook. She suggests a vegetarian alternative of aubergine and lentils. Lentils make me bloat. I need to say this out loud but do not. Meal prep has not yet begun. She selects a steel cutting knife to chop butternut squash and celeriac into wedges. It is so large compared to the vegetables it is going to chop, and so shiny, I can barely take my eyes off it. They oscillate between the knife and the clock. It is not yet midday. If we can work and eat – or cook, work and eat – I can head straight to the theatre from Caitlyn's and meet Mum there.

The recipe Caitlyn is following makes her think of her time in Morocco, she tells me.

'Have you been?'

'No.'

'The souks are just out of this world, Sika. Absolutely amazing!'

She struggles to recall the name of her tour guide, was it Nadim or Nabil? What he didn't know about Marrakech was simply not worth knowing. Her only wish is that he had warned her about the early-morning call to prayer which had her certain, at 4.45 a.m. the morning after she arrived, that she was late for work. The idea of waking up before sunrise to pray every day had Caitlyn convinced that Moroccans share the same devotion to prayer as her Pilates class to core strength: unshakeable.

The recipe directs that the blitzing of coriander, lemon zest and green chilli should come together in a vivid green paste, about which Caitlyn asks my opinion.

'Looks good to me.'

She decides that an extra ten seconds is needed to blend the mixture to perfection, before clothing her hands in gloves to handle the lamb. Caitlyn does not enjoy touching raw meat. I do not enjoy watching her effort. She likes to keep her protein sources varied. She says that this is important, and that I should do the same. She talks like someone who has been limited to her own company all morning. A person who suffers the solitude of a large house outside office hours and needs to purge herself of it. A person who has it all and yet is still searching. Her engagement ring is brilliant under its cover of latex.

'Right, we need to slow-cook the lamb.' I can't tell whether she is talking to me or herself.

'Okay...Just to let you know...It's just...I'm taking my mum out for her birthday this evening, so as long as I can make it to town for 7 p.m., that would be perfect.'

'No problemo!' Caitlyn says.

Her reassurance allows me to relax.

Slow-cook. The lamb cooks so slowly in its cast-iron dish that by the time we sit down to eat it is almost 2 p.m. And we are no closer to starting on the pitch. I am relieved when Caitlyn asks, 'How does another espresso martini sound?'

It is not as effective as a double espresso, but it makes me less conscious of the time and my hunger. Or the fact that I am not with Mum on her birthday. It holds my guilt at bay.

'It sounds great, thank you.'

I got home after 10 p.m., the tickets to the Tina Turner musical wasted. Mum did not want to go without me, despite my pleas on WhatsApp for her to take a friend. She was up in bed reading, hair tied and ready to sleep, when I knocked on her bedroom door.

'I'm so sorry, Mum.' My voice caught on tears that took me by surprise. 'I was really looking forward to spending the day with you.'

'It's okay, Sika. Don't worry.'

The tears ran slowly down my cheeks and wet my lips with the taste of salt. 'There was nothing I could do.' I say it knowing that the fear of falling foul of Caitlyn's favour stopped me from putting Mum first. I am plagued by thoughts of the shoulda woulda coulda kind. Sure, I understand that work isn't done until it's done, but it would have been done about three hours ago if I didn't have to watch you slow-roast a lamb before we could make a start!

'It's okay, Chou Chou. It's okay.'

The look on her face made my insides ache with guilt.

'Oh! So you didn't get to see the Tina Turner show?'

'No,' Mum laments.

'Sika wasted her money on the tickets for nothing.' Auntie Larjey kisses her teeth for longer than I thought possible. When I think she is coming to the end, because she will soon need to draw breath, she holds it for longer still. 'What nonsense!' she says, cutting her eye at the idea of Caitlyn flexing her muscles of authority in that way. 'Because she has nothing to do on a Sunday, she thinks you must suffer with her?'

'And pay out of her own pocket to go on weekend team building trips, Tough Mud or whatever it's called,' Mum adds.

It confirms the idea Auntie Larjey had already started to form about Caitlyn: she doesn't think about others as much as she thinks about herself.

'There is more to life than work and Prada, Sika. Don't let anyone convince you otherwise.'

TOUGH MUDDER

'I don't know where to start, Julian. It's like something out of *Grand Designs*. Her office is at least the size of the boardroom. The light – well, it's not a single light, it's like a galaxy of spotlights suspended from this gold fixture with nine bulbs—'

'Urgh, it sounds grotesque!'

'I mean, it is excessive.'

Julian is grateful that Caitlyn has never asked him to make his way from east London to north under the guise of working on a Sunday.

'I don't know what I'd say to her. I've got better things to do with my time than watch her play *MasterChef*. Where was Mr Caitlyn?!'

'No idea. Playing tennis?'

'All day? Playing for peace of mind, more like!'

We are enjoying freshly pressed coffee before the office comes to life and the chaos of the day begins. Early birds.

An email from Caitlyn with the subject line *Team Melon Does Tough Mudder* flashes simultaneously into our inboxes. A link leads to a website that showcases people with highly sculpted bodies which they are clearly committed to maintaining. They look like people who train for triathlons every quarter and restrict their carbohydrate intake with impressive discipline. Like those who spend at least one evening every week with a local cycling club and run a distance of eight miles to work and back the other days.

'I don't get it. Does she want us to do that?!'

'I bet they can do hardcore cardio and speak at the same time. They are so out of my league!'

'Oh my God, she made me watch her do a Peloton session while the lamb was in the slow cooker!'

'Is that a joke?! Firstly, do you know how much those things cost? Secondly, what the actual—'

'"It's about encouraging the permanence of endorphins in your body, Sika."'

Like a compass, the cushioned seat of her Peloton bike indicated the city of London via her manicured garden. I struggled to picture her in rubber gardening shoes, secateurs in hand in lieu of designer athleisure wear and neon orange 'can't miss me if you try' trainers.

'The garden was giving South Beach vibes.'

'She obviously pays someone to maintain it.'

'Obviously!'

'Obviously.'

'She says I should come over so we can train together. That we can take turns on the Peloton. Can you imagine?'

'Excuse me while I sweat like a bitch and prepare a pitch for you at the same time? As if!'

I am processing the image when an email notification from Tristan Clarke flashes up on my screen. He has finally decided, after changing his mind eight times, that the original font for the word 'classic' is 'the one'. I suppress the urge to write *Are you effing kidding me?* and take a deep breath before pressing Send on a one-liner: *Brilliant choice, Tristan!*

I scroll back to Caitlyn's Tough Mudder email. She has signed everyone up: the creative, account management and strategy teams. The website sells the experience as 'a team-building opportunity' which boasts 'world-class obstacles'.

'What does it actually entail? Are we talking *World's Strongest Man* or a *Crystal Maze*-type thing?'

'I have no idea.'

The obstacles have names like 'Electroshock Therapy', 'Arctic Enema' and 'Block Ness Monster'. Julian's forehead creases as I read from the website. He is quite comfortable tap-tap-tapping into the office in the cleats and Lycra uniform of a cycling enthusiast with all the gear and no idea. But at the likening of an obstacle course to stool evacuation at freezing temperatures he draws a line: 'Count me out!' He stands beside me as we examine Caitlyn's email. It is capitalised in places that don't require emphasis and bold in others that are immaterial. Understanding it is perhaps part of the challenge.

team melon does toughMUDDER!!!!!! NO EXCUSES!!!!!!

Caitlyn avoids the use of certain words. If she is talking about an event and says 'Let's represent Team Melon!' we know attendance is mandatory. 'I know I can count on you guys' means we have to be there. 'The Agency are going to have people there' means Melon must too. She will rarely say 'you must come' or 'you have to be there'. But you need to know there is a subtext beneath everything she says. Her subtlety is part of her success. We reread the buzzwords in the email: 'teamwork makes the dream work' and 'let's kick ass!' We know from the way the email is worded that participation in Tough Mudder is mandatory.

The people on the website are covered from head to toe in mud. Their experience looks analogous to pigs rolling in shit. They are not just caked in mud, they are smiling about it. Brilliant Colgate smiles like they have won the Game of Life. They are wearing headbands and French plaits and smiling while standing thigh-deep in bog water. They are wading through it in their trainers.

'Why would anybody waste a good pair of trainers like that?!'

The smile seems contagious. It's the kind of smile you see from people who dodge a parking ticket or finish work early on a Friday. Their colleagues are cheering them on at the sidelines.

There are testimonials from previous participants:

Tough Mudder will challenge you physically and mentally in ways you have never been challenged before.

'Is that something I want or need in my life though?'

Get ready to go to the brink of human capability!!!

'Is that really necessary?' Julian asks.

The participation pack includes headbands, a T-shirt and a celebratory drink. A photograph suggests that at the end of the obstacle course there is some sort of shower orgy from which everyone emerges with clean skin, wet hair and unravelled braids.

'Christ, it's £120 a person!'

'£120?!!'

Caitlyn asks us to transfer funds to the company account by the end of the week.

We think about the excuses we could make to justify our absence. Whether a case of hypothermia in June would be believable. Perhaps pneumonia would be more appropriate? If a sprained ankle could heal over the course of a weekend, putting us out of action for Tough Mudder but back in the office for Monday morning?

'I bet you can't get to Ghana quick enough!' Julian says.

I have counted down the months, weeks, hours and days.

'Two weeks away from this madness. I'm so jealous!'

'I just hope two weeks gives me enough time.'
'I hope so too.'
'Have you tried to broach the subject with your mum again: Project Reset and Retry?'
'I've tried, but she just shuts it down.'

Mum says that Dad's family treated her with such contempt before she left Ghana that she does not know which of them she could ask to sit down and talk upon her return. That if they could not show compassion to her then, when she was a new mother and recently widowed, what kindness would they show her now? That if they could see a newborn baby, the child of their son and brother, and not do everything in their power to love and protect me as one of their own, what could they offer me as an adult? They have done nothing to be a part of our lives in twenty-seven years. So it is not us who will go to them, cap in hand, begging for their hearts.

'She's not having it, Jules. She won't entertain the idea that things might be different now. That they might have been blinded by grief and unable to see beyond it. Or that they might want to move forward. I think I'm going to have to find a way to do it without her. I don't think I have any other choice.'

'Sounds like you've got your work cut out. But it's got to be worth a shot. I'll be cheering you on, you know that, don't you?'

'Thanks, Julian, that means a lot.'

'Whatever you do, please don't waste time thinking about Melon. Work can wait. Your inner peace cannot.'

He names the thing that represents finally understanding why the shape of my nose is so different to Mum's. The genetic coding that gave me front teeth without her distinctive gap. The person responsible for half my features: my narrow feet, my belly button, the shape of my hands. Do I have aunties and cousins who are flat-chested and rectangle-shaped like me? Are they left-handed too? Inner peace. I want to meet it. To know it. And to hold it close.

'I'm so excited for you, Sika!'

'I'm really excited too!'

I am also stuck on the worry of what I am going to do with my hair for Tough Mudder. Mud and water? Said no black girl ever.

GYE NYAME

The soporific effects of lunch have taken hold and I need to lie down. Auntie Larjey opens the door to a large room. In the centre is a four-poster bed protected by mosquito netting. It would be perfect for a girl child. But Auntie Larjey doesn't have a daughter; she is a mother to two boys. From a table next to the bed, she picks up a remote and presses a button which causes the air conditioning unit to let out a gentle hum as it starts to circulate cool air. Auntie Larjey's voice is like mood music, intentionally soft and gentle.

'These buttons control the temperature, okay? Don't worry, there are no mosquitoes in here. Do you want to bathe before you lie down?'

I do. She opens another door to reveal an en-suite bathroom. Fresh white towels hang in readiness. She points out a toothbrush in its packaging and a tube of unopened toothpaste. A dressing gown hangs on the back of the bathroom door. She opens a cabinet to show me body cream, deodorant, powder.

'What else do you need? There are sanitary towels in here if you need them. I stopped using them a long time ago.'

She opens a cupboard to show me the selection. I don't have the heart to tell her that I wear tampons and that I've been thinking about switching to a menstrual cup. I smile at her smile. She shows me how to operate the shower. Or would I prefer a bath?

'A shower is perfect; thank you, Auntie.'

'Okay, rest. I'll be downstairs when you wake up. Uncle Papa will be home soon. He will be so happy to see you.'

The bed is made from beautiful dark wood. Its white bedding harmonises with the room, which has a calming simplicity to it. Auntie Larjey opens the door quietly to let herself out, as if I am already fast asleep. I have just let my hair down from the top of my head when I remember.

'Oh, Auntie, do you have Wi-Fi?'

It has not been as easy to switch off from work as I wanted it to be. And I have realised that being online, being connected, being reachable, is as much a physical act as it is a mental one. Like cigarettes to a smoker, it is as much about the nicotine as it is the physical act of holding the white stick between the index and third fingers, raising it to the mouth and taking a drag before exhaling. It is seeing the flash, hearing the beep, feeling the vibration. It is about knowing what is happening, when it is happening and not after the event. It is about being connected. In Ghana, I know I have not been. The nature of the internet connection has made that a challenge outside my control.

'Of course!'

In *Settings*, she shows me which of the four Wi-Fi options is hers.

'GyeNyame, all one word, capital G, capital N,' she tells me when the password prompt appears. 'You know what it means, don't you?'

'Receive God?'

'Yes, that is the literal meaning. The expression means: Except for God. It reminds us that God is omnipotent, omnipresent and omniscient.' She points to the decorative carved stool in the corner of the room. 'That's Gye Nyame.'

'I've seen that symbol in so many places.'

'Yes, it's the most well known of the Adinkra symbols. I will show you some more after your nap.' She throws her contagious smile and I catch it. 'Rest well, okay? You are at home.'

'I will. Thank you, Auntie.'

Before she shuts the door, I need to ask her one more thing. It is something I have tried to ask Mum. Something, I have realised, that I need to do without her.

'Auntie Larjey, I really want to... While I'm here in Ghana, I was hoping...'

Auntie Larjey stands by, a fairy godmother ready to grant my any and every wish.

'I understand why Mum doesn't want to... Or can't...'

Ready to step into Mum's shoes and fulfil any maternal role she is called for.

'But I really want to try and find...'

'Yes, sweetheart?'

'I really want to meet my family. On my dad's side. My aunties and uncles. My cousins. I don't know where to start. Not without Mum. Will you help me?'

Speaking those words into existence allows me to exhale with the full capacity of my lungs. It causes my muscles to soften and my shoulders to relax. It articulates the dream that has followed me across the Atlantic, and brings me within touching distance of realising it.

'Mum says that Dad's family made it clear that they don't want anything to do with us, but...'

Auntie Larjey pushes the door closed behind her with the palms of both hands. The features of her face straighten in a way I have not yet seen. She is concentrating on my words. Listening intently. I feel relief in the seriousness with which she receives them. That she understands my longing and my need.

'She says that it is not after twenty-seven years that she is going to knock on their door, but I...'

Auntie Larjey moves her hands from the door to her face. The shape of her mouth is concealed behind gold and diamonds. She offers an automated nod from where she stands, her body otherwise still.

'What if they want to move forward? What if they've been looking for me too? What if they don't know where to start? I just want to try, you know?'

'Okay. Okay. Okay,' she says. Whispering. 'Okay. I see. Your dad's family...You want to see them? To...meet them? Okay. Okay. I'll...I'll help you. I'll speak to your mum. Okay?'

I feel gratitude take over my features and tears of relief gather behind my eyes. 'Thank you, Auntie! Thank you, so much.'

She closes the door softly behind her.

I wriggle in the soft sheets of the bed freshly bathed and free of the dust of Pokuase. Propped up with hope and an excessive number of soft pillows, I reach for my phone. I know that the blue light of the screen is supposed to interfere with sleep. Perhaps it is the production of melatonin or the softness of the sheets, the fullness of my stomach or the laziness of my eyelids. Perhaps it is one of those things, or a combination of them all. Maybe it is being away from Melon, and London, and the constant demands on my time. Or because of the bofrot and the sound of Auntie Larjey's voice. Perhaps it is the way she makes me laugh. Or the fact that she is going to help me find Dad's family, that I can no longer fight sleep. I am already drifting. I am already there.

I wake up to a harmony of baritone and soprano laughter. It

dulls the sound of WhatsApps, iMessages and email notifications that illuminate my phone screen and send a familiar jolt of adrenaline flushing through my veins. Waking up in this bed feels so far away from the violence of being pinged awake in the middle of the night by a message miscategorised as urgent that I want to stay here forever. It is an alarm clock of dreams. I open my eyes and stretch, a full-body stretch. I have snoozed two hours away in rest and reverie. I draw back the mosquito net once I have found the opening, and drink from the bottled water on the bedside table. The tiles feel cool against my feet.

I scroll through my inbox and open electronic envelopes. Nothing is urgent and yet everything is. The to-do list awaiting me on my return is growing rapidly.

Caitlyn: *SIKA, JEAN-JACQUES HS INVITEd melon to pitch for Green Gable – in PARIS!!! U cming with!! Ned strtegic plan to revieww by Thrsdy. We gping to Paris!!*

I read the message three times over, my heart leaping between beats.

Me: *Jules, she's asked me to pitch with her for Green Gable in Paris!*

Julian replies with the speed of the faithful: *Get it gurl!!! <3*. And follows with an update of his own: *she's making me go to the Berlin expo with her. you know I love a bit of German sausage but FML. would rather be going with you!* And another: *come back soon, can't cope without you!!!*

We abuse emojis because words are surplus to requirements.

Jules: *How is Ghana?*
Me: *Hot but amazing!*
Jules: *Project RnR update please?*
Me: *Auntie Larjey is going to help me find them! x*
Hope flutters in me like the wings of a phoenix.

JULIAN

Julian, was two years old when he appeared at his mother's bedside with a cluster of nuts and bolts in his hand. He wore cartoon pyjamas and a smile of accomplishment on his face. It was before sunrise.

Mandy opened her eyes to see her sweet boy standing at her bedside staring at her with big hazel eyes, loose blonde curls framing his face. The prize in his hand and his pride in showing her. He had undone the nuts and bolts of his cot and let himself out because he was patient and because he could.

As patient as he is, there are things Julian does not have time for, that he cannot stand. What is completely unacceptable to him, and beyond the limit of his tolerance, is for Caitlyn to call him into her office under the pretext of urgency, only for her to ask him to look through options for a summer house. Not when he is about to leave work for the day. Not ever.

'Sika, I couldn't give a flying fuck!'

Oblivious as he sat beside her. Eyes glazed. Toe tapping. Late for his date and simmering with anger while the threat of retribution kept him in place. To excuse himself would have carried a sentence disproportionate to the crime: the denial of career-building work opportunities. She would make him pay.

'So I cancelled.'

'Oh no! You didn't meet him?'

'Nope. I couldn't turn up forty minutes late! What kind of first impression would that make? "Sorry, I had to help my boss choose the wood panelling for her summer house..."'

'Yeah, that sucks.'

'It's not great for a first date, is it?'

'It's not, but you can reschedule. Remember, if it's for you it won't go by you. Isn't that what Mandy says?'

'Does Mandy know I haven't had a shag in eighteen months? Does she?!'

'I hope not, Jules. For your sake and hers.'

'But seriously, how am I ever going to meet someone when I'm in a relationship of servitude with my boss?'

'What do you mean? It sounds so attractive! A man in control of his life. What's not to love?'

'Urgh. I actually had a good feeling about this one.'

'What's his name?'

'Fred.'

Speaking the words out loud causes us to realise how absurd our lives have become through working for Caitlyn. We don't know whether to laugh or cry.

'I'd love to come, but I have to watch my boss peel a carrot.'

'If I didn't have to count the hair follicles on my boss's upper lip, I'd be there...'

'Sounds great, but I have to navigate my way out of my boss's arse without the benefit of a compass, so I'm otherwise engaged.'

Julian is my work husband. We started at Melon within a week of each other and are bound in a way that colleagues who share an office space, work together and keep each other sane can be. Our working days are not nine to five. They can be eight to six. They can be nine to nine depending on the client and the campaign. But Julian is more than a colleague, he is a constant in my life. We have seen marketing graduates come and go. They arrive bright-eyed, bushy-tailed and confident. By week two they are crestfallen and uncertain. They have failed to understand the way Caitlyn works. That she relies on your ability to read her mind and deliver what she has not yet asked for.

'Can you think more outside. And bigger box?'

That she might ask you to do something specific for a client and then change her mind once you have dedicated an entire day to doing it. That you have to be reactive, because she asks you to do things urgently and gives you an impossible turnaround time. That you will lose a night of sleep doing exactly what she has asked, only for her to ignore the work you produce. That something even more 'urgent' will crop up that will require you to repeat tasks at a significant cost to the client. And with no less enthusiasm. They don't understand that at times there is no logic to the workings of Caitlyn's mind: you just have to get it. And get on with it.

'How about less flesh, more backbone?'

It means running on adrenaline with little respite. Not everyone can do that; most people can't. Not as a way of life. And if that's the case, they can't succeed at Melon. Because Melon and Caitlyn are one and the same, synonymous and indivisible. Julian's laughter sustains me, and mine, him. That's how we are able to breathe life into her vision. But it requires determination and intentional decision-making on our part. It means living to work, because the reward fills the cup from which we drink. It means that one day I can have my own portfolio of clients, and market products I really care about. Ethically sourced products, like cocoa beans from Ghana. I can work with cocoa farmers and give something back to their communities. I can have my own business and honour Dad's memory in the process. I can continue his legacy. I can make him proud.

'How is Mandy? We're due a coffee date soon, no?'

'I don't think Mandy needs any more caffeine, do you?'

Julian worries that I confuse his mum's chaos for enthusiasm. He does not recognise, it seems, that they are two peas in the very same pod.

'Oh God, I agreed to go shopping with her on Saturday. "A few things for my holiday." Is it ever? Absolutely lost her mind in TK Maxx. So I thought I'd do myself a favour and take a walk, maybe see if I could get a haircut. Did I mention we were in Brixton? Well, we were. So I didn't have to go far before I came across a black barber's. And I'm thinking, if you can cut an Afro, you can cut this, can't you?' He runs his hands through his hair, disturbing loose curls held with wax. His hair, once blonde, has evolved to a light brown that matches his hazel eyes.

'Brixton? That's a long way from Hackney!'

'Don't I know it! And I mean, going to the barbers can be intimidating at the best of times. But Sika, I'm a man in charge of my life, right? So I walk in. There are about five men in chairs, chatting away as they're getting cut. A little boy in some kind of toy car designed to make the experience less terrifying. There's a football game playing on the wall-mounted TV. You've got capes flying, clippers buzzing, hair falling. There's a whole vibe, right—'

'Where's this going, Jules?'

'Patience, Sika. So I've walked in and I'm standing at the door, waiting as you do for somebody to acknowledge the fact that you exist. I'm waiting long enough for Crystal Palace to score a goal. Three-quarters of the barber shop pause to celebrate and watch the replay. There's the commentary, on- and off-screen. And there I am, still waiting. It's only when play is resumed that the guy who looks like he's in charge stops the fade he's working on, looks at me and asks, "Can I help you?" At this point I'm wondering what's so wrong with TK Maxx that I couldn't have just stayed there. They do good toiletries and a nice sports range. I could even have browsed the kitchenware. I could, quite frankly, just have kept Mum company. Asked her about her holiday plans. Why she needs to top up her fake tan before she goes. Anything. But I needed a trim, didn't I? So I ask him, "Can I have a quick trim?" Sika, on Mandy's life. He looks me up and down, straight in the eye, and says, "Sorry, we're closed."'

'What? No!'

'On Mandy's life! He looks me straight in the eye, and that's what he says.'

'No!'

'And obviously I'm much better value than the football match at this stage, aren't I?'

'Wait – because you're white?'

'Well, it's not because I'm bald, is it?!'

'Oh my God. Julian, stop! I feel bad for your soul! What did you do?'

'What did I do? Sika, I said, "Thanks mate, no worries." Called Mandy and asked if she wanted to have a look in Morleys afterwards.'

It's always laughter. That's where we end up. At a place of breath-defying laughter from which we struggle to return.

UNCLE PAPA

I head in the direction of the laughter drifting upwards, past the spiral staircase and into my room. My appearance at the living room door causes a pause of thought, gestures and conversation. It is celebrated as a long-awaited event.

'Sika, did you sleep well?'

I scan the room for Auntie Larjey, whose enquiring voice calls me to her. But it is Uncle Papa who my eyes find first. He is wearing a dark-green trouser and shirt set, perfectly pressed, and trendy leather sandals. His arms are outstretched. 'Hello, sweetheart! Welcome to Ghana! How are you?'

Uncle Papa's smile could make a grieving man forget his loss. It reveals itself despite, and through, his neatly trimmed beard, which is speckled with silver disguised as grey. It radiates across his face and shines through his eyes. It draws you to him like a warming fire on a cold winter's day. And makes you smile from the inside out.

'Sika, do you know that Uncle Papa was supposed to be in an important meeting this afternoon?'

'I told them to finish fast fast because I had a visit from some important dignitaries: an international delegation from the UK! Well, it's true, isn't it?'

When Uncle Papa is sitting in an air-conditioned office on a swivel chair with a high back, I imagine there is nothing he can ask for that he would be denied. At home, it is Auntie

Larjey who wears the trousers, Uncle Papa happily acquiescing to her directions. I note the way they share sentences, or rather how she completes his. How he trusts her to do so. Instinctively and intuitively.

I fall into his embrace. It is a warm embrace. A loving one. An embrace that smells of amber and oud and cedarwood, musky and masculine, like a dad. It feels safe here. It feels like home. His beard grazes the top of my head and with a firm but gentle touch, one that communicates love and protection, he pats me on my back like you would a baby. I am soothed this way, by the rhythm and his touch. The moving parts of my chest are stilled. In this moment, I wish he was my dad and that I was his daughter. Love could keep me here forever and a day. But the guilt of betraying Dad brings me back to myself.

'Didn't I say she was beautiful?'

'She is. The spitting image of her mother!'

He speaks softly and gently. Everyone is smiling: Mum, Auntie Larjey, Uncle Papa. There is a familiarity between the three of them that goes back to a place in time when I did not exist. But I am also part of them, their love for me heavy like a weighted blanket.

'Your cousins will be excited to meet you. Larjey, have you spoken to the boys?'

It is a rhetorical question, because there is not a day that goes by when Auntie Larjey does not speak to her sons. Whether they call her or she them.

'Yes, they are fine. They are excited to come home. We are just counting down the days now. To have all our three children home under one roof. That is what we have longed for all these years.'

Mum's hand finds Auntie Larjey's and squeezes it. Auntie Larjey holds her chest and tells us that her heart is full.

From the cocoon of Uncle Papa's embrace, I reach for my ankle, which is hot and itchy.

'Sika, what is it? Have you been bitten?'

'I think I was, earlier today.'

An alarm registers on Auntie Larjey's face that causes her to hitch her boubou at the knee, stand abruptly, and walk towards me with purpose and haste.

'Bitten? In this house?'

She is on the floor, level with my ankle, telling me to put my foot on her lap so she can take a proper look.

'I'm not sure where. It might have been at Auntie Edem's, or in Pokuase.'

'Esi! Es-iiiiii!!!'

She cannot see properly without her glasses. Uncle Papa has his, which she asks him to give her. They are not the same prescription, but this is apparently an irrelevant detail.

'Esi!'

'Auntie, it's fine, honestly.'

'Are there mosquitoes in this house?' Mum asks from her seat.

I look up to realise that Auntie Larjey, Uncle Papa and Mum have established a Mosquito Inquiry for my benefit at the same time as I notice the two men sitting opposite us.

'Sorry, Sika. Let me introduce you. This is Uncle Sammy,' Uncle Papa offers.

'Welcome to Ghana.'

The Mosquito Inquiry disbands while Auntie Larjey goes in search of a miraculous anti-itch cream that she swears by and Uncle Papa swaps one pair of glasses for another.

'Hello, nice to meet you.'

'You've been bitten?' Uncle Sammy asks, seeking to contribute his own findings to the Inquiry.

'It's fine. I'm fine. Thank you.' I offer my hand and surprise

Uncle Sammy, and myself, when I click my third finger and thumb against his in the customary handshake that identifies one Ghanaian to another. He returns the greeting with a generous laugh.

'Sika, Uncle Sammy is an ecologist. He is developing an ecolodge in Ada and we are exploring opportunities to work together. I'm considering what we can do to bring environmental consciousness to some of my developments.'

'That sounds really interesting. I'd love to learn more about it.'

It has not been lost on me that as we have crossed the motorway linking Tema and Accra, or driven through the back streets that lead to Auntie Edem's house, I have seen piles of burning rubbish on sideroads, their fumes burning into and confusing the daylight. That although we have sipped from innumerable bottles of water, there has been nowhere to recycle them and no chance to reuse them before they are thrown out with general household waste. It has not escaped me that plastic bags are used without restriction. That there is no 20p surcharge that would encourage the use of bags for life. Or that so much could be made of the sunlight gifted in the form of solar energy. It could be transformative. But I am also conscious that I have been in Ghana for five days, and in the grand scheme of understanding how things operate, I know close to nothing.

There is nothing more irritating than the newcomer who steps into a space and starts to critique it without understanding the reason behind its features. Yes, it would be better if the floor was even, but the reason it's not is because of subsidence. And the new owner has not yet had a chance to assess the structural damage caused by the subsidence. The subsidence needs to be assessed before the problem can be addressed. And actually, the owner spent all her money buying the property in the first place. Her husband, the father of her children, said he would help her, but he didn't; he upped and left. No alimony. No nothing. When she realised she could not depend on him, she started to save. She worked and saved worked and saved worked and saved for years to buy it. And she did. She bought the property all by herself. Spent every last penny she had. So, she is going to have to work hard and save some more before she can think about sorting out things like subsidence. And with the current cost of living, that is going to take time.

'Sika, did you know that Ghana is the most proximate country to the centre of the earth?' Uncle Papa asks.

'No – but I'm not sure I know what that means?'

I do know that time is passing quickly, too quickly. Sunrise into sunset and night into day. Here, where longitude zero degrees meets latitude zero degrees.

'The Greenwich Meridian runs through the ocean to the equator, so technically speaking, you are at the centre of the world!'

As Auntie Larjey administers anti-itch cream to my ankle, I wish I could slow it down, that I had more time with Auntie Larjey and Uncle Papa. In this place that feels so wholesome and familiar. In this place that feels like home.

DANSO

The young man next to Uncle Sammy stands to introduce himself. His beard covers a large part of his face and shines with a brilliance that suggests attention to grooming. He sips from a bottle of Coca-Cola while Uncle Papa holds the floor. Until there is an opening, a space for him to fill.

'Hi, I'm Danso.'

He does not wear a generous smile. Or share the effervescence of the other adults, their excitement at my presence. He does not attempt to click my finger with his but offers, instead, a firm handshake. It introduces formality to our exchange.

'Sika.'

'Nice to meet you.'

Spoken with words but not body language. He does not welcome me to Ghana with the enthusiasm to which I have become accustomed, or enquire as to my experience so far. He is tall, and I have to shift my position to make eye contact with him.

There is a moment in which the adults, a number in which I do not count myself, fall silent. Danso does not rush to speak in the way a person who assumes responsibility for another's comfort would. It is not that I think he should go out of his way to make me, a visitor to his country, feel at ease. But his indifference agitates the status quo, the foundation of care everyone else has worked so hard to lay down. The relaxed position of his shoulders and slackness of his hands beside his torso. The loose grip of his phone in his right hand. The interest he displays in the inanimate objects in Auntie Larjey's living room and around me indicates that he is free from discomfort. I follow his lead to land on the photograph of Auntie Larjey and Uncle Papa on their wedding day. We examine it, side by side, opposite the floor-to-ceiling windows that frame the setting sun.

The silence abates when the adults return their gaze to each other and resume their conversation. Talk of politics, the 'old days' and the diaspora animates the space around which Danso and I are stood in a silent vortex. They speak in a mix of Ga, pidgin, Twi, English and whatever else they want. Sounds of agreement and discord appear between skilled code-switching. Every sentence throwing more laughter into the air.

When Danso speaks again, it is after the delivery of an ultimatum by Auntie Larjey to Uncle Papa, the headline of which is: 'Unless you learn to dance salsa!' This elicits a raucous mix of baritone and soprano laughter into which Danso adds, but does not project, his voice.

'Sorry?'

'Sika is a beautiful name.' He speaks with a straight face and neutral expression.

'Oh, thank you.'

Uncle Papa has taken Auntie Larjey by the hand and is manoeuvring her like a mannequin in the middle of the room.

'Isn't this salsa?'

'What type of salsa is this?'

She resists his moves like a rigid doll. This encourages

him to showcase additional dance moves which, although sensational, are unrelated to salsa.

'Selom, have you ever seen salsa like this?'

'Papa, have you been watching *Strictly Come Dancing*?'

Uncle Papa pretends to bite his lip in concentration, and directs Alexa to play salsa music at volume eighteen. 'I've won competitions,' he says.

Auntie Larjey tries, half-heartedly, to free herself from his hold. 'Which competition have you won?!'

'So, you are Ewe?'

'Sorry?'

'Your name, Sika. It's an Ewe name, no?'

'Oh. My mum is Ewe, yes.'

He speaks a little louder this time, to send his voice over the pantomime being performed in front of us. 'Do you want to sit down?'

'Sure.' I would love to be in reaching distance of the snacks on the side table that Esi has set down.

Uncle Papa takes a seat next to Uncle Sammy on the opposite side of the room after a grand finale in which he leans Auntie Larjey so far back it threatens the placement of her wig. 'Papa, don't be silly!' she manages, the hair struggling against gravity.

When Uncle Papa instructs Alexa to play Kojo Antwi, he chooses their song 'All I Need Is You'. The song Mum and Dad used to dance to. I don't know what it will do to Mum to hear it like this, without warning or preparation.

The song forces Mum out of her chair and towards Auntie Larjey with static footsteps and an unsteady gait. I hold my breath until I know Auntie Larjey is close enough to catch her if she falls.

I know all the words to their song.

'So, how long are you here for?'

'Just ten more days.'

I could do with silence again to focus on Mum, to make sure she's okay.

'Oh! Why so brief?'

'I have to get back for work.'

'Ah, okay.'

Sat on the same sofa, it is easier to hear him. And I have a clear view of Mum.

'What do you do for work?'

'I'm in marketing.'

'Oh, nice.'

Auntie Larjey has her by the elbows.

'What about you?'

'I'm working with my dad at the moment.'

A nepo baby. It makes sense.

'Cool.'

But is it? To grow up without having to work for your future? Secured against having to do any real work by the financial security provided by your forefathers. To have no ambition or pursuit of your own?

'Well, my background is in environmental engineering, so it's exciting to be able to put theory into practice.'

I have to lean forward to hear him, because my concentration on Mum is heightened. Her limbs are moving unpredictably. Her body. She is…dancing. Mum is dancing! She and Auntie Larjey are showcasing a catalogue of moves from their younger days. Seeing that Mum is okay allows me to exhale deeply, sit back in the chair and enjoy her dance moves.

'Oh! That sounds interesting.' I'm not sure what it is exactly, but it does sound impressive.

'What are you doing tomorrow?'

'We'll be going back to Tema at some point but I'm not sure when.'

'Oh, okay.'

He turns his attention to his phone and allows silence to fall once more in the small space between us. Mum is fine. She is better than fine with Auntie Larjey by her side. I take the opportunity to eat a handful of achomo from the snack bowl. They are sweet, crunchy and cinnamon-rich. So good. I explore the contents of the bowl while he explores the content on his phone. It beeps and pings with a volume louder than his speaking voice. It is the kind of sound that would grate in a quiet room. The kind of sound that after two minutes would force me to ask, 'Sorry, can you put that on silent, please?'

Uncle Papa looks away from Uncle Sammy and over in my direction. He senses my discomfort. A father can sense things like that. It is his protective instinct at work. I stand up, grateful for him, wishing he had always been there. Present in my life. I am one step closer to him when Danso finds his voice again.

'The daytime is tricky for me, but if you are free in the evening, we could go for dinner tomorrow?' He speaks at the volume of a person who is shouting to be heard over loud music at the very moment the loud music ends. It catches me by surprise. He is standing now, and I have turned to face him.

I haven't so much as opened my mouth to form a sound before Auntie Larjey responds on my behalf: 'She is free!'

Mum's hand is in hers. They are dancing the dance of old Ghanaian ladies everywhere. Their hands closed in gentle fists, their hips swaying to move their lower bodies. They tap their feet at a different beat to their hands but keep a perfect rhythm.

'Pick her up at 7 p.m. She is free!'

MORNING HAS BROKEN

I wake to the sound of nature's alarm clock, a chorus of crickets chirping loudly outside my window. In close proximity, a cockerel announces daybreak every forty seconds. Morning has broken. Praise for the singing and praise for the morning. So announces her voice as Auntie Edem enters my room. She walks towards my bedside table and rests her iPad against the bedside lamp to free her hands. 'Sika, good morning!' she says, arranging and rearranging the bedcovers.

'Good morning, Auntie,' I manage through a yawn.

The Prophet beams through the iPad screen. 'It's a live stream,' Auntie Edem says, in an exaggerated whisper.

I hear in her words thanks for the technology that allows her to reach God via a wireless network. And understand through her early-morning wake-up call a gesture for togetherness. It is 6 a.m.

I sit up against the headboard, a pillow propped against my back. Sunlight streams through the gap between the bottom of the blinds and the windowsill. It does little to convey the impending heat of the day.

Online, the Prophet is dressed in a purple shirt and black trousers. There is a silver 'H' that marks the middle of an expensive-looking belt: 'H' for Hermès. He is flanked by the two Prayer Warriors who strong-armed me. They walk with focus and purpose beside him, sometimes creating with their arms a protective barrier for the Prophet to pass through, like personal bodyguards. So many people want to touch him. Or a piece of his clothing. So many people, and he is just one. Or three. I don't know whether Auntie Edem is connected to God, the Prophet, the Church of Incredible Miracles, or all three. I don't know if there is a distinction. Or whether they represent a trinity of sorts: one and indivisible.

The Prophet stands in front of stacks of paper on which causes for prayer have been written and printed. They contain requests from all over the world. There is no border or sea or man-made obstacle that can defeat the power of the Prophet's prayer. For a contribution of some $10, $15 or $20, worshippers can receive dedicated blessings from the Prophet himself. They type their testimonials in the live chat function on YouTube as he preaches.

'An incredible miracle?'

The contribution does not have to be restricted. Not at all. People donate in the hundreds and even thousands. What is the size of the miracle you are asking God to perform? All credit and debit cards are accepted. Payments can be made by PayPal and Apple Pay. Or even in instalments via the buy now, pay later service of Klarna. There is no logistical barrier to accessing God. Not in the Church of Incredible Miracles.

'I said, an incredible miracle?'

'Is happening right now!'

The Prophet talks at the pitch of a scream, and Auntie Edem responds along with the live-streamers whose responses flash on the screen in quick succession. She sways on her feet, her arms reaching for the ceiling. I wonder if she can lower the volume, just a little bit. But I am reluctant to ask. To break her trance. There is something about the Prophet's voice that moves her but stops me.

The face of a woman from Maryland replaces the Prophet on the screen and reduces him to a rectangle in the top right-hand corner. She is a living embodiment of an incredible miracle that happened in this place. She appears to give her testimonial. To explain that she went to hospital after finding a lump in her breast. The doctors told her she had 'a cancer'. On receipt of this news, she knew that an agent of evil was conspiring against her. She took this to the Prophet and laid her worries at the foot of the cross. The Prophet told the cancer to 'Get away, by fire or by force!' The woman prayed with fervour and devotion to this end. The next time she went to hospital, the doctors told her the cancer had disappeared.

'This is the miracle of God!' the Prophet screams at the story's end. It is indeed extraordinary. So extraordinary that it causes him to jump up and down in his shiny shoes and speak in tongues. The agents of evil who conspired against the lady in Maryland will feel the vengeance of God! He is agitated by a spirit so powerful it moves him across the stage like a Tasmanian devil and causes him to sweat from his temples. No mercy shall be shown!

I am wide awake now. The light blanket I used to sleep is gripped between my closed fists and pulled towards my chest. I want to open the blinds and let the sun's rays into the room, but I don't want to disturb what is happening. I am scared. I cannot lie here for three hours, not like this. Mum would save me before then. She is probably downstairs, on the phone or reading. I'd like to call out for her and to begin my day. Before the sun reaches its zenith and the heat becomes unbearable, I want to escape this room.

Loli appears at the door as Auntie Edem opens a red pouch containing moon-shaped wafers wrapped in cellophane and individual cups of a dark-red liquid in small plastic containers. She hands me one of each.

'Take it. It's communion.'

She places the wafer on her tongue and drinks from the plastic container in one go to finish its contents.

'It's the body and blood of Christ.' She opens closed eyes and speaks encouragingly.

I copy her actions. The red liquid looks like cough mixture but tastes like Vimto. I swallow it like a shot of sambuca. When I open my eyes, she is standing next to the bed, looking at me. Smiling. I try my best to smile back.

Loli has just woken up and is drunk on sleep. My eyes are happy to see her, this and every morning, but particularly right now. She crawls into bed with me and offers a grounding cuddle. I release my grip on the blanket to allow her under. The noise has stopped. Auntie Edem has ended the programme on her iPad and opened the blinds. It is over.

Loli runs her hands over my face and hair and looks deeply into my eyes. My ribcage expands with a deep intake of breath. She reflects my smile to reveal her baby teeth, a perfect set of porcelain, that precious gap between her front teeth. Her eyelashes curl enthusiastically, and I can see from the fullness of her bottom set that she probably inherited them from her dad. Mum, Auntie Edem and I share the unhappy genetics of having no lower eyelashes. It is a feature I do not know how to remedy. I trace the neat partings in Loli's scalp with my finger, which makes her giggle. It is a nice sound after the Prophet's screaming.

'Oh, I f-f-forgot something!'

'Loli, talk properly! Oh!' Without taking her eyes away from her iPad, Auntie Edem issues a correction that is by now familiar. Loli's stammer, a characteristic of her speech that her mother is determined to correct.

I watch Loli crawl out of bed, her eyes trained on the floor, her cartoon pyjama bottoms gathered above her left knee. Her feet are so dinky. They carry her out of the room with an anxious patter. She reappears before long, clutching a doll. It is half-dressed in a dutch wax top with no trousers. She is unfazed by the doll's nudity and carries it by one leg.

'This is my baby.'

'Oh! What's her name?'

'Her name is...'

Loli pauses – she has forgotten something else. I flick through my WhatsApp messages while she goes to retrieve it.

Julian and Fred are in a bar somewhere. They are grinning at the camera with the look of two people who have just received a tax rebate. But it's better than that. I sit bolt upright in my bed. Fred is holding Julian's left hand in front of the camera. On his fourth finger, he is wearing an unapologetically large stack of Haribo rings. Underneath the photograph, the caption reads: *I said YES!!!*

My fingers tap aggressively at the screen. *OMG OMG OMG! WHAT WHEN HOW?!!!!* Trust Julian to get engaged when I am halfway across the world!

Haha! Knew that would get you! ;) We've decided to take the plunge and move in together!

JULIAN!!! My heart was in my mouth!

He is typing when Loli returns clutching her doll and a miniature bottle.

'Is your baby hungry?'

'She wants you to f-f-feed her.'

Auntie Edem is taking her time to fold clothes that I have discarded with reckless abandon around the room.

'Oh, don't worry, Auntie. I'll sort it out when I get up.'

She does not stop.

'Won't you come for breakfast?' she calls when she has tidied to her satisfaction and opens the door to leave.

'Yes, Auntie. Just getting up now.'

I am relieved when she closes the door behind her and I can give my full attention back to Loli.

'Okay, I'll feed her. What is her name?'

'Her name is…Her name is…Sika.'

'Sika? Wow. She has the same name as me!'

Loli smiles her beautiful smile and hands me the baby.

'Hello, baby Sika. Do you want your bottle?'

I feed her for no more than ten seconds before Loli announces that baby Sika is crying.

'Oh no, why is she crying?'

'You have to hold her like this and pat her back f-f-for her.'

She claims her baby with rough love and asks her if she wants to go on my back.

'She wants you to back her.'

'Oh, okay.'

'Where is your cloth? You need your cloth to back her.'

Concern spreads across Loli's face when our eyes dart around the room to no avail.

'I f-f-forgot something.'

In her brief absence, I take another look at Julian and Fred. Julian looks like he has eaten the sun for breakfast. He is beaming from the inside out. He has even cut his hair.

Loli returns with her mum's cloth and, with surprising dexterity for a five-year-old, helps to secure the baby on my back, directing me to fold the cloth above my boobs and at my waist. I am pleased at the result of our joint effort.

Loli smiles. 'She is happy now.'

On the dressing table is Loli's family portrait. It is an impressive effort. We are holding stick hands and smiling broadly, Auntie Edem, Loli, Mum and me. She has given Auntie Edem a ruby-red smile and rosy cheeks that suggests an appreciation for lipstick and make-up she does not have in real life. And made Mum's fashion frames the defining feature of her face. She has even tried to draw, in their smiles, the gap between their teeth. Her attempt at braids has turned me into Medusa, but I am her Medusa according to the title of her picture: 'My Family'.

The picture is as notable for the people missing as it is for those who are present. Do you miss your dad? I wish I could ask her. I miss mine too.

DINNER TOMORROW

Outside, Danso's face is illuminated by the white light of his phone. He is distracted from the screen by the sound of my sandals against the concrete of the courtyard. They are hidden by the wide legs of a halterneck jumpsuit. The gold of my sandals matches the creole earrings I have reclaimed from Mum. As I walk, my hand reaches for the back of my hair to make sure my braids are in place. I touch them more than is necessary in the short space that separates us, and run my tongue against the front of my teeth to remove any lipstick that may have transferred. I am multitasking like the kind of person who wants to make a good impression.

'Hi.'

The soft hair on his arms, exposed by his short-sleeved shirt, brushes my skin as we exchange a kiss, cheek to cheek. Comfortable in the evening heat, he wears jeans with sandals, and on his wrist a black knotted bracelet. Seemingly at ease with silence, he doesn't rush to fill it.

'I'm glad you found the house okay.'

'A friend of mine lives close by, so I had a rough idea of where I was going.'

'Oh good.'

Away from the main road, the quiet is profound. I wish Auntie Larjey were here to fill it with her laughter.

'Okay, well—'

'Are you ready? Shall we go?'

'Sure.'

As we prepare to leave, I question whether it was sensible to wear white. Is it practical? Bridal? Is it too late to change?

'Where did you say we're going?'

'I didn't.'

'Oh. Okay—'

'It's a surprise.'

'Okay.'

'You look beautiful,' he says.

'Thank you.'

He says it is best not to stand outside for too long. The lack of sun, decreased wind and humidity of the evening are ideal for mosquitoes. He has citronella spray in the car in case I need some. It is distilled from lemongrass and acts as a natural repellent.

'And it smells nice.'

'Thank you. I keep getting bitten.'

'Oh, sorry!'

He opens the passenger door and reassures me, before I take a seat, that the interior is clean. In the back seat, I note the hard hat and high-vis jacket he must use for work. He lowers the music that plays as soon as the engine starts and with one hand on the steering wheel pulls away from the kerb. I turn around as he manoeuvres and catch a glimpse of Mum at the gate. She blows a kiss and waves. She waves until we turn left at the corner and disappear from view.

I am happy for the company of Davido and Burna Boy, KiDi and Tiwa Savage as we drive around potholes and through backstreets that take us into Accra. I wonder if Danso was raised in one of those 'do not speak until you are spoken to' homes and, if so, why Auntie Larjey volunteered me for this silent retreat. He speaks more with his hands than he does his voice, gently tapping the steering wheel to the music as he drives. I understand his silence as a challenge and decide to match it, curious to know whether there is a point of discomfort which he will not cross.

I run my hand along the new bites between my wrist and elbow. The ones I have been scratching since we left Auntie Edem's. Danso's hand rests on mine to prevent me from scratching and catches me by surprise. I take my hand back, more abruptly than intended.

'I know it's hard, but try not to scratch.' He switches on the car's interior light. 'Can I take a look?'

'It's fine. I'm fine, thank you.' I blow gently to interrupt the heat escaping the raised bump on my skin. Outside the car, Accra is bustling and the traffic slowly building. My eyes find his before amber turns to green.

'Sorry, I didn't mean to—'

'No worries, it's cool.'

A cacophony of car horns tells him that it is time to move.

Danso parks outside the gates of a hidden heaven in central Accra. There is a valet to park the car if it would be convenient for him to do so. Danso greets the valet, kindly refuses the offer and slips a discreet tip into his hands to thank him all the same. The street lights bathe us in a warm glow which highlights the squareness of his jaw, his collarbone, the oil in his beard. He guides me to an entrance concealed by white walls. It is staffed by two men dressed in brown shirts and trousers, who greet him as we pass.

'Mr Danso, good evening.'

'Good evening, Madam.'

We are ushered past a small queue of people to stand on the threshold of some wonderland. The count of candles before me rivals the number of stars in the sky. To the centre left is a large square bar where light dances on glasses which hang from a suspended ceiling. There are bottles of red wine whose vintage year predates my birth. And against a mirrored wall, every bottle of every spirit I can name – and those I can't – are stacked. I try to take it all in, this incredible space. To the right, there is a stylish display of gold cylinders which hang from the ceiling: a beautiful, inanimate detail. It is clear every feature has been carefully considered. I am sold on the beauty of the place. And the idea that light can be used to create this feeling of life and love. The bar staff move in sophisticated choreography behind the bar, the underside of which is also lit. They dance the familiar two-step of those who give pleasure to pleasure seekers, replenishing cocktail shakers and glasses in quick succession, making a complex craft look simple.

Danso pulls out a leather bar stool for me to sit down. 'What can I get you to drink?'

The menu offers, in beautiful calligraphy, a selection of cocktail options from which I struggle to choose.

'A lychee martini?'

'Good choice.'

I follow the panoramic light show as Danso orders a whiskey sour, lychee martini and two bottles of water.

'It's so beautiful here.'

'I'm glad you like it. Have you seen the water feature over there?' He points in a direction which my eyes follow willingly. The sound of water falling slowly but surely, gently but steadily, transforms the space into a soothing oasis.

'I wasn't expecting anything like this.'

The interior walls are decorated with palm trees and plants which grow from beds of woodchip underneath. The white walls are rendered brilliant by the haloed bulbs that light them from the ground. The candles, lights, gold and glass features. The movement of people in and around them. It does something that slows the passage of time.

'I love it.'

Danso looks different sat next to me at the bar than he did in the driver's seat of the car. His skin is the colour of dark mahogany that has been polished to perfection. He doesn't speak to hear the sound of his own voice, or even to quieten the nerves of his company. With a neutral expression, he scans the space above and around me. I return his silence with a steady examination of his hands. His rounded nails are clean-cut, with smooth cuticles.

'I should have asked you if you like sushi.'

'Sushi? Well, it's not that I don't like it…it's just that I'm allergic to it!'

'Oh shit!' The features of his face rearrange themselves as he realises his error. And I see his mind work at pace to try and reformulate the evening's plans. 'I should definitely have asked you. That's a complete oversight on my part.'

'With things like seafood, it's always worth checking…' I let the logic of the point sit in the air and marinate.

'Man, I'm sorry! I got carried away with the idea of surprising you.'

I try to remember the last time anyone tried to surprise me, and come up short.

'Okay, here's what we can do. Why don't we have a drink here, and then—'

'I'm just joking, Danso. I love sushi!'

'Wait, what? You're not allergic?!' He expresses relief with the downward adjustment of his eyebrows, relaxation of his forehead and the slow spread of a smile across his face.

'Okay. Okay. You got me!' He concedes to laughter, flashing the whiteness and straightness of his teeth. It is the most expressive I have seen him since we met.

'On a serious note, I am a pescatarian.'

'Yeah, sure! I'm not buying it.'

I am giggling because I have set myself up for this fall.

'I'm serious, I don't eat meat!' The more I protest, the more unconvincing my case sounds.

'Fool me once...' He is animated now he thinks he has caught me in a lie. It is a situation of my own making. I am happy for him to order for us.

'Chale, what dey happen?'

'Chale! How far?!'

Greetings fly over and around me. Fingers click. Smiles flash. Laughter chimes.

'Kobi, this is Sika. She's here from London.'

'Hi, nice to meet you.' I extend my hand to shake his.

'You are welcome.'

'Thank you.'

'How are you enjoying Ghana?'

'I love it!'

The woman by Kobi's side is dressed in a bodycon dress and stiletto heels. She greets me by nodding and mumbling through pursed lips. She is unfriendly in an enigmatic way.

'The food here is amazing! Hakkasan vibes. Enjoy!'

'Chale, next time!'

They click their fingers – until next time.

Kobi's hand finds the bodycon woman's waist as they head towards the exit and out of the gate. Danso shakes his head.

'You're a popular guy.'

'Not really. I'm pretty shy actually. An introvert, I guess.'

'I thought it was my company,' I say dryly.

He laughs at the suggestion, which he reassures me could not be further from the truth.

Danso consults the waiter's opinion on some new dishes, before ordering a selection for us to try. He rubs his beard with his thumb and index finger before he speaks, a gesture for thought. At other times, he bites his bottom lip in concentration.

'That's a lot of food!'

'I know. I hope you're hungry!'

He seems like the kind of person who offers to those in positions of servitude deliberate acts of kindness: the valet, the barman, the waiter. Small, subtle acts. Gestures that are almost imperceptible unless you are watching him as closely as I am. Remembering a name, shaking a hand, an encouraging smile.

'Are you comfortable?' Danso asks when the waiter has taken our order.

I take the lychee off the cocktail stick and enjoy the vodka-infused fruit before it is swiftly replaced by another. It feels less awkward now I have seen and heard him laugh. It causes me to look at him again. To examine the filter through which I have viewed him.

'I am, thank you. Very.'

THE ECOLODGE

The waiter walks towards us wielding colourful plates of sushi and a selection of steaming hot dishes. He balances the weight of the order with poise and sets the dishes down with the precision of an artist. The food is a sensory charm, impressive for its aesthetics as well as its smell. Lobster dumplings. Scallop and crab shui mai. King prawns with black garlic. Royal king crab. And on and on and on. I look down at the white of my outfit and wish myself luck.

'Massa, no shito?!'

Danso's question forces me to pause my survey of the food and look him dead in the eye, pupil to pupil. I can think of few things that shito, the condiment of champions, would not taste good with. I wouldn't say no to the blended ginger, dried fish, prawns, garlic and spices with chips, for example, or pasta. Give me fish pie and shito any day of the week: delicious. I wouldn't judge someone for eating shito with a baked potato, cheese and beans on the side, or with eggs royale for breakfast. But shito with sushi? Instead of soy sauce? You wouldn't eat sushi and ketchup. Or sushi with mayonnaise, would you? So the very idea of sushi and shito… Sushi and shito? I mean…I mean…Actually…

'That is genius!'

'Massa, don't worry, I'm bringing it right now.'

After the first mouthful, I decide to put etiquette to one side.

'Danso, please don't judge me!' I arrange my napkin like a backwards cape to protect my dignity from sushi and shito.

'Yes, Sika!' He follows my lead and tucks one side of the napkin into the open front of his shirt.

'Oh my God. This is so good!'

'Right?'

'I'm sorry. I can't talk right now!'

My enjoyment is reflected in the upward shift of my eyebrows and the widening of my eyes. It's a gastronomic feast and I have to make an effort to maintain an air of civility while eating.

'Do you know Auntie Larjey called me this morning to ask where I was taking you and at what time? Had I filled the car with fuel? Was I taking my car or my father's car? What time would I drop you home?'

'No!'

'She called me three times. I must remember to get down and greet your mum before we go out. I shouldn't play my music too loudly in the car. I must remember that a good driver is not a fast driver. Am I nervous? I should just relax and be myself. Anyway, do I want her to come with me? She could sit discreetly at the back of the restaurant.' His laugh is deep and gravelly and contagious.

'Stop! What was the third call about?'

'To check that I was leaving at the time I said I would!'

I understand Auntie Larjey's meddling as a demonstration of her trust in Danso. Without her say-so, there is no way I would be in his car at sunset, heading to an unknown destination, with Mum waving us off at the gate. Without her interference, there is no way I would be sitting in this beautiful place opposite this shy and introverted, generous and kind guy, eating sushi with shito.

I am in no hurry to be full. But when I near that place, when my breathing becomes laboured and my jumpsuit snug around my waist, I am ready to pick up where we left off.

'That was delicious, Danso.'

It is safe to remove the napkin now the food is within and not outside my body. I burp into my fist like someone with no manners.

'Sorry! I'm so full!'

'Me too.'

The calm and content energy of the well-fed washes over us like a wave. It breeds familiarity and encourages eye contact.

'Hey, I want to know more about your ecolodge.'

'The ecolodge? Hmmm. Where to begin? Okay, well…I lost my mum when I was eight—'

'Oh my God, I'm so sorry—'

'No, don't worry…I mean, thank you.'

'It's not easy to lose a parent. Especially at such a young age.'

'Yeah, it was brutal.'

He starts a journey down memory lane, and I feel bad for leading him there.

'She was sick when I was younger, but nothing prepares you for being motherless.'

'I can't even imagine.'

Danso remembers the feeling of his heart breaking when she died. 'And afterwards, a heavy feeling on my chest that wouldn't go away.'

It made it hard for him to breathe. He remembers feeling permanently dazed. Feeling that he would never be able to navigate life without her. That he was, quite literally, lost. She was the centre of his world.

'She started having these episodes that would make her cough and wheeze. There was nothing overly alarming about them in the beginning. But then they got worse. The episodes got longer. The cough deeper. The wheezing relentless. Until she was struggling for, like, twenty minutes at a time, half an hour, sometimes longer.'

There was something badly wrong. At seven years old, he knew that much.

He arranges his chopsticks neatly on his empty plate, the only legacy of the meal we've just eaten a trace of black vinegar glaze.

'The first time she went to the doctor, he listened to her chest and diagnosed asthma. She came home with an inhaler, but the episodes continued.'

He became an anxious child. Distracted at school by thoughts of her. Impatient to get back home at the end of each day. To be close to her. Just in case.

'I don't know what I could or would have done. But I just wanted to be there.'

His focus shifts to the wall behind me, where water cascades into the beautifully lit pool. I cannot tell him that at the age of seven I still slept in Mum's bed. That she would indulge me by rubbing my back to help me sleep. That when I was little and refused to eat she would put jollof rice in a cup, turn it upside down on my plate, put a toothpick with a piece of paper that said *Sika* on it and tell me it was a sandcastle. That she decorated my plate with 'trees' made from broccoli. That if she was desperate, she would arrange chicken strips on my plate to resemble birds in the sky. That she would pour my apple juice into a wine glass while she drank chardonnay and we would cheers before I accepted the food on my plate.

'I remember the feeling of fear. It was like fire in my chest, you know?'

I do not know. The idea of life without Mum makes me feel heavy and hollow and helpless. It's always been the two of us. Mum, the safety net into which I have never been afraid to fall. My heart hurts for him.

'Please don't feel you have to talk about it. I had no idea...I don't want to upset you.'

He says he is fine and that it is good to talk about these things.

'One day, she went to the market with her friend and the same thing happened. But instead of going back to the doctor or getting a second opinion or even going to the hospital, she went with her friend to church. The woman said she had a powerful pastor who was known to perform miracles. That he could cure people of AIDS and cancer, serious stuff. Unbelievable stuff. Literally.'

Danso turns his palms upwards to examine the lines that make them. I wonder if there is an intersection of the heart and fate lines. An indicator that at some point his life would be irrevocably altered. A time when his fortune would collide with the maternal relationship upon which his seven-year-old life rested. I lay my palms on the white tablecloth to steady a rising fear.

'She became convinced over time that these episodes were...'

He pauses then. To overcome something. Something that is difficult for him to put into words.

'...demonic possessions. That each time she had a coughing fit and had to fight for breath, she had become...'

His voice quietens before it trails off. Before he raises his eyes to meet mine.

'...possessed.'

He is searching for meaning in the truth.

'Possessed by a demon.'

His voice, just louder than a whisper.

'The pastor said that the demon had to be exorcised if she was ever going to be cured. So that's what he did. He exorcised the demon from her body, sending her eyes rolling to the back of her head. Making her writhe and convulse under his commands.'

I did not know where Danso's story would take us. Or that it would interfere with the passage of time. That it would ring a bell of familiarity and cause heat to flush through my veins. Nausea rises in the pit of my stomach along with an anger, red and rousing. I don't know if shito with sushi was such a good idea after all. I don't want to throw up in this beautiful place.

'I saw it all.'

I see tears gather in his eyes and sadness take over his features. I want the story to have a different ending. For something to have happened to save her, or for someone to have intervened. I want to rewrite for him the end to this chapter of his life.

'The exorcism didn't cure her. Of course it didn't. The episodes got worse and worse. There were times when the pastor would decree an abundance of demonic activity against which spiritual warfare must be waged.'

During those times, local waste burned close by and black clouds gathered in the sky. They made the air heavy with the smell of exorcism.

I find my right hand covering my mouth and my left holding his. 'Danso,' is the only thing I manage. It comes out in a whisper. 'I'm so sorry.'

He became environmentally aware as he watched his father navigate the different stages of grief. Distracting himself for fear of staying still. Tidying litter, organising waste. Collecting the plastic and wood his neighbours would otherwise incinerate. The steel wire discarded after use. He would trade them for whatever the family needed at the time. Food, clothes, toys for Danso and his sister. He didn't realise until he was older that the benefit of this distraction was multiple; his father was recycling, monetising his efforts and reducing local pollution. It was survival in every sense of the word.

'I saw how the distraction brought him a kind of peace. So the association of doing these things became a positive one for me as a child. That's where it all began. Sorry, did you ask for the long or short version?'

'Danso, I...' I am lost for words.

'Would you like another drink?' He comes to and looks around for the waiter while I consider the emptiness of my glass.

'Water, please,' I manage. 'Thank you.'

I take the empty cocktail glass in my hand and examine the single drop of lychee martini at the bottom.

'I understand,' is what I am able to offer him.

Because I do.

I know what it is like to lose a parent.

A MIRACLE

I was born with determined nostrils around which my features had formed so similarly to Mum's, it made me her carbon copy. That's what the midwife said when she delivered me. It wasn't her first remark. Her first observation was that she had never seen anything like me. Mum would have preferred 'healthy'. 'Healthy' would have gone some way towards calming the anxiety that pressed on her throat after nine hours of laboured breathing. It was an anxiety she had learned during pregnancy, one so powerful it could turn sweet food sour. It made her palate reject childhood favourites like tatale for unripe and unsweet green plantain, which she had never enjoyed. It could cause her to feel her heartbeat in her throat. It was an anxiety that intensified in the days leading up to my birth. That it expressed itself in a physical language of abdominal cramps and heart palpitations had led her, more than once, to confuse Braxton Hicks for early labour. It was an anxiety she says you can only understand when you have life growing inside you. It is an anxiety that never leaves once you bring that life into the world.

The midwife, could have described me as a miracle instead. That might have explained her expression when she first laid eyes on me. Before she held me up to meet Mum's gaze. Her mouth fixed in the 'o' of wonder. Mum never imagined that when she saw me for the first time it would be through the casing of my amniotic sac. My legs folded in front of my body and feet against the translucent veil. My eyes yet to behold the world.

'Wow! Look at this!'

And yet she couldn't. Too weak to prop herself up by her elbows to see me for herself. Her mouth dry from the unrelenting labour of labour. Her heart yet to find its resting beat.

'Is she okay?'

'She is more than okay! She is one in a million!'

An exaggeration – in reality the number is more like one in eighty thousand – but a rarity none the less. I was the midwife's first ever en caul birth. Mum had never heard of such a thing. The sight of a baby gift-wrapped in nature's original offering was such a rare event it warranted the calling of other midwives into the delivery room to behold.

'What a blessing!'

'A gift from God!'

It was only after multiple eyes had been laid upon me, born but unborn, that the midwife took a silver instrument in her hand and snipped away at the sac that held me. Fluid escaped in the way Mum had expected her waters to break before contractions started to ravage her body. It gave no other sign that she was in labour. But it wasn't Braxton Hicks this time; it was the real thing. She called the office to reach Dad when he didn't answer his mobile.

'It's happening now. She's coming!'

'Your waters have broken?'

'No! But I'm having contractions. Hurry!'

And he did. Dad told his boss that his wife was in labour, and he was excused. He left work just after 3 p.m. to make his way home, telling her, 'Be calm, okay. I'm on my way. I'm coming right now!'

Mum refused to leave without Dad. It was only when the spasms were so strong that they threatened her ability to walk unaided that she agreed to go to the hospital.

The office confirmed that Dad had left for home. She continued to call his mobile; it continued to go to voicemail. Over and over and over and over and over and over again. Why wouldn't he pick up?

It was Auntie Edem who took her to the hospital in the end, baby bag in hand and tears in her eyes. This had not been the plan. Mum approached the midwife's station with slow steps and as much urgency as she could manage. With her right hand she gripped her lower abdomen; with her left she clutched the bag she refused to let anyone take from her. She took short breaths through tense lips, sweat gathering above them and at her temple. Where are you? she thought. This was not the way it was meant to happen. Pick up pick up pick up! She needed Dad by her side.

'Congratulations, Selom! A beautiful baby girl! Well done!'

When she took me in her arms and saw the likeness for herself, Mum was filled with an effervescent gratitude. God, in his absolute benevolence, had given her a baby who no one could deny was hers. Her body was hostage to a searing hot pain from the laceration between her legs. And yet she was grateful. Even as she lay in a pool of her own blood, red and fresh and bright and warm, she was grateful.

'Oh dear! I told you not to push!'

She doubted her ears when the midwife, having surveyed the damage, highlighted her error. Had she given birth herself? Had her vagina parted like the Red Sea and slid the baby into the hands of a smiling midwife poised and ready to catch it? Had it done so without incident or tear? Had her bowels betrayed her in the process? The glare of the light between her legs, still in stirrups, brandished her mistake.

To explain the depth and extent of a mother's love, Mum would retell the story of my birth over the years, tailoring it according to my age. A fairy tale fit for a four-year-old was modified during adolescence when the start of my period convinced her that I would be able to manage more detail. I was not.

'That is the most disgusting thing I've ever heard. You shat yourself?'

'Wait till it's your turn.'

'That's so gross.'

'You think that was the worst part?'

My face contorted so violently on understanding the meaning of a perineal tear that it made Mum laugh her kikikiki laugh.

'It is the only trauma you would choose to go through for the end result.'

'There are no circumstances in which I would risk a tear from my vagina to my bumhole, Mum. Thanks, but no.'

I was nineteen minutes old and learning how to latch on when he finally answered his phone. The anger she had felt when trying to understand how a man who knew his wife was due to give birth at any time could lose his phone had dissipated when she laid eyes on me. She lost herself there. In me, in my eyes. As she fed me and counted my fingers and toes. When she touched the soft part of my head and realised how delicate I was. When she examined the texture of my hair. The stump of my little belly button. The folds of skin at my neck. When she traced the rims of my ears with her finger and understood the shade of brown I would become.

Her daughter. It had given way to a sadness that sat in her swollen belly. That Dad, who was already besotted with me, a precious baby girl, had missed my birth. She was more sad for him than she was for herself. Sad for the experience he would never get to relive. Sad he wasn't there to witness the moment, all the more special because—

'She's here! She is here! Safe and sound. And healthy. I've been calling you for hours! Where are you?!'

The voice on the other end of the line. The man who answered. The person who spoke.

It wasn't Dad.

A FATHER

In her second trimester Dad surprised her with a wooden bench easel, two weeks after she started to complain of back pain.

'Let me rub your feet,' he would say when he came home from work. 'Raise your legs when you are sitting down. It will help with the swelling.' He would move them onto his lap and use lavender oil to knead them like soft dough.

'Hmmm. That feels nice.'

'Don't be spending too long on your feet, okay?'

'I've been taking breaks.'

'Yes, but maybe travelling to the arts centre so often isn't a good idea?'

Her hands started to swell soon after. But because art was her passion and her peace, Mum refused to stop painting. She would continue – at home. Dad bought the easel so she could sit to do the thing she loved most. When he hauled it through the door, Mum complained that he was bringing unnecessary things into the house.

'This place is getting cluttered!'

He had started doing this in preparation for my arrival: bringing things home. One day he returned with a wooden rocking horse. His boss offered it to him, saying his own children had outgrown it and he wasn't planning to have more. It was beautiful. A white rocking horse with a brown mane and bronze studding along the bridle. He set the easel against the window in the brightest room of the house.

When they found out that they were expecting a girl, Dad could not contain his excitement. He told everyone! The barber, the petrol station attendant, the woman at the motorway tollbooth... Mum said it was only the bofrot seller in Community 14 who had not heard the news. 'There is no greater protector of a girl than her father,' Dad would say.

Mum knew Dad would protect us both. Knowing that gave her a comfort which helped her find sleep despite the painful stretching of her skin and the somersaults in her stomach. I was incapable of keeping still and refused to sleep when she did. She worried that he would spoil me, and it made her laugh to think of herself as the disciplinarian of the two. She who was so softly spoken and mild-mannered.

She started craving hot cocoa before her spine began to curve and her belly swell. Dad said it was no coincidence. His daughter knew her father and where he came from. Before I was born, I knew that Dad once rose at dawn to harvest ripened pods from the trunks and branches of trees in the forests of the Volta region. That he used a sharp blade to cut through the stalk of the yellow fruit for a clean cut, taking care not to damage the branch. That for pods high on the tree he would use a pruning hook, with a handle on the end of a long pole to detach it. I knew that if he wanted to check the fruit's ripeness, he would shake the cocoa pod and listen for the movement of beans. If there was no sound, he knew they were still attached to the inside of the husk and needed more time.

He learned that the best time to open the pods was ten days after harvesting. And that the discarded husks could be returned to the soil for fertilisation. He would use a wooden club to strike the yellow fruit at its centre and split it in half. A machete used without care could damage the fruit. He was not one to take unnecessary risks. Once the pod was open, he would remove the wet beans by hand before they were fermented, dried and bagged for transportation. He learned that drying was a slow process. That if it was rushed, or carried out incorrectly, the chemical reactions set off by the fermentation process would not be allowed to finish properly. This would leave the beans with a bitter and acidic flavour. But if dried too slowly, mould and other bad flavours could develop. It was a careful balance to strike. Dad knew this. There was nothing about cocoa, or the harvesting of it, that he did not know. So it was no coincidence that Mum craved Milo. I was growing inside her. And I was my father's child.

Dad was working at Ghana Cocoa Board when they met. After years on the plantation, he had worked his way up to an administrative role, seizing the first opportunity that presented itself. He was happy to sit in the cool breeze of the air-conditioned office after years spent under the heat of the sun, his skin toasted under its rays. He was happy to swap his T-shirt and sun hat for a shirt and trousers, pressed with starch, and his weathered work boots for black office shoes he could polish and shine. The promotion meant he could move from the boarding facilities at the plantation and rent a small two-bedroom house where they could live together.

When the cravings started, Dad made Mum a mug of hot Milo every morning before leaving for work. The chocolate powder to which he would add hot water was a world of processing away from the plantation. In its refined form, it bore little resemblance to the cocoa beans from which it originated. The raw beans were bitter and sharp to the taste, nothing like the green tinned sweetness of Milo. They would eat their breakfast together – Milo with egg and bread, or koko with bofrot – and listen to the radio before they parted ways. Dad would leave for the office and Mum for the arts centre.

Milo was like a switch that would wake me up and keep me active until about lunchtime. Was it a sugar rush, or was I going to be one of those energetic babies who would deny her parents rest and sleep, Mum asked herself. After a lunch of banku and tilapia, kenkey and fried fish or omo tuo, I would fall asleep just like Dad, and give her peace until dinner time.

There was something beautiful about the way Dad cared for Mum during her pregnancy. The way he worried about whether she had eaten enough, rested enough, smiled enough during the day. The way he would stop any task and run to her when she said, 'The baby is moving, come!'

'Where? Is it here?' he would reply, moving his hand gently across her stomach.

'Shhh. Just wait.'

He would wait, quietly and eagerly, until—

'There!'

'I felt it! Hello baby, do it again!'

He encouraged Mum to dance if she hadn't felt me move for a while, to wake me up. He would switch on the radio and make her laugh with exaggerated dance moves, her swollen belly jiggling with the spectacle. She would protest, initially, that she was tired. Her feet were swollen. She couldn't get up. But he would stretch out his hand for hers, and help her. She would join him in the small square of their living room to dance on their makeshift dance floor to highlife music.

Kojo Antwi's 'All I Need is You' was their favourite song.

The first time he felt me kick, his eyes filled with tears. If tears for a kick, what then for fatherhood?

In choosing him to be my dad, Mum knew she had already given me one of the greatest gifts a parent could give her child.

FIFI

The preparations for Auntie Larjey and Uncle Papa's wedding anniversary are in their advanced stages. Mum sits on Auntie Larjey's bed and watches her friend try on one wig after another. The bed is big enough to sleep eight people. The room, light and airy and spacious. Neutral walls and warm lighting communicate tranquillity and calm. Mum is committed to the task of fashion adviser. The options are narrowed down to a fiery blonde piece that channels Tina Turner, a wavy bob that says Viola Davis in *Ma Rainey's Black Bottom*, or a Diana Ross number, which is my personal favourite. In the dressing room attached to her and Uncle Papa's bedroom, Auntie Larjey turns 360 degrees to examine herself from all angles in the full-length mirror. Her reflection fires questions at me.

'Sika?'

Glance behind the shoulder, look to the left, a step to the right.

'Auntie?'

'I'm waiting for my report.'

Strike a pose.

'Your report?'

'My report, Sika!'

Handbag on the inside of the elbow, lifted up to the shoulder.

'The filla!'

'Auntie?'

Strike a pose.

'Your dinner with Danso? Ah!'

Brief pause from modelling to express exasperation at my slowness to spill the highly sought-after beans.

'Oh!' I laugh at her efforts, her eagerness to know. 'It was so nice!'

Mum is a silent but invested observer.

'We went to this amazing sushi place! The food was—'

'Eh heh. And how was Danso?'

Find matching shoe, wear it for full effect.

'He was nice.'

Strike a pose.

'He is nice.'

Reverse turn on catwalk to look me in the eye.

'We're going to go out again.'

Auntie Larjey expresses satisfaction with the update in a broad and glittering smile, before directing her next question to Mum: 'Or is this one better?'

Mum's feedback is a score of different sounds which carry meaning that Auntie Larjey alone is able to understand.

The floor space of the bedroom allows Loli to run around without fear of knocking into sharp corners or breakable fixtures. She has found a new friend in Fifi; where one goes, the other follows. There is apparently no limit to the number of times they can run around Auntie Larjey's bed. From one bedside table to the other and back again. Bare feet and paws pattering after each other. I am at the centre of a sound battle. Breathless laughter of a five-year-old meets high-pitched barking of an overexcited dog meets fashion critique from an impassioned panel of one. Mum and Auntie Larjey are sufficiently distracted by the task of positioning the Viola Davis wig 'just so' that no one sees Loli take the Tina Turner wig and wave it in front of the dog like a matador. Manic movement at the periphery of my vision distracts me from contributing to a discussion about the pros and cons of the *Ma Rainey's Black Bottom* look, Auntie Larjey's final offering.

'It makes me look old, enu shi shi?'

It is the pitch of Loli's laughter and the frenzy in Fifi's barking that finally shifts their attention. Loli has fixed the front of the wig on top of her single plaits, where it sits lopsided. Her hand flicks the fringe from the right side of her face, where it interferes with her vision. Again and again and again. Her new game with Fifi involves intense head-shaking and body-spinning, so taken is she by the novelty of hair that moves when she does. The excitement causes her to blink frequently as she loses herself in a state of delirium. It causes Mum and Auntie Larjey to suspend their fashion critique to focus on the spectacle before them. Mum is laughing her kikikiki laugh, and Auntie Larjey has started to cough from the pantomime of it. She bends down to scoop Fifi up in her arms with tears in her eyes.

'Heh, Lololi! Are you wearing my wig?'

'Loli, you think your auntie's wig is a toy eh?'

'And you, Sika, you've been sitting there watching her?!'

'Have you been drinking Uncle Papa's akpeteshie, or?'

Loli loses her balance to the power of gravity and only becomes still when her limbs make contact with the floor. The Tina Turner wig, no longer attached to her head, lies inanimate beside her. The episode has caused Fifi to become demented. She runs towards the wig from all angles, baring her teeth and challenging it to a fight. That the threatening thing is unresponsive seems to provoke her further.

'Loli, smile!'

Loli looks at me, right hand on hip, knee bent and on tiptoes, and flashes that smile of hers.

Auntie Larjey did not want a dog in her house. She told her sons as much when they came home from school, aged seven, and tried to convince her of the brilliance of their idea.

'Mama, please!'

'Corey, do you know how to look after a dog?'

'Of course!' Corey, ever impulsive, answered without giving the question proper – if any – thought.

'We will learn!' Casey said. He was the more considered of the two.

'Corey, you convinced me to buy you and your brother walkie-talkies just a few weeks ago? Do you know where they are?'

'Mama, it's not my fault! Jojo asked to borrow them and he didn't bring them back!'

'So you are blaming your cousin?'

Auntie Larjey examined the pleading in their eyes before surveying the altered state of the school uniforms in which she had dressed them for school, freshly washed and ironed. The shine of the shea butter she had applied to their elbows, knees and growing limbs was long gone. In its place was the dry skin of football tackles, chasing, falling and incessant play. They held themselves like their father. They had his mannerisms, his ambition and his sense of fun. If she didn't know better, their doe eyes could have made her weak enough to succumb to their pleading.

'Go and ask your father for a dog.'

'Daddy doesn't like dogs!'

'He won't let us have one!'

And there Auntie Larjey rested her case. As if it was Uncle Papa's decision. As if she could not say to him over dinner one evening that she would like a dog and he would not buy one for her the very next day. As if she were not married to a man who made his wife's happiness his daily business. As if he did not understand that she was the sun around which his family orbited.

But Auntie Larjey did not want a dog in her house. She had told Uncle Papa as much when the boys left Ghana to study in America and the house assumed a quietness she had never known. That big house with the playroom the boys and their friends had claimed with enthusiasm as their own. The room Uncle Papa had agreed they could paint any colour they wanted and had helped them decorate with layers of Midnight Blue.

The room to which Auntie Larjey brought drinks and snacks, more regularly than was necessary, to make sure everyone was fed and watered. In which she spoke pidgin with her sons' friends to show them she could. In which she showcased her azonto dance moves because she knew them all. The playroom was a place of laughter which would echo throughout the house. A place of happiness and togetherness, the very heartbeat of their home.

She could weather their absence at boarding school because she could visit them anytime she chose. And she did: she frequently stopped by unannounced with an offering of home-cooked food. Food she had cooked herself with ingredients that included a mother's love. Dishes exchanged on successful interrogation of personal lives, school programmes and general well-being. She could weather the separation of boarding school because she knew that during the holidays the house would become a home once more. But America? America was not boarding school. America was so far away, too far away.

*

'What am I going to do with a dog? Please, Papa, I don't have time for that.'

But Auntie Larjey did have time. A lot of it. That was the problem. Uncle Papa knew his wife had lost some part of herself when the boys travelled across the Atlantic to pursue their careers and lives as young men. She had not told them what subjects to study or what paths to pursue, but they were their father's children. They had seen his hard work, vision and social conscience; they were inspired by it. Had Auntie Larjey been surprised when Casey told her he was going to study medicine? Or when Corey announced that he was going to become a civil engineer? Of course not. She could barely find the words to communicate her pride. Uncle Papa knew that once they left, her days, which used to be spent caring for their energetic sons, had become long and empty. She now spent too much time dusting things that were already clean, rearranging furniture that was perfectly positioned and getting under Esi's feet in the kitchen before he came home from work.

Auntie Larjey's maternal heart ached for someone to care for. That's why Uncle Papa, ignoring her protestations, had returned home from work the day before her birthday with a white ball of fluff weighing five pounds tucked under his arm. She wore a pink bow he had chosen for her and doe eyes that caused Auntie Larjey's heart to thump against the walls of her chest.

'Papa! What is that?!'

Uncle Papa did not need to answer the question, because Auntie Larjey had already taken the puppy from his hands to examine it in hers.

'Papa!'

'Esi is collecting her food and crate from the car. She has a food bowl and a water bowl and some toys.'

'Papa!'
'Yes, sweetheart?'
'Has she eaten? Is she okay? Oh, my dog!'

SOMETHING SMALL FOR THE BOYS

Auntie Larjey's driver walks across the courtyard as if avoiding hot coal in bare feet. His grimace suggests a bee sting and his uneven footsteps a poorly masked fear of being bitten by the tiny dog at his heels.

'Ah! Fifi, what is that?!'

Fifi is unmoved by his authority and ignores his familiarity. If he looked her in the eye to plead mercy or compassion, he must now realise he did so in error. She refuses to negotiate. Is it better to stand still or try to walk away? Whatever he does, he knows he should not run. The dance of a scared man and the dog who scares him should not be a thing of comedy, and yet he is six feet tall, well fed, and hostage to an ankle-high Bichon Frise who terrorises him.

Auntie Larjey enters from stage left as pack leader and scoops Fifi into her arms to bring the performance to an unscripted end. She is immune to the high-pitched sound of Fifi's barking in a way no one else is and swears blind that the dog is 'just protecting the house'. Our ears are relieved when peace is restored.

'Thank you, Fifi,' Auntie Larjey says. 'Elvis, are you okay?'

The shaken man says he is very okay. And I swear I see a grin on Fifi's face.

'Elvis, we are going to the nail salon. But let's pass the dog parlour first.'

We pile into the big car, thankful for its air conditioning against the heat of the day. From the moment the electric gates open, I witness from Elvis an attention to details of safety with which Yaw was unfamiliar. It allows me to take in a silently moving world through the soundproofed interior and tinted windows of the SUV. The billboards dedicated to a rice brand, a hair relaxer or a mobile phone network. Notices of luxury developments in central Accra. An image of the perfect Ghanaian family enjoying a perfect bowl of jollof rice cooked in a perfect new rice cooker. There are official stops where people wait for tro tros to ferry them to and from various destinations and unofficial stops where tro tro drivers pause to allow for a convenient pickup or drop-off. Countless taxis feature in the busy afternoon traffic, overtaking hawkers who offer goods between invisible car lanes and at traffic lights. People with perfect posture carry loads on their heads with babies strapped to their backs. Children move their hands between their mouths and car windows, begging for money to buy food. A disabled man uses a skateboard to manoeuvre from A to B, chale wote on his hands to navigate the challenging terrain.

Elvis knows where traffic will be building at this time and which route to take to avoid it. If you ask him, he will tell you about politics, the cost of living, inflation and the government's building of an expensive cathedral while people struggle to find money for food to eat. But his eyes, even when he talks to you, are always fixed firmly on the road. The car tyres cushion us from the potholes in a way that many road users do not experience, and the rhythm of stopping and starting in unrelenting traffic sends Loli into the soft sleep of travelling children.

We are flagged down as we approach a checkpoint by a police officer dressed in an unforgivingly tight black uniform. He is restricted at the waist by an elasticated belt to which a baton is attached, constricting his bulging gut. He wears boots that cover his ankles and a felt beret on his head. I think the colour and design of his uniform unsuited to the climate in which he works. But I am distracted from that thought by the sight of the gun in his hands. It is trained downwards but very visible. He motions to Elvis to roll down his window; Elvis complies.

'Good morning.'

'Good morning, officer.'

'Where are you going, please?'

The officer does not look at Elvis as much as he looks past him and into the car. From the passenger seat, Auntie Larjey pierces him with steely eyes.

'Good morning, Madam.'

She does not respond to his greeting.

'Please, where are you coming from?' He directs the question to Mum and me, who are now the subjects of his gaze, hidden from the exterior behind the darkened windows of the car. His curiosity pauses the blinking of his eyes.

'Cantonments.'

Elvis is calm. Unflustered.

'I see. Licence and registration, please.'

Auntie Larjey reaches for the glove compartment and hands the documents to Elvis in a silent transaction. The officer barely glances at them before returning his gaze to me and Mum in the back seat. His eyes are laser-focused.

'Where are you coming from?' the officer asks again, this time fielding his question directly to Mum with an upward nod and a point of his index finger.

'Me?' Mum asks, pointing inwards, her voice dripping with disdain.

'Officer, the documents are in order—'

He cuts through Elvis mid-sentence. 'Madam, where are you coming from?'

The silence that follows the officer's question is ominous. Mum meets his gaze and raises him with her own unblinking skills. Meanwhile, Auntie Larjey stares through the windscreen. Simmering.

'She is coming from Cantonments.'

Elvis is the only person to recognise the officer's probing effort. The officer's eyes remain fixed on Mum and her defiance as he flexes his muscles of authority, staring at her with eyes yellowed by jaundice. Auntie Larjey will not acknowledge the officer's existence. Mum wants to erase it.

He returns the documents to Elvis. Slowly. Oblivious to the simmering within the car, unfazed by it.

'Officer, is that all?'

'Something small for the boys?'

It is his response to Elvis that makes the simmering energy boil.

'You say?' From a place of muteness, Auntie Larjey has found her voice. She asks the question in a way that suggests unreliable hearing.

'Something small for the boys?' the officer asks again. His audacity produces a stench which infiltrates the car. It ignites a firework display he is not prepared to see.

'SOMETHING SMALL FOR THE BOYS LIKE WHAT?!!!'

Auntie Larjey is the gunpowder. She tests the belt lock of the passenger seat as she stretches against it – and Elvis – to deliver her message to the police officer. She blasts the man with insults that rain on his head and through his body. Sharp words in Twi, quickly spoken. Words that question how he was raised and by whom. How he can look at himself in the mirror. And how he is able to sleep at night. Words that interrogate the pride his parents must feel for him and the example he is setting for his children. Words that dare him to ask again for something big or small, near or far! Something! Anything! For the boys or the girls or whomsoever! Her anger makes the car shake. Mum looks out of the window. It is her turn to be silent.

The officer walks away from the car when its shaking suggests an earthquake of increasing force from which he must seek cover. And the risk of staying seems to outweigh the unlikely reward of a bribe.

'Something small indeed!'

Mum watches the back of the officer as he retreats and leaves Auntie Larjey's insults trailing behind him. When she turns around to face the direction of travel, she is wearing a discreet but distinct smile on her face.

'Eiii, Lady Justice!'

Elvis waits until Auntie Larjey kisses her teeth before indicating and pulling out slowly to join the cars on the main road.

'Loli, we're here.' I call her name softly and rub her hand to bring her out of her nap.

'Are we here?'

'We are!' I help her get out of the car and navigate the descent to street level.

At the nail salon, we are greeted by uniformed staff who appear used to Auntie Larjey's custom. They offer glasses of prosecco on arrival and the tired smiles of the hard-working.

'Good afternoon, Ma.'

Auntie Larjey communicates our need for four manicures and pedicures while holding up her old gel manicure to the light. There is collective appreciation of how well it has lasted. 'This is the only place I get my nails done,' she shares with

Mum, who is already holding the glass of prosecco to her lips.

'Excuse me, do you have Wi-Fi?' I ask.

'Yes, please.' A uniformed woman hands me a laminated card with the login details before showing us to our seats and demonstrating the massage function.

'Thank you.'

'Make sure you scrub the bottom well.'

'Yes, Ma.'

Auntie Larjey issues instructions to the girl doing her pedicure while enjoying the vibrating function of the massage chair. The girl sits down with some effort and takes a grater to Auntie Larjey's foot, hesitating and rearranging her body before pausing once more. She fidgets in the manner of the distracted. A person unable to find comfort.

Auntie Larjey appears fluent in body language, enough to understand what the girl feels but does not say. 'You have cramps, eh?'

The girl nods as she pats her stomach. Her mouth downturned, her body overwhelmed by pain. Mum is searching through her bag for the painkillers she always keeps on her. At the same time, Auntie Larjey is rummaging through hers. Mum has changed bags, which means she has nothing on her. They settle for the next best option. Cedis are discreetly handed to someone with the direction to find a pharmacy to buy painkillers, quickly. In less than ten minutes, the girl is on her way to a recovery borne of Auntie Larjey's compassion, for which she wants neither acknowledgement nor thanks.

I lie back in my chair and enjoy the massage it administers to my back. Meanwhile, an excited Loli struggles with the tickling sensation of having her feet rubbed. Auntie Larjey and Mum run through the list of final preparations for the party. She has confirmed the final menu with the caterers.

She has reminded them that they need to bring tablecloths; sometimes they assume the host will provide these things. Why would she pay them so much money if she wanted to do half the job herself? The nkate cake lady's husband had a stroke last week, so she has had to find someone else to do it last minute. She has seen the work of the new nkate cake lady and thinks she is even better than her original choice. The marquee people will set up on Thursday. She has told them she wants them to finish by 2 p.m. They better not be late. Because the lady who is doing the decorations has another party on Saturday, and she doesn't want her to rush the job or to squeeze it in last-minute. She decided to let Papa choose the DJ. She told him and the boys that the music is their domain. Apparently these days they can even create a playlist on something called Spotify. She hopes the DJ is going to do more than press Play on a laptop and stand there fiddling with his phone. That's not the type of DJ she has in mind.

'Heh Sika?'

'Yes, Auntie?'

'I hope you've brought your dancing shoes? On Saturday we are really going to dance!'

THE FIRST BITE

I am in the comfort of deep sleep and on the brink of REM when something violent startles more than stirs me. It is the kind of alarm that punctures peaceful sleep.

In the darkness, my right hand reaches for the skin between the knuckle and joint of my left ring finger. There is a change in the texture and sensation of the skin there. The application of pressure to it dulls a sting. The sting is the cause of my waking.

I reach for my phone. It is 2.46 a.m. The torch shines a spotlight on a raised bump on my finger. There is another on the inside of my wrist. I have been bitten.

I know I am sharing a space with a buzzing thing. I can hear it. The high-pitched sound whose frequency offends the ear. I sit upright in bed to search for the flying insect against the dim light into which my eyes are squinting. It is like searching for a needle in a haystack, but harder. This needle moves.

At the puncture points, discomfort makes its home. My body has identified a foreign body and is staging a resistance. The itching intensifies. Sleep remains outside my reach while I look for the mosquito to neutralise the threat. My search eats into the night as the sting spreads.

Despite my promise to stay awake, I abandon vigilance. My eyes fail to see the mosquito. And my ears no longer reliably hear it. I lose the war I have attempted to wage and surrender to the stillness of the night.

I wake to the call of crickets, the cock's crow and three more bites: on my ankle, forearm and the side of my ear.

The sun has only just risen when Danso arrives to pick me up. Auntie Larjey announces his arrival in her dressing gown and a quiet voice I have never heard her use before. Mum is asleep.

'Here – in case you get peckish on the way.' She takes charge of my departure, handing me a food parcel for the both of us and two flasks for the journey. 'Your mum said you wouldn't eat breakfast at this time.'

'No, it's too early for me.'

'Well, it's there when you people are ready: bofrot, vegetable pie and achomo. Is it okay?'

'Amazing! Thank you, Auntie.'

'Should I quickly fry some kelewele for you?' She is ready to turn on her heel and set about the task.

'Auntie, we are fine,' Danso assures her with a smile.

The thought of Auntie Larjey chopping plantain and seasoning it with ginger, cayenne pepper, nutmeg and salt to make kelewele, while Danso and I wait for her to fry it, makes me wrap my arms around her and squeeze. 'We don't need kelewele, Auntie. We're fine. Promise.' The croakiness of my voice reveals that I am out of the habit of waking up early and trying to emerge from a sleep cycle.

'Coffee with milk. Is that how you like it?'

'Perfect, thank you.'

She presses my trainers at the toe, the way Mum used to when she bought my school shoes, to check they are comfortable. I offer my hand to help her stand and confirm that I am not scared of heights before she releases her hand from mine.

'Okay. Enjoy yourselves!'

'See you later!'

Auntie Larjey issues instructions in Ga to Danso, who nods and returns sounds of affirmation.

'Okay. Drive safely.' Her hand rests on his open window. 'Call me if anything, okay?' She looks left and right, surveying the length of the road for obstacles or hazards in our path.

'Of course. Don't worry, Auntie, I'm a careful driver. I'll let you know when we arrive and when we are about to leave.'

Auntie Larjey steps back from the car and waits by the gates until we have fastened our belts and driven off into the morning mist.

The quietness in the car matches the reverie in the streets around us. Accra is gently stirring. I pull down the passenger mirror to see the state of me. My eyes are puffy and red. Rubbing them releases a burning sensation.

'You're tired, eh?'

'I'm okay.'

An involuntary yawn suggests otherwise, forcing me to cover my mouth to preserve the mystery of my tonsils. When my eyes meet his, laughter escapes us both.

'I'll be fine after a coffee!'

'I know it's an early start. But we've got a bit of a drive, and I want to avoid the traffic.'

'Are you going to tell me where we're going this time?'

'We're going to a park.' He says it with a casual smile as he navigates backstreets to get to main roads away from the city and in the direction of the Central Region. 'How have you been?'

'Good, thank you. I kind of wish I was staying for longer.'

He looks at me with a knowing smile.

'What about you? How's work?'

'Work is busy! It's nice to have a day off from chasing people!'

I can relate without difficulty. Time off work has allowed me to meet and spend time with my family. And to begin my search for the other half of me, with Auntie Larjey's help. It is the most special collection of days I have ever had outside the world of Melon. I want it to last so much longer than the short time I have left.

'Who doesn't love a day off?!'

'I'm telling you!'

'I'm so annoyed. I got bitten in the middle of the night.' I hold out my arm to reveal the raised bumps on my finger and wrist and fold my right ear to expose another.

'Oh, sorry!' His voice is quiet with concern and deeper than I remembered.

'They really feasted on you!'

'It woke me up in the middle of the night.' I decide against slamming my leg on the dashboard to show the swelling on my ankle. He gets the point.

'Once I know it's in my room, I have to find it and deal with it.'

With his left hand on the steering wheel, Danso reaches across the gearstick, hesitating briefly when he gets there. I give him permission by leaning closer to the centre of the car. Gently, he takes my right hand in his, and with his thumb examines the raised bump on my finger. He turns my hand over to do the same to my wrist.

'I tried! But I was so tired I fell asleep.'

'Sorry, sorry. You're taking antimalarials though, right?'

'Yes, I've been taking them religiously.'

'Okay, good. As long as you take them you'll be fine.'

The road ahead is clear and free from potholes as far as I can see. So I don't tell him to stop. Or to hold the wheel with both hands.

'Have you taken an antihistamine?'

'I meant to take some this morning, but I was half asleep when we left!'

'Don't worry, we can stop at a pharmacy.'

'Okay, thank you.'

'That should take the heat and itch out of it a little.'

'Thank you. It's so hard not to scratch.'

'I know.'

He takes his eyes off the road briefly to look at me. My eyes meet his when he does.

'Do you get bitten?'

'Rarely. I'm boring to them.'

At the traffic lights, he seems to know when the lights are about to change from red to green. He holds my gaze until they do.

'I'm not. My blood is like nectar to them!'

Danso's hand reaches for mine again when the traffic lights get fewer and fewer. When valleys start to appear in the road ahead of us and hills on the horizon.

I wake up as the car slows to a stop some three hours later.

We are at a park.

Kakum National Park.

It is a park in the tropical rainforest.

THE RAINFOREST

We are so high up that the clouds touch our faces and graze the tops of our heads. It is an intangible thing, a cluster of clouds. It does not feel like you imagine it will, like soft cotton wool. It feels like nothing disappearing in the space between my fingers. And yet I can see there is something there. We are walking above a rich, evergreen canopy that extends further than our eyes can see. Trees upon trees upon trees upon trees. We are passing rivers and ravines so far beneath us that we cannot hear their current or even guess their depth. It is unlike any place I have ever seen.

The rainforest boasts a complex landscape of roots and branches, tangled and intertwined. Colonies of creatures, large and small, concealed below and in between. They are camouflaged, hiding in plain sight. Inhabiting a world to which I am a first-time visitor. A secret place that only the privileged know exists. It is a world of vegetation and foliage away from the world I know. A world that showcases the entire palette of green, in every scene, down to the wingspan of the parakeets to my left and right and flying overhead. I feel full of wonder in this place. So small, so insignificant.

We are not alone in the forest; we are in the company of nature's most precious offerings. Things that grow from the earth and are nourished by it. A chorus of sound emanates from the world below and around us. Chirping and squawking, hissing and humming: a range of expression that speaks to languages without words. Sounds so far below us, and so high above, that we are caught in between them. Others at a pitch and frequency the human ear cannot register. We are in a place that takes my breath away, one that could be described as celestial.

We are also behind a large American tourist who is in a state of regret.

'Why is the bridge shaking like that?'

'Don't worry, Rhonda! Keep going, girl!'

'Madam, it is normal. You are very safe!'

The attempts of our tour guide to reassure Rhonda are in vain.

'Is it supposed to shake like that?'

'Madam, you are very safe. Advance. Don't stop. Come.'

The tour guide beckons her towards him but Rhonda is slowing down to the point of stillness.

'I can't do it, LaToya! I can't!'

Rhonda has reached a point of hysteria which has sent her into full-body paralysis a hundred and thirty feet in the air. She is a third of the way along the canopy walkway that hangs above the trees linking one platform to another. Danso and I are behind her.

'I don' wanna die!'

'You ain't gon' die, Rhonda!' LaToya calls out as she continues to inch forward, her friend's paralysis not inhibiting her own progress.

Danso and I are stuck on the walkway behind the large bottleneck that is Rhonda's backside.

'Please, Madam, keep moving.'

Rhonda cannot or will not move. She is also unaware that the trembling she is experiencing is coming from her shaking body. Her hands are gripping the cables of the hanging canopy so tightly that their movement has transferred to us all. Her unsteady legs cause the wooden boards to creak beneath her.

'Father God have mercy!'

Rhonda must have missed the warning that advises tourists that the canopy trail might not be enjoyed by those with a fear of heights.

'I don' wanna die! Oh God, I don' wanna die!'

When we have been stuck behind Rhonda for more than twenty seconds, an eternity when you are waiting at cloud level, my mind turns to the physics of our situation. The tour guide assured us that the canopy can hold the weight of eight tonnes, or two big forest elephants. He did not specify whether that weight had to be distributed evenly across the canopy to manage it. What happens if the weight is concentrated in one section?!

Rhonda has started to sob.

'Madam, the canopy is safe for everybody, no matter how heavy you are or what your weight is.'

'Can it take 236 pounds?'

Rhonda's histrionics are entertaining until I realise that I do not know how many pounds are in a tonne, or the size of the elephants the tour guide was referring to. Male elephants can weigh twice as much as female elephants can't they? LaToya has made such headway that her words of reassurance are now distant. If Rhonda can hear them, they are having little effect. Her sobbing intensifies. A nervous energy starts to spread through the bottleneck. People are getting impatient and agitated.

The development requires the tour guide to take action. He walks back on himself, towards Rhonda, and slowly, carefully but confidently, takes one of her hands in each of his before walking backwards to assist with the movement of her legs. Like a child, he coaches her forwards.

'Don't worry, nothing will happen to you. You are fine, please. I am here. Walk with me. Can you see the birds? Look at the birds, Madam.'

Rhonda is not looking at the birds. She is not looking at anything. Her eyes are now closed. She is blind to the skill of the tour guide as he walks backwards while guiding her. And the birds that dance above us in the cloud-filled sky.

'The walkway has been here since 1994, and there has never been an incident or casualty.'

I want to ask how the walkways are maintained, but decide to save that question until we are back at ground level.

'Can you see the birds? Beautiful birds.'

He walks with the confidence of someone who knows the secrets of the rainforest and the canopies that hang above it. The confidence of someone who wouldn't be scared if night fell and he was forced to sleep there, alone.

'Come. You are almost there, Madam. Come towards me. Keep walking.'

He tells us about the wildlife beneath us. The elephants and buffalo and antelope, the monkeys, crocodiles and more. The birds who soar above the treetops. He knows their migration patterns and wingspans. He knows the distinct sound of their calls.

'Smile!' Danso turns around and captures me against a panoramic view of Kakum National Park, which is only slightly tarnished by Rhonda's presence. Squatting down in front of me, he takes a selfie of us both. 'Caption?'

'Prisoners of Rhonda?' I whisper.

I am caught off guard when I turn around to catch up to the group and hear Danso's voice:

'Oh shit!'

'What?'

'Shit!!'

'What is it?'

'I dropped my phone!'

'No!'

His face flushes with a panic that I share.

'Where did you drop it?'

There is no helpful information my question can elicit. Danso's phone is already a thing of the past. A device for the entertainment of the forest's wildlife, never to be seen again. I survey the area below with no recovery plan in mind.

'Cute, you've got dimples!' His voice draws my gaze upwards, where I see not only his smile but also his phone in his hand under a steady grip. His beard bobs up and down as he chuckles.

'What?'

'We're even now!' He is pleased with himself, and I am relieved enough to smile.

'Is this payback for Sushigate? Danso! I felt so bad for you!'

'Seriously, I haven't noticed them before.'

'What?'

'Your dimples.'

Rhonda heeds the guide's advice when we descend from the first canopy, and she decides to give the next part of the tour a miss. She will see if she can get some plantain chips to eat while she waits for LaToya. She needs to settle her stomach.

On the drive home, we entertain ourselves with reenactments of *Rhonda on the Canopy: A Play*, developing elaborate storylines that end in her being carried off by the guide and LaToya, her so-called friend. The group having no option but to step over her prostrate body and leave her to the mercy of the birds. Her trembling causes a tear in the canopy rope that sends us catapulting through the rainforest like orangutans. We roar with laughter when we imagine the news reaching Auntie Larjey.

'I can actually see her running through the rainforest with a raised cutlass in hand—'

'—cutlass in one hand and an offering of kelewele in the other—'

'—a rescue party of one!'

Her love for us is a palpable thing. And her comedy, a gift that keeps on giving.

'Can I see the pictures you took?'

'Sure.'

Our fingers touch as he passes me his phone from the holder and unlocks the screen with his eyes. The selfie of us captures more than our smiling faces. It captures the heads of the trees behind us and the ropes of the canopy. In the bottom right-hand corner is Rhonda's left foot, clad in a Reebok trainer and matching white sock. Top left is a flock of transient birds. The ones we heard but could not see.

We enjoy Auntie Larjey's snacks as we move between a standstill and snail's pace in the build-up of Accra traffic. In a wordless exchange, I replace the lid on Danso's water bottle when he hands it back to me.

'Are you tired?' It has been a long day of driving for him.

'No, I feel good! I had a great day with you.'

'Me too. Thank you for taking me to the rainforest. Best park ever!' I flash a smile at him and reflect on my trip so far. 'I wish I'd come to Ghana years ago. Being here is like finding the missing pieces to the puzzle of my life and holding them in my hands. Does that make sense?'

'Definitely. It allows you to join all the dots together, right? To understand not only who you are but why you are?'

'Exactly!'

'I get that.'

I understand his contentment from the smiles he throws in my direction whenever the traffic permits. The way he sings softly to the music that plays at low volume as we inch through Accra. He pauses briefly between tracks before studying the scene framed by his window.

'I dreamt of my mum last night,' he says the next time the traffic brings us to a stop. His head rests against the headrest and his eyes are fixed on the road ahead. 'For the first time in a long time.'

Maybe it's because of our conversation the other night. Telling me about her probably brought his mum to the forefront of his mind.

In the dream, they were playing basketball in the courtyard of their family home. He was eight years old and in his school uniform. She was in her cooking clothes, her hair wrapped in a scarf as she bounced the ball like a pro in bare feet. She was running rings around him as he tried but failed to get the ball off her. She had skills like Kobe. He grew breathless trying to keep up.

A misstep. An invisible stone or fumbling foot sent him crashing into contact with the concrete of the courtyard. She abandoned the ball and ran over to him, calling his name. It was only when he tasted the salt of his tears that he felt the burn of his shin, stripped of its outermost layer. She reappeared with a bottle of perfume in her hand and sprayed it onto his exposed skin. Directly onto the pink dermis. The pain sent fire flushing through his body and sweat to his forehead and temples and the back of his neck. The basketball had bounced to a stop next to the flower beds and the guava tree.

'I could smell her when I woke up. Her old perfume. It was like she was right there with me. It was as if she never left.'

He was moved by the believability of it all. The dream. The fragrance. That brief moment when you think it's true, before you wake up and realise it's not. Before you understand that it was a dream. Just a dream.

If I am moved, it is because I have had the same dream. I have had it every night on the eve of my birthday, ever since I can remember. A dream in a home that is not my own. A home in a country I have never before known. A dream where Mum, heavily pregnant, waddles around on the threshold of labour. Where she picks up the phone before replacing the handset in order to make a mug of Milo first. Where she tidies her paintbrushes before she dials his number. Or waits for one more contraction, just to be sure. A dream where Dad leaves work thirty seconds later, or even ten. Where they say 'I love you' before they end their phone call. Where there is more traffic on Dad's way home. Or less. Where he runs into an extra red light. Or misses a green one. A dream where he arrives at the hospital with seconds to spare before I am born and finds Mum in a state of sweaty labour, about to push. The penultimate push. A dream where he gets there just in time to see my birth. To meet me and I him. Only, in the dream, I never get to see his face. And I never hear his voice.

'I have dreams about my dad too. The same dream at the same time every year. But I only ever see his silhouette.'

We are parked at a junction where our losses meet. It is at the end of Auntie Larjey's road.

'How did he die, your dad?'

'He collided with an HGV on the motorway. On his way home from work. A forty-foot lorry. Hauling concrete breeze blocks to Tamale. It weighed thirty tonnes. His skull went through the windscreen of the car. He didn't suffer. He died instantly.'

CUSTOMS AND TRADITION

The news of Dad's death made Mum doubly incontinent and caused her to forget the mechanics of speech.

Auntie Larjey arrived at the hospital within hours – or was it minutes? – of hearing the news. She paced the corridors in search of her best friend, her heart thumping against the walls of her chest. 'Selom Akollor?' she interrogated the midwives at the nurses' station. 'Where is Selom Akollor?'

She found Mum in Bed 6, slumped at the waist and lost in the valley of the shadow of death. How had this happened? Auntie Larjey held me, her eyes wet with tears, her mouth moving in silent prayer. She held me because Mum couldn't. How could this have happened? She held me as Mum shivered with a shock that moved her head from left to right in disbelief, as she was blinded by tears and betrayed by her senses. As she stood up from her hospital bed and sought support from the ground beneath her. When she opened her mouth, Mum released a sound which made the hairs on Auntie Larjey's arms stand on end.

The noise coming from Mum's mouth found a new pitch when she visited Dad's people. It shook the air around her and the ground beneath. It travelled through me and made me cry, softly at first. The soft cry of a newborn baby yet to discover the capacity of her lungs. But with every tremor I discovered a new range of vocal ability until Mum's shaking made me hysterical and Auntie Edem took me gently from her arms. Auntie Larjey guided Mum to her seat so she didn't collapse there and then. So she didn't shatter into so many pieces they wouldn't be able to put her back together again. Tears streamed from her eyes, red and swollen, down her face.

Auntie Larjey's tears were for her best friend. For the pain that ravaged her body from the inside out. For the love she had lost and the life she would have to navigate without him. She cried, too, for her best friend's baby, a beautiful baby girl who would never see her father's face, hear his voice or feel his love. They took their seats amongst other members of Dad's family before Uncle Klenam said in a deep voice, breaking with sorrow, 'My brother is no more.'

Plastic chairs were brought to the house and set up in the living room for visitors. Mum struggled to recognise their faces. Aunties, uncles, neighbours, friends. All dressed in black. They shook hands with Mum, Dad's family and the visitors who had arrived before them. Some cried loudly as soon as they arrived. They leant on pieces of furniture or the wall to steady themselves and control their grief. Others cried quietly. Speaking the same words, over and over again. Why why why why why? How how how how how? They asked the questions to anyone and everyone, but mostly to God.

Uncle Klenam and Mum did not laugh and joke in the friendly way they used to when Dad was alive. When Mum arrived at the house with Auntie Larjey and Auntie Edem, he did not greet her in his familiar way, by shaking hands and clicking his thumb and middle finger against hers in the way they always had. It was as if they were meeting each other for the first time. Instead of talking about someone they had both loved, it felt like they were discussing politics, Uncle Klenam a supporter of the New Patriotic Party and Mum a supporter of the National Democratic Congress. It was a discussion in which neither could agree on the existence of bribery and corruption in government, or who was responsible for it. They could find no common ground on the best strategy for international development or economic growth. There was no accord to be found on the correct approach for investing in rural areas or the public health service. There was no middle ground on which they could meet. The ceiling fan of the living room provided little relief from the heat of grief. It was a still and stifling and slow-circulating heat. The motorised blades did little to cut through the tension.

'Selom, have you heard of a funeral in December before? Nobody buries the dead before Christmas like that.'

It was only recently that an Ashanti land chief had been buried after a family dispute around the identity of his legitimate heir had dragged on for years. Mum said that she would not leave Dad's body in the morgue for six years like those people, who could not decide amongst their family members who was the chief mourner.

'This is not a matter of not knowing who is, or who is not, the chief mourner. But you know we must consult our people. Our mother is in Lomé. She cannot travel to bury her son, but we must find a way to discuss the burial with her. Whether that is to send a representative or a delegation, we must decide. We do not want people to say that we buried our brother rush rush and not in the way he deserved.'

Dad had not deserved to die, but Uncle Klenam didn't say that. If Auntie Larjey had looked at Mum the way she looked at Uncle Klenam when he was talking, Mum would have stopped and closed her mouth. But Uncle Klenam did not know the language of Auntie Larjey's eyes.

'You know our people can bury between three months to a year after death. That is not what we are asking of you, Selom. Two months is all.'

Uncle Klenam's voice sounded strange the louder it became. He spoke as if he was in a hurry. As if he did not want to be caught by Dad being a politician and using weapons of politics against the mother of his child. They had not even done a knocking ceremony, so what say did Mum think she had? Uncle Klenam was doing what his brother would want by including her. But the matter was not up for discussion.

'You know our custom and our traditions. You know that my brother's family is more than you and his child.'

It wasn't fair that Uncle Klenam said this. When was the last time he had visited them and left without asking for something? Now he had come to take his seat as chief mourner and decide that Dad would spend Christmas in the refrigerator at the mortuary. There was nothing Mum could say to change his mind. She kept quiet in the meetings that took place after that. Meetings in which details were discussed and plans made. As if it was Uncle Klenam who knew Dad better than everyone and not she, who was his best friend.

'To bury him before February would be an abomination. People will talk.'

Uncle Klenam spoke firmly to help Mum understand that his word was final. It made Auntie Larjey's jaw clench to see Mum hushed like a child who had not yet learned the ways of the world.

Uncle Klenam gave directions for the next steps.

'We have not yet begun preparations for the funeral brochure – that can take time. We must arrange for the house to be painted so that we are ready to receive guests. There are so many preparations that have not even started. And all these things cost money.'

He would visit the funeral home every day before the burial as a witness for the family, to make sure Dad's body remained intact. And that nobody used any part of him for rituals.

There was no suggestion of dancing pallbearers. The circumstances of Dad's death did not allow for that. He had not lived to see the birth of his first child, the daughter he had dreamt about and longed to meet. He had not even lived to see old age. There was nothing to celebrate. There was nothing but grief.

Auntie Larjey found it hard to let me and Mum go back home. She did not want us to be in a place where she could not care for us every second of every day. She did not want Mum's tears to wake me at night, or for mine to wake Mum in the early hours of the morning when she had found sleep after hours of searching. She did not like to see Mum wander from Dad's record player to their bedroom like a woman who did not know the rooms of her own house. To sit on their bed like a person lost and smooth the sheet over and over and over again long after its creases had disappeared. To hold the things he used to hold and turn them over in her hands: his records, his watch, his handkerchief. Mum had made of their bed an island on which she was shipwrecked. Auntie Larjey pleaded for time, but Mum insisted. She wanted to go home to feel close to Dad.

Auntie Edem and Auntie Larjey visited Mum while she navigated the corridors of grief in the house she and Dad used to share. They cooked for Mum and comforted her and sat with her in silence and sadness. In the beginning, Mum would raise her lowered head and part her lips as if...

as if she was going to say something. But just as slowly, they would rearrange themselves in a straight line and her body would deflate with a sigh. She had lost half of herself. Her right arm did not know what to do without the left. She stored the food they brought her in the freezer. She did not care to eat.

It was lucky for Mum that she had me. When she could stand again and bear her own weight, she understood with clarity that I was her most precious thing. After the torrent of her tears had slowed, she cared for me like a jewel she was scared to let out of her sight. She fed me even though she did not feed herself, and dressed me like a delicate doll. She did not know how she could be both Mum and Dad to the daughter they had imagined raising together. Or that she would ever be enough, alone. But she loved me because I was the last part of him. She loved me because I was both of them. She loved me. And I was her reason.

CHRISTMAS

Mum saw Dad in the funeral home and touched his cold body. On his face, he wore new features. Lacerations across his forehead, cheeks and nose, marked by a map of dried blood. A cut across his lips had appeared since they had last danced together. It had sliced his mouth diagonally and unevenly. Bruises shadowed the land of the face she knew so well. Soft matter once protected by an unfractured skull was distended beyond the point of repair. If he could have smiled, his mouth would have exposed spaces where his teeth had been before the impact of the crash dislodged them and sent them flying in different directions across the tarmac. With the arc of his swollen lips pointing downwards, he wore a sad expression. He was sad because he had not been ready to leave this world. He had been too young and too happy and too excited about life. About me and what the future had in store for us. The fingers on his right hand were bent and stiff. When Mum tried to straighten them, Uncle Klenam told her to stop. The room smelled as if air freshener had been sprayed to mask the smell of death.

A blue rosary hung around his neck, against skin which had turned an unfamiliar shade of brown. It was a colour she had never seen worn by the living. On top of it, someone had dusted him with a powder that made his complexion ash-like and transformed his whole being into a spectacle.

The make-up on his face hid the colour, but not the texture, of the skin the windscreen had taken from him. She wanted to know who had painted him like that. Had they seen him when he had lived and breathed and danced? Did they know him as he stood at the threshold of fatherhood? Did they know him at all?

There was a dent in his collarbone. It appeared just above the cloth they had dressed him in. She wondered what other parts of him were broken. What other parts were shrouded in cloth purchased for a corpse. Were there pieces of him on shards of glass swept to the side of the motorway? Mum asked Dad if he could hear her, but he didn't answer. The AC was on full blast. She shivered as she stood at his feet.

'Is it fine?'

Mum raised her head and saw the face of the woman who had painted Dad's face like a stranger. She wore an expression that was eager to please, to know that in preparing his body to be viewed she had done justice to the deceased. But there was no amount of make-up or concealment that could make the situation 'fine'. And there was no justice that Mum could find to dull the ache of her broken heart.

'Heat is not good for the body,' the woman said. 'It speeds up the process of decomposition.'

Until then, Mum had not thought of maggots eating Dad's flesh.

Uncle Papa arrived from America to be by Auntie Larjey's side so she could be by Mum's. He came before Uncle Klenam arrived to take his seat as head of the family and chief mourner without whom the preparations for the funeral could not begin. He came before Dad's younger brother landed from Togo and his sisters boarded a plane from Maryland. He came before Dad's cousins and extended family arrived from the Volta region. Before the news of Dad's death had spread around the Knights and Ladies of Marshall and the whole of Community 6 like wildfire.

By the time Uncle Papa arrived, Mum had refused to eat for three days, and Auntie Larjey had started to spoon-feed her.

A large announcement with Dad's face on it was fixed to the gate at the front of the house like a billboard. Beneath his name, it listed the day he was born and the day he died. The announcement made a lady from the Knights and Ladies of Marshall fall to her knees and wail like a child: 'You have left us, our brother! Why have you left us?!' Her voice went up and down like someone who was learning a new song and did not know the right register to sing it in.

Mum sat in the courtyard with Auntie Edem, Auntie Larjey, Uncle Papa and the rest of Dad's relatives. The air was still under the shade of the canopy that had been erected at speed to provide cover from the sun. Relatives who had travelled to the house would eat, sleep and bathe there. They wore T-shirts and wrappers to sit and mourn in the heat. It was quiet under the canopy, apart from the sound of loud tears. Auntie Larjey held Mum in ways that would allow her to draw strength from her friend's body. She would remove her hand from time to time to dry her eyes with a handkerchief she kept in her bra. Later, when the wailing had quietened, the drummers arrived.

A woman interrupted the order of the compound when she ran before seated guests to perform a loud song and dance of grief. She ran with her hands on her head, dragging her feet along the ground as if her chale wote were made of lead. The talking drums started to tell their stories about death and to narrate Dad's journey to the afterlife. The beat of bare hands against the taut skin of the drums claimed the same beat as the hearts of the grieving and quietened others. The woman's ululations sent them into a frenzied beat, causing tears that had settled to flow once more.

'What is that? Is it she who has lost her father?' Auntie Larjey frowned at the demonstration. The loudness and brashness of it.

The woman's performance lasted for longer than it should have. It demonstrated that grief was not a linear experience but a thing that ebbed and flowed. As soon as it seemed that she had found a composure which allowed her to lift her feet from the floor and walk with a heavy heart, one foot in front of the other, hysteria would catch her once more and hold her hostage in the middle of the compound. It would flail her limbs in the air and bend her body at the waist. It would cause hot tears to flush her face and make a striking performance of her grief.

When more guests arrived, they made their way around the courtyard to greet those who were already seated. To Mum, Auntie Edem and Auntie Larjey they offered 'Baba na mi', 'Sorry'. By the middle of the afternoon, almost two hundred people had gathered.

Dad had left the land of the living. He was no longer of flesh but of spirit. Had Mum not seen him at the funeral home the day before, she might have screamed to see his body lying in the living room like a statue at night. She had been to plenty of funerals, of course, but there was a difference between attending a funeral to pay her respects or catch up with friends, and seeing the father of her child lie in state in his family home.

The outside of the house had been painted in preparation to receive guests. And fairy lights bordered the white silk cloth that hung from the walls inside. At a different function, a birthday party or a wedding, the lights could be set to slo-glo, slo-fade or to twinkle and flash. At Christmastime, they could even be turned from white to multicolour. Mum sat in a chair by Dad's side, her hands clasped together in prayer mirroring his. When guests arrived throughout the night, they circled the coffin to see him one last time.

Mum fell asleep to the sound of the talking drums just before dawn. They had been telling their stories about Dad's journey to the afterlife for hours and hours. The stories followed her into sleep.

That night, she dreamt that she was carrying me on her back through the cocoa plantation after a drought which had destroyed many of the crops. Dad was afraid there would be nothing to harvest and that we would have little food to eat. Mum walked for hours to get to the plantation with me on her back. She did not tell Dad where she was going. While she was walking, she prayed to God for rain. She offered to sacrifice the two goats they had, and the chickens that roamed the courtyard. She would even pour libation if that was God's wish. If that was what was needed for rain to fall from the heavens to quench the arid land and save Dad's crops. The trees were tall but their leaves were yellowing, threatening the fruitfulness of the harvest. She untied me from her back and set me down on the ground. I took the soil in my hands and played with the fallen beans that were within my reach. As I played, Mum walked, her arms outstretched to the sky. She walked towards the cocoa plants, praying to God for the drought to end. As she walked, the leaves started to obscure me. I dipped in and out of her sight until they swallowed me completely. I started to cry for her to come back. She didn't hear me at first. But when she tried to follow the sound of my cry, she couldn't find me. I sat there on the ground where she had left me, earth between my fingers, waiting for her. That's when the heavens opened.

As she looked for me amidst the trees and the leaves, it started to rain.

In the morning, Mum wore the black-and-red cloth Dad's family had ordered from the textile manufacturer for the Saturday burial. They did not wear white and black like they had for Grandpa's funeral, when they had been able to celebrate his ninety-four years of life. The red in the cloth represented the tragedy of Dad's passing, the pain of their losing him. His blood. At the cemetery, they walked past tombstones like they were dodging potholes in the road.

The sound of traffic from the main road quietened as they entered the belly of the cemetery, until it disappeared altogether. Mum looked at the hole that had been dug for Dad. It was dark and eternal, like the death that had taken him. The priest who officiated at the graveside said, 'God's timing is the best timing.'

Mum found no comfort in those words. She did not cry until they lowered Dad into the ground and threw flowers and dirt on top of his coffin. They left him in the cemetery to sleep there alone.

Back at the house she stood on the veranda and watched guests drink Guinness and eat suya kebabs. The drummers gathered in the centre of the compound once more and beat their drums with a fervour that made the guests step from side to side. A group of women removed handkerchiefs from their handbags and bras, and shoes from their feet, and stood to form a circle that did not know how to be still. A trumpeter created brass notes to accompany the voices of the people. The music sailed above their heads and into the blue sky. The women shuffled their bare feet in the red sand and bent at the waist to shake their bums at the same speed as their fast-moving handkerchiefs. They met in the middle of the compound to sing and dance, to entertain and enjoy. Mum stood at the periphery, pain burning within her like a searing flame. She wished the rain would come to extinguish it and to wash away her grief. Even women who did not have handkerchiefs stood up from their seats to join the moving circle and to dance the borborbor.

After the funeral, Uncle Klenam kept Mum outside the circle of Dad's family. Perhaps he blamed her for the circumstances that had led to Dad's death. Perhaps he blamed me. Perhaps he blamed us both.

AFEHYIA PA
Ah-fee-shi-ah pa

Auntie Larjey fires questions at me from the left-hand side of the bed as I walk towards her from the bathroom under the spell of sleep. She is propped up against soft pillows in silk pyjamas and a headtie. The digital clock on the bedside table reads 6.13 a.m. The cockerels have long ago started their call, but it feels too early to wake. The left side of the bed is Uncle Papa's side. His overnight trip to Kumasi created for Auntie Larjey a perfect hostage situation.

'You will sleep in my room tonight!'

'Is it by force?'

'Yes!'

'Eiii, Larjey, do you still snore?'

'Selom, tell the truth. Is it me who snores, or you?'

I am the piggy in the middle of their sister sandwich. Mum returns her phone to the bedside table as I climb over her to reclaim my place between them.

'Did you sleep well?'

'I'm still asleep, Mum.' My voice is croaky for lack of use. I close my eyes in the hope that I can return to sleep. It is a misplaced hope.

'Sika, I haven't slept,' Auntie Larjey complains with the frustration of the restless.

'Did Mum's snoring keep you up as well?'

'That's a lie!' Mum's attempt at righteous indignation rouses me.

'I'm still waiting for the filla!'

'What filla?'

'Hoh! What did you say when you came home yesterday?' There is no attempt by Auntie Larjey to speak in the soft voice she used when she waved me and Danso off in the direction of Cape Coast some twenty-four hours ago. Today, she speaks like a woman who does not know how to whisper.

'Oh! Yesterday with Danso? It was amazing. We went to Kakum National Park.'

She assumes the deliberate withholding of information is to deprive her of joy. 'Eh heh. And? Do you want me to beg, is that it?'

Auntie Larjey's levels of enthusiasm on subjects which hold me at their centre makes me laugh. It also makes my heart full of love for her. I want to ask for an update too. Has she had a chance to talk to Mum about the thing we spoke about? About Dad's family, and me meeting them? Will we go to them or will they come to us? How soon can we meet? But I cannot do that with Mum on one side of me. I cannot speak about it until I can speak to Auntie Larjey alone. Navigating Project RnR without Mum makes me realise it is the biggest thing I have ever kept from her. I hope she will forgive me for excluding her. I hope she will understand.

'Were you easy in each other's company? Did you make each other laugh? What was the vibe?'

'Eiii, the vibe?'

Auntie Larjey's enthusiasm persists. She wishes she was a fly on the wall before shifting her focus to the future: 'When will you see him again?'

'He's coming to the party, so I'll see him there.'

'I see.'

I assume I have given her enough nectar, because she smiles when she hears it confirmed: Danso is coming to the party. We will be at the party, together. I abandon my attempt to fall back to sleep when I realise I am here to entertain, not to rest.

'Sika, how much red red did you eat yesterday?'

Red red for the ripe plantain and black-eyed beans, cooked in red palm oil Esi made for me on request.

'The beans were repeating on you all night!'

'What?'

Mum makes the sound of an untuned trumpet playing a staccato sound through pursed lips.

'Mum, stop!'

Auntie Larjey joins in, adding another brass instrument to their improvised orchestra.

'Sika, you were on fire!'

'I'm glad you went to the toilet.'

'I went for a wee!'

They kikikiki laugh together as I concede the remote possibility that the black-eyed beans may have given me gas. We are in no hurry to get out of bed.

'So will you book your ticket today or tomorrow?' Auntie Larjey is determined that I book a return flight to Ghana before I leave the country. 'Why don't you come at Christmas! Christmas in Ghana is fun! Selom, am I lying?'

Mum reserves a special smile for Auntie Larjey's rhetorical questions.

'Christmas in Ghana was always fun.'

At Christmastime, Mum remembers, her mother would use the deep freezer to store the slaughtered goat from which she would make delicious meals over the festive period: fufu and light soup, banku and okro soup and tuo zaafi.

The freezer would be so full she would have to dig to find things that had become buried: the diced beef the butcher had sent, the kelewele that was too much to fry in one go, spring rolls, samosas and other titbits. Guests would pass through the house from the middle of December until the first week of January. They would leave with full stomachs and promises to visit again before the end of the festive period.

Family friends would come for the nkate cake Mama would make from peanuts and melted sugar, or her famous cakes and biscuits. And the house would shake with the speakers of the sound system Dada would arrange in the courtyard. Christmas was a fun time. There were so many things to organise: music, hired tables and red ribbons to tie on the backs of plastic chairs. Mum would hang the paper chains and snowflakes she had made in school, and on Christmas Eve, Mama and Dada would throw a big party for their friends. The photographer and videographer would capture the night: the visitors, the music, the Christmas tree and the memories.

When they went to church, Dada would always suggest they leave a little earlier to see the parade in Accra and listen to the musicians play. Mum never forgot how scared she was when she saw the performers for the first time, the ones who wore masks that made them look like spirits, dancing in their colourful costumes of white, green, pink, orange and blue.

'The way they surrounded the car when it was stuck in traffic!'

Mum had cried like a terrorised child. Edem, being fearless, wasn't fazed.

'It was the masks that scared me.'

She had been too young then to understand that behind

the dark eyes of clowns and monsters and ghouls were people celebrating the festive season, people just like them. Her terror seemed to please the masqueraders and send them into a frenzy. When Dada rolled down his window, Mum feared she had taken her last breath. She had never even seen snow.

'Imagine my shock when he gave them ten cedis and they moved past our car and on to the next!'

Dada told her not to be scared, but his words fell on deaf ears.

The parade was one of those things that instilled terror until it didn't. When she grew older, Mum would beg to go to Accra to see it.

'Mama, can I have a costume like that next year?'

'You? You who used to cry in the car thinking they would come and get you?'

The memory makes her smile. 'Christmas in Ghana was always fun.'

Apart from the year Auntie Edem was sick and stayed in bed on Christmas Eve, Christmas Day and Boxing Day, moving only to throw up the contents of her stomach.

'That year Edem did not eat Christmas lunch.'

She did not eat at all. She didn't even get up to open her presents. Mama diagnosed food poisoning. On Christmas morning, Dada said he was surprised there was anything left to throw up. But Auntie Edem continued to be sick, throughout the day and in the morning on Boxing Day. A fever established itself that made her shiver and sweat at the same time, groaning as she clutched her stomach and writhed on her bed. By the afternoon, Dada was no longer persuaded by Auntie Edem's claims that she was starting to feel better. Mama insisted that they take her to the hospital. But by the evening Auntie Edem started to take fluids: small sips of water that required great effort to swallow. By morning, the vomiting had slowed down.

'Apart from that year, Christmas was always fun.'

THE MAN IN BALMAIN

The man sitting at Auntie Edem's dining table has a shrill laugh that travels from the living room, along the corridor to the bedroom, and down the length of my spine. Outside the window are three Mercedes, still shiny from the showroom. In the first, the driver caresses the steering wheel as if tracing the curves of a woman. The man in the passenger seat watches the scene, tempted by the sleek leather on display. The windows of the car are rolled up to guarantee the circulation of premium air conditioning. Four men from the second vehicle peruse the inside of the courtyard, while another four patrol the outside perimeter. They are dressed in suits notwithstanding the heat of the day. I leave Loli with paper and crayons and head over to investigate the cause of the noise.

Mum sits at the living room table opposite a man wearing Balmain: a jacket and matching joggers. They are not cheap rip-offs or black market goods. The newspaper in front of her is closed; a blue biro lies beside it.

Hehehe, the Man in Balmain laughs again.

Mum is uncharacteristically quiet. I cannot tell whether she has missed the punchline, or whether she has simply refused to catch it.

The man sips from a glass of whisky, greedy gulps from a glass that will soon need to be refilled. He pours from a bottle within his reach. It is brand new. It is the first time I have seen alcohol in Auntie Edem's house. Mum's glass is empty. I know the Man in Balmain by his voice. It is so shrill I know I am not hearing it for the first time. It is the type of voice you register once you have heard it, the type of voice you do not forget. He is both familiar and unfamiliar.

Auntie Edem walks towards us carrying a tray of fufu and steaming light soup. What I dislike about fufu is its texture, the feel of it in my mouth and against my tongue. It is so close and yet so far from its cousin, banku, which I could eat with okro stew every day for the rest of my life. Auntie Edem's movements suggest that she is serving the Prince of Zamunda, and that she will soon be readying to bark like a dog and hop on one leg out of servitude to him.

'An incredible miracle?'

'Is happening in this place!'

'Amen! Amen! Amen!'

The call and response forces a violent realisation as I recognise the Man in Balmain as the Prophet! Away from the Church of Incredible Miracles, he is a man in designer clothes! Mum speaks slowly as my mouth opens, shuts and opens again like a fish.

'Sika, Auntie Edem's…the Prophet…has come to eat.' She hesitates to call him by his self-appointed title. It is one which suggests divine power and implies a level of deference she is unable to afford him.

'Prophet, you are welcome,' Auntie Edem says as she walks towards him, smiling before bending at the knee.

The Prophet eyes up the food she sets before him like a king. His eyelashes, like a broom overpopulated with bristles, fan his face as the spiciness of the soup catches his nostrils. They are incompatible with the steeliness of his other features: his angular cheekbones and hard-set jaw.

His stern eyebrows which arch like an upside-down v. The peppeh catches my throat and makes me cough.

'Sister Edem, you are spoiling me!'

Auntie Edem laughs in a way that transforms her from an adult, somebody's mother, into a shy little schoolgirl. After serving him, or prostrating, or both, she straightens at the hips and rubs her hands down the side of her wrapper. She is wearing a T-shirt. On the front, the face of the Prophet beams under the now familiar words THE CHURCH OF INCREDIBLE MIRACLES. He smiles a wide smile. The smile of a blessed man.

'Hi,' is all I can manage. I do not know how to address him in Balmain clothing or in this context.

'Sika! Our visitor from London! You are highly welcome!'

Auntie Edem is the only person who responds. 'Sika, won't you offer the Prophet another drink?' she asks at the same time she unscrews the cap to the bottle of whisky – an action the Prophet has already shown himself capable of – and pours a generous amount into his glass.

'This is my favourite whisky!'

'I bought it especially for you, Prophet.'

The glass hardly grazes the table before the Prophet sweeps it up in his hand and decants a third of the contents into his mouth. I cannot understand why Auntie Edem has shelled out for a bottle of premium whisky for this man, or why she is wearing a T-shirt with his face emblazoned on it.

'Sika from London! How is it?' He is unable to speak at normal volume, so used to addressing crowds he must be.

'Fine, thanks.' I remind myself to close my jaw and remove it from the floor.

'Your auntie is a righteous and highly favoured woman. She has prayed and fasted and sacrificed for this very moment. When she would be with you and your mother under the roof of her house. You see how God works?!'

His voice takes on a pitch which makes my hair follicles itch.

'Do you see how God works?!'

Repetition in the absence of response.

'Amen, Prophet. Amen.'

The Prophet's hands are in the bowl of soapy water Auntie Edem has brought to him. I watch as he rubs them, one against the other, soapsuds sticking to the diamond clusters of his pinkie ring. He holds his dripping hands over the bowl before taking a cloth held out for him to dry them.

'Sister Selom, won't you join us?'

I don't know who the Prophet is referring to when he says the word 'us'; he is the only one eating. Auntie Edem stands to the right of him in readiness to respond to any wish he might convey, any need he might have. I glance to my left. The downturn of Mum's mouth shows little sign of straightening. And the fold of her arms communicates something else altogether. The Prophet does not wait for Mum to respond before taking a portion of the pounded cassava root with his fingers and scooping the fufu and light soup into his mouth.

'Sister Edem, I don't know anyone who makes light soup like you do. Heh! This is one of your best!'

His enjoyment of the meal is something I see as well as hear through the machination of his mouth. Meanwhile, Auntie Edem smiles like someone who has discovered the Holy Grail.

'Oh, Prophet, I just made this one quickly because I know you like it.'

Mum looks at Auntie Edem and enquires with her eyes if she is okay.

'Mr Asamoah, let me leave you to enjoy your meal in peace.'

The Prophet starts at Mum's use of his government name. 'Not at all! It is you London people I have come to bless after all!' He sounds like he is about to choke on her audacity, but at the last minute decides against it. He has tucked the tip of the dishcloth he used to dry his hands into the collar of his T-shirt so it hangs like a napkin against his chest. Mum breathes deeply and leans back in her chair, her arms still folded at the chest. The Prophet takes this as a cue to begin his story:

'There are some invisible demons working in our community. You people must beware!'

The rise and fall of Mum's chest implies an agitation that neither the Prophet nor Auntie Edem appear to recognise. Her eyebrows furrow.

'Prophet, the woman who had maggots crawling from her vagina lives less than four kilometres from here!'

At this, Mum and I react in unison. Our necks turn abruptly to look at Auntie Edem as she points in a direction we do not attempt to follow with our eyes.

'It is a very serious matter,' the Prophet replies.

'That woman had been raped by a demon. Do you know what that can do to a person? To the children they will bear?'

Mum does not kiss her teeth discreetly. And the Prophet does not register the act. He strikes me as the type of person who is more attuned to the sound of his own voice than the voices of others. Like a faithful fan, Auntie Edem tells of the powerful preaching the Prophet exercised over the possessed woman. The way she writhed on the floor as the demon fought her from inside. It was only when the Prophet stamped with his right foot on her vagina and commanded the demon to out that the woman found stillness.

'What next, an anointed penis?!' Mum asks at raised volume. She excuses herself to go to the toilet, taking her phone with her.

'Heh, that demon was stubborn,' the Prophet says, between mouthfuls of fufu and sips of whisky.

'Stubborn!' Auntie Edem echoes.

'Maggots from her vagina?'

'Don't worry, Prophet will bless you for protection.'

The Prophet lifts his bowl to drink the remainder of the light soup, before wiping his mouth in satisfaction. Sweat has gathered below his nostrils and above his lip. I feel nausea when he belches loudly and unapologetically, rubbing the pot belly underneath his clothing. I understand his smile as a grimace and his voice as dark noise.

'Heh! I haven't seen Loli! Is she not here?'

'Oh! Prophet, she is here!' Auntie Edem shakes her head as if she is coming to, out of reverie and back to reality. 'Loli! Lololi!' she calls from the living room. 'Lo-liii!'

When Loli appears from her mother's bedroom, green crayon in hand, the Prophet smiles and calls her to him. 'Heh, little girl, where have you been?' he asks, pinching her right cheek in a way that can only be painful. I start with the desire to protect my little cousin as Mum rejoins us. 'Didn't you know that Prophet was here?' he asks.

He can only speak of himself in the third person to encourage others to do the same. It can be of no consequence to a five-year-old that he has visited her house to eat and drink her mum out of pocket, his entourage waiting for him outside.

'Loli, didn't I tell you that when the Prophet comes, you must come and greet him?'

Loli has lost the power of speech. She stands in one spot, still as a soldier called to attention, and looks to her mum for the answer to the question she does not understand.

'How are you?' the Prophet asks, looking her up and down.

'F-f-fine, thank you.'

I want to hold her hand or sit her on my lap.

'God is watching you from where?'

'From a d-d-distance.'

'Good,' the Prophet responds. 'Come and take my bowl for me.'

When I realise he has called Loli away from her colouring to ask her to dispose of his used bowl, a plea for Mum to intervene escapes my mouth. I stand up instinctively, incredulously. Before I have finished calling her name, Mum is out of her seat. This triggers Auntie Edem to start. The quick succession of movement introduces a new tension to the room. We are all standing: Mum, Auntie Edem and me. Our eyes move between Loli and the Prophet; he looks only at her.

'Sweetheart,' Mum says to Loli. 'Come, let's finish your picture.' Without another glance in his direction, she takes her niece by the hand and leads her back in the direction from which she has come.

I follow Mum into Auntie Edem's room, my heart beating furiously in my chest. There is so much to say and yet I don't know where to start. Angry tears form in the corners of my eyes and I struggle to give words to my feelings.

'Loli, what is your favourite colour?' Mum asks.

'I like pink.'

'Pink? Pink is my favourite colour too!' she says as she hands a crayon to Loli and watches her draw.

The pink nail varnish from two days ago has been removed from her fingers and toes.

After her bath, Loli fights the sleep that weighs down her eyelids and turns her smile into a yawn. I fall asleep beside her in an unintentional act of solidarity.

When I stir, it is to the raised voices of Mum and Auntie Edem. Loli is fast asleep, her legs in tree pose, her arms in mountain. I cover her with the blanket she has kicked off and prop myself up on my elbows. They must be in the kitchen. Obstructed by the corridor and a closed door, it is hard to make out what they are saying. But in the exchange of muffled words, I understand a charged energy in the space that separates us. Loud words ricochet between the walls. It is the kind of heated discussion I imagine belongs to siblings. One in which I have no place to intervene. I tiptoe to the bedroom door and open it gently.

'For God's sake, Edem. She's a child!'

When I hear the movement of bodies, I close the door and try to interpret through the medium of wood. They are not speaking in raised voices; they are shouting at each other. No. Mum is shouting at Auntie Edem, her voice like a sword.

'What world are you living in?!'

It cuts down any offering Auntie Edem makes. Her pitch ascends and her words fall like shards of glass.

'Have you ever thought of anyone other than yourself?!'

My heart beats louder and louder until I am worried it will wake Loli.

'The truth hurts, Edem!'

I am an only child. I do not know the rules of sibling warfare. I do not know whether to go to Mum or stay put.

'You are living a lie!'

I can't leave Loli. What if she wakes up to hear my mum call hers a hypocrite and a liar? I do not recognise Mum's shouting voice.

'Sister? You?'

I startle at the sound of footsteps coming towards me along the corridor and nearing the bedroom. I climb into bed with Loli and close my eyes.

'With a sister like you, who needs enemies?!' Mum shouts as if it is news for public information. 'You are no sister of mine!'

Before she opens the door to the bedroom and steps loudly into the dark.

THE PARTY

On the day of Auntie Larjey and Uncle Papa's party, the sun refuses to set. It shines a warm glow on Mum's face as she takes her turn in the make-up chair, her face contoured to perfection. Hints of ember in her red locks catch the evening light, while fake lashes add a detail of glamour that befits her. A mulberry blush accentuates the angle of her cheekbones and a red pout draws attention to the radiance of her smile. I sit on the bed and watch her beauty magnify.

Our matching, mint-green lace cloth, free from its protective polythene, hangs patiently in front of the wardrobe waiting for a body to adorn. Measurements taken by Auntie Larjey's seamstress have been used to transform six yards of beautiful fabric into handmade couture. The workshop, an atelier where nimble hands make magic happen. Cuts of fabric scattered like stars underfoot. Sewing machines and foot pedals and large cutting scissors in constant motion providing a hum of industrious activity. The seamstress's ability to hold in her mouth any number of pins while speaking both a hazard and a skill. Her ability to realise my abstract description of a 'cross-halterneck-pencil-skirt-dress-type thing', before tailoring it to fit like a second skin, causes me to wonder at her talent. Auntie Larjey, creative director, providing a running commentary as the seamstress takes in a 'tiny bit here' and lets out 'a little bit there'. Finished pieces are ready to be collected.

Mum looks glorious in her balloon-sleeve, off-the-shoulder design. She concedes that the thigh-high slit was the right choice; it shows the slenderness of her legs. In her devotion to Auntie Larjey's party preparation, Mum is bridesmaid, best friend and chief organiser.

Corey and Casey have arrived from America to complete our collective sense of family. They fill any quiet moment with laughter. And despite standing at six foot two, they allow Auntie Larjey to mother them as if they are still small boys. We are more excited about the party than we know how to manage, because they are here to celebrate with us. They are experts in teasing their mum and making her smile from ear to ear in the process. That they are taller than their father and dwarf their mother is something Mum cannot get over. The boys are gentle giants, apples which have fallen close to the parental tree. Sometimes Auntie Larjey looks at them and doesn't even speak. She just beams like an object charged with pride.

The sun shines its rays on tables decorated with beautiful floral displays of pink and white and lilac. They have been set on brilliant white tablecloths by hard-working hands. Groundsmen survey the lawn and fountains for any foreign objects and ensure that candles and fairy lights are placed as directed. A gardener inspects the flora to check the perfect pruning of flowers and manicure of the lawn. The valets familiarise themselves with the designated spaces where cars will be parked. Meanwhile, caterers fill chafing dishes under the direction of a no-nonsense chef. The waiters have their instructions. The DJ looks like a man well versed in the art of making still feet move and stationary bodies dance. He has set up speakers and turntables under a shaded spot, and is ready to play.

THE PARTY

On arrival, guests carry a wave of audible excitement across the threshold of Auntie Larjey's house. Polished faces gravitate towards each other like poles across a magnetic field. They collect champagne on arrival and take pictures against the perfect backdrop of the garden. A puppet show of selfie-taking phones and a roaming photographer combine to ensure that people, outfits and moments are captured for posterity. The light of the setting sun seems custom-made for the evening.

Introductions are made between new people and reunions held among old friends. People engage in conversations where intrigue to know competes with impatience to tell. Uncle Agape is delayed as he makes his way from the entrance gate to the epicentre of the party, navigating his way around and through the guests and their kinetic happiness. If he is in a hurry to see Mum again, his walk does not betray his urgency. He is interrupted by handshakes and hugs, stopping for laughter and pleasantries en route. I note the rise and fall of his chest as he draws closer to Mum, approaching her from behind. He recognises her frame or some other feature, it's hard to know which. Whatever he says to her when she turns around is quietly spoken. It has the effect of introducing a special smile to take up residence on her face. It is accompanied by an inward glow sourced from joy, a display of dimples and a brilliance in her eyes. Her arms refuse to let him go.

When the MC announces that we should be upstanding for Mr and Mrs Baden, we rise to our feet and arch our necks for an early view of splendour. Auntie Larjey has thought of every detail, and it shows: in the precision of her pencilled eyebrows, the extension of her lashes and the bounce of her Viola Davis wig. Hand in hand, Auntie Larjey and Uncle Papa dance past and between the tables where their guests are waiting to welcome them. A view of twenty-five years of marriage. They are dressed in matching kente in the predominant colour of white. It boasts patches of gold, with a pattern of gold diamonds in its foreground. Stripes of red, blue, black and green feature throughout. Corey and Casey are less identical as adults than their childhood photos would suggest. They wear long shirt and trouser sets in blue and green, chosen by Auntie Larjey: with or without their consultation. Their sunglasses do little to hide their smiling eyes as they walk behind their parents. Specimens of excellence. And of course Fifi is tucked under Auntie Larjey's arm, boasting freshly coiffed and lightly perfumed corkscrew curls. She will soon be enclosed in the quiet of the house but is not to be denied her entrance.

Auntie Larjey's priest says that the dance floor is lonely, and that it will be necessary for us to keep it company for the rest of the night. 'But first, let us bow our heads in prayer.'

I scan the scene before lowering my head to examine the height of my heels and the blades of grass underneath them. Like a child preparing to blow out the candles on her birthday cake, I close my eyes to make a wish.

'We thank God for Auntie Larjey and Uncle Papa, their love for each other and their commitment to the vows they made twenty-five years ago. Theirs is a faith that has stood the test of time. It is a faith they have called upon to navigate the challenges life has placed in their path. They have been richly blessed by God. And they have shared those blessings with the people they love and those in need. Today is a day for celebrating the strength of their union and giving thanks for their presence in our lives. It is also a day for eating, and dancing. And enjoyment! Amen.'

'Amen!'

A collective response from guests. The opening prayer

is short, sweet and succinct. I conclude that Auntie Larjey knows her priest well. And that she likes him for his message, delivery and good humour. When he takes his seat and loosens his collar, I understand that Father Darku is as excited by the aromas escaping the open chafing dishes as the rest of us.

Voices replace the quiet reserved for prayer as music and mingling are restored. I look around again and see a queue beginning to form at the buffet table. Mum and Uncle Agape are lost in conversation. I have never seen her this way, so committed to the company of a man. So content in it. She squeezes his arm in mock play as they go back and forth in Ga. He looks dapper in his burgundy cloth and shorts combo; the colour compliments her outfit beautifully. When he puts his hand to his lower back and feigns the walk of a man much older than his years, it makes her laugh with her whole body. He pours wine into her glass and invites her to cheers. When they clink glasses, they look into each other's eyes for longer than is customary.

I am surprised by what the butterflies in my stomach do when I turn around and see Danso. He is late, but he is here, smiling as he walks towards me, the cut and fit of his suit on full display. He looks so different to the casual Danso who took selfies with me on the canopies above Kakum National Park. A cousin to the smart-casual Danso who ate sushi and shito with me against a backdrop of candles and fairy lights.

'Hey babe, you look stunning!'

He speaks quietly. And with his head bent to kiss my cheek, I am caught by the scent of his fragrance. It is captivating. It makes the butterflies in my stomach flutter to my heart. So irresistible it is almost edible. It makes my tongue catch on my words when I open my mouth to speak. I want to stay here and breathe. And maybe lick his neck – too much?

'Hey...' I steady myself against his arm and feel the strength of his muscles under the fabric of his shirt. I wonder if he can feel the pounding of my heart in the palm of my hand.

'Seriously, you look incredible, Sika!'

You look fit as fuck, I think, but stop myself from saying it. 'Thank you. You too!' I say instead. Seriously fit.

Danso pulls my chair out for me and makes sure I am comfortable, before taking his seat beside me.

As the sun sets in the west of the sky, I head with Danso to the black-and-white checked tiles of the dance floor because our bodies can no longer ignore the hits the DJ is dropping. We pass Mum and Uncle Agape dancing old-people moves under the glitter ball Auntie Larjey insisted on. Its spherical shimmer animates the space where dancing feet find the irresistible beat. Somebody's grandfather is doing the moonwalk from one side of the dance floor to the other. His Michael Jackson moves make Danso and I lock eyes with each other and laugh before we find our own rhythm. There are so many bodies, and so much movement. So much fun and so much laughter. But once we are in our space, I see only him.

I didn't know it was possible to slow-dance to Afrobeat but it is, and we do. My hands find their place at the back of his neck, and his arms, my waist. We dance that way because there is a magnetic field of attraction between us which we cannot deny. It is invisible but undeniable. One of us is north, the other south. There is only one direction of travel.

POOLSIDE

I seek the sunlounger next to the pool which offers the best view of the dance floor when we have danced so much my feet have earned a rest. It is cool and quiet here, pretty as a postcard. Danso sits beside me to watch guests who are still partying into the night. An old man with a solid gold ring in the shape of a crab on his pinkie finger and a penchant for a three-piece suit is doing a one-legged dance across the diagonal length of the dance floor. He is applauded for his efforts. Another guest has understood the MC's direction to 'get down low' as a personal challenge and is now relying on the help of friends to stand up from the squat she has attempted with an unreliable knee. If only those people could stop laughing. The expressions on the faces of some suggests a focus reserved for exams: furrowed brows and tongues clamped in concentration while extraordinary dance moves are executed with flair. Dancing is a serious matter; it is a matter of serious fun. Some of the moves threaten to cause injury. Our laughter gets louder as the risk increases.

I kick off my shoes and raise my legs onto the sunlounger to relieve the burning sensation in the balls of my feet.

'Come.' Danso beckons with his hands before taking my feet in his lap.

Suddenly feeling shy, I pull my legs away. 'They're so sweaty!'

'Gross!' He pretends to draw back in disgust before he smiles and beckons again. 'Come.'

He says it in a way that makes me concede. I concede because his hands cool the fire in my feet and feel like the sweetest balm on my skin. I concede because his touch is one I didn't know I needed until now. It takes me to a place where my heartbeat accelerates and becomes an audible thing. He must be able to feel it when he interlaces his fingers with mine and studies the intricacy of my palms. When I run my hand from his forehead over his hair and down to the base of his neck. He must hear it when he puts his head against my stomach and his hands find their home on either side of my waist. Because it is thumping against the wall of my chest and in every other part of my body.

Danso's hands are gentle where the bite on my ankle has become swollen. He takes my feet one at a time and rubs them as if he is kneading precious dough. He rubs them until the blood starts to circulate again and I can bear to stand. But I don't stand. I don't move. I am happy where I am.

When he has finished with my feet, he takes my hand. The one with the mosquito bite on my wrist and finger. He turns it over to examine the damage.

'You need to wash your hands!'

He takes this as an invitation to rub them along the length of my arm and laughs at my disgust. 'You've really suffered, eh?'

'I have.' The bites are still raised and warm and itchy. I have scratched them so much that I have broken the skin.

'Sorry, sorry.'

He learns the plane of my arms with his hands, moving from my wrists to my elbows to my shoulders. My shoulders to my elbows to my wrists. He blows gently on the bites before he brings my hand to his lips. One by one, he kisses them. With lips that are so soft against my skin. And a kiss that is so gentle.

'Why are you laughing?'

'It tickles!'

His pupils familiarise themselves with mine. Slowly. Deeply. Intimately.

'Should I stop?'

I look at him to communicate, without words, that tickling is a side effect I am willing – no – wanting to bear. 'No.' It comes out as a whisper.

He continues. With soft lips and gentle kisses. Up the length of my arm, along my collarbone and across the part of my neck where the nerve endings are so sensitive it makes my head dive at the sensation. It is only when my back starts to arch and our breathing becomes audible that we pull away from each other, remembering where we are.

My heart beats over the music that has people fixed to the dance floor. It creates a pulse in parts of my body that aren't supposed to pulse. And in other parts, where pulsation leads to desire. The party is in full swing and the outdoor lights have come on to join the glow of the moon. I am lost in the pattern of his irises by candlelight, and he in mine. It is hard to keep count of how many tributaries run through them, but it is not for want of trying. I rest my head on his shoulder to return to a resting heart rate. There, his fragrance assumes control of my senses.

'Sika?'

I love the way he says my name.

'Danso?'

'Sika.'

And his voice. It is deep and soft: velvety.

'Danso.'

'I really like you, Sika.'

I willingly follow to the place he leads. 'I really like you too.'

The exchange draws an exhalation from us both. It is an exhalation that communicates relief at the reciprocity of our feelings. And a happiness that we have put those feelings into words. It expresses sadness that we only have a short amount of time left together in Ghana. And concern for what happens when I leave.

'I want to see you again.'

'Me too. I want to see you again too.'

'Okay, so we have to make a plan.'

'Okay.'

Our lips find each other's with closed eyes and little effort as we surrender to tenderness and touch. The Law of Attraction at work.

'Danso?'

'Yes?'

We are whispering now, our voices lost in the corridors of intimacy. He searches me with his eyes as I pull away.

'Are you okay?'

'Yes. It's just…Danso…'

'Sika?'

'I really need a wee!'

His beard bobs up and down as he laughs. It is black and lustrous and beautiful.

'I can't hold it! I'm sorry!'

I am laughing too, because there is timing and then there is timing.

THE BATHROOM

The tiles of the guest bathroom in Auntie Larjey's house are so cool against the soles of my feet that I don't want to move. The decor is impeccable. Gold finishings. Fluffy towels. Luxury hand cream. I know Auntie Larjey wishes the sunloungers outside were always occupied, by Corey and Casey and their partners. And the pool one day full of laughing grandchildren, splashing and swimming between inflatable pool toys. Feasting on home-made snacks. I hope for her that one day it will be. Theirs is not a house or a garden or a pool area designed with two people in mind. Seeing how happy she is with the boys back home, and Mum and I visiting, makes me wish for her that this was the status quo.

When I think about Danso, my stomach fills with dancing butterflies and my breath catches in their flapping wings. The feeling makes me forget the urgency of my bathroom break. And then remember it again with sudden and threatening urgency.

I am drying my hands on the softest hand towel I have ever felt when I hear Mum's voice. It is not the kind of towel you wipe your hands on and then leave on a rack for someone else to come and use. No. It is a towel from a stack of clean, white, neatly folded towels that you put in a wicker basket when you have finished. The used towels will be collected by someone long before they grow in number.

They will be washed and replaced smelling of patchouli and jasmine, summer or spring. And the next person to use one will marvel at the way Auntie Larjey cares for her home and her guests. I put my towel in the basket provided and examine my face in the gilded mirror. I look untidy but in a way I don't mind, my hair disturbed by the movement of his hands. My lipstick faded by his kiss. I reapply it, knowing there is little point in doing so, and leave my hair as it is.

My hand hovers over the lock of the door and pauses when Mum speaks again. I don't recognise her tone at first. It is hushed and heavy with emotion.

'I wanted to say goodbye, Agape. Believe me, I did.'

'Do you know how I searched my mind for answers? Did I say or do something wrong? Did I imagine it? Was any of it real?'

The doorknob looks like it is made from gold. Or brass, I'm not sure which. It is cool against my palm.

'I never stopped loving you, Agape. If only you knew. I loved you then and—'

At the mention of love, my interest peaks. Mum was in love with Uncle Agape?!

'You were seeing someone else before you left, is that it?'

'No! Of course not. I would never do that to you!'

Someone else? So they were 'a thing'? They used to date?!

'I see. If I didn't make you happy, you should have said as much. We could have ended things properly and gone our separate ways.'

I knew there was something between them. When they laid eyes on each other in Pokuase, after so many years apart. Now it makes sense!

'The happiest times I ever had were with you, Agape.'

'Yes. You were so happy that you were able to move on with your life as soon as you arrived in London.'

I try to place Uncle Agape into the chronology of Mum's life. Did she love him before or after she fell in love with Dad?

'Agape! What are you saying? No! Ours is not a love that you can just replace or recreate. Please don't say that!'

It could only have been before Dad?!

'It is no more, Selom. The love that we had. It can never be again.'

'Agape, I—' Mum's voice catches on her tears.

'You think I haven't done the maths? You think I haven't understood that you must have been expecting before you left Ghana or very soon after?'

I don't turn the handle.

'She is not my child, that much I know.'

Uncle Agape's words stop my breath.

'You are right. She is not yours—'

'Please, Selom. I have suffered enough.'

'Agape, it is not what you think.'

'You could not so much as pick up the phone to call, Selom? And you swore Larjey to secrecy and silence. Is that who you are?'

'It wasn't you, Agape. It was—'

'I married twice and divorced, do you know that? I never saw my life taking that path, but I was never able to settle after you left.'

'Oh, Agape!'

I struggle to find it again. My breath. I am struggling.

'The plans we made. The life we were supposed to live together? I would never have thought that you could get up and leave me like that.'

'You think I wouldn't have preferred to stay here in Ghana? To get married to you and start a family? The dreams you had of us together, I shared them, Agape. No one has ever compared to you.'

I am lost now. Blindsided and lost.

'What's done is done, Selom.'

'Agape, please—'

'What do you want from me? All these years later?'

'I don't want anything from you.'

'You turn up at Pokuase with no notice or warning and pretend as if nothing has happened. As if you didn't break me. As if we could just pick up where we left off. Do you know what seeing you like that did to me?! What that kind of thing can do to a man?!'

'Agape, please. It wasn't easy for me either. Believe me. Please let me...I want to...I want to explain—'

'Please do. I would love an explanation. What did I do to you, Selom? Please, tell me.'

I am frozen where I stand.

'You are right. I was pregnant when I left. I was.' She is close to hyperventilating.

'Eh heh! So you were seeing someone else? When we were together? How?! How could you do that to me – to us?' His tears join hers. The release of a deeply buried sentiment given new life.

'Why would I have done that to us? Do you think I was building dreams with you for fun?'

'I don't know. I don't know what you are telling me.'

'I didn't choose to become a mother, Agape.'

'What?'

'The pregnancy – I didn't choose to—'

'The person you were seeing behind my back? How long did it go on for?'

'I wasn't seeing anybody else, Agape! There was no "person behind your back"! Please don't make this any harder than it already is.'

'You think it was hard for you? Do you know how I

suffered? How my mind raced day and night, reliving every second we had together? How my heart ached and my dreams disappeared? How I struggled to find stillness and peace? Do you know how my body longed for you?'

'If I could do it all over again, I would have—'

'What? You would have what?'

'What I'm saying—'

'Do I know him?'

'Who?!'

'The man you left me for? Do I know him?'

'What I am saying, Agape…What I am trying to say…to explain to you…is that… I fell pregnant because—'

'Because what?!'

Uncle Agape's anger spikes and the question leaves his mouth loudly, abrasively. He speaks in the tone of a man robbed of his dreams and left with no means to rebuild them. A man exhausted by thoughts of what could have been, and the grief that took its place. It is the violence of the past visiting his present and knowing that the two cannot be reconciled.

'Because I was forced—'

'You were forced?'

'I fell pregnant because I was raped, Agape.' She says it quietly, whispers it, her voice so faint that I doubt the function of my ears. I wonder if the music from outside the house has muffled the sound of her words.

'What?'

'I was raped.'

'What are you saying?'

'Agape, I was raped.'

'Raped?'

'Yes. I was raped. And I fell pregnant.'

'I don't understand…I…I…Selom?'

'I didn't know what to do.'

'You were raped? You mean…Oh my God. Oh my God, Selom. Selom. Raped? God have mercy. Selom.'

I do not know if I am inside my body or outside it. If I am dreaming or awake.

'Why didn't you…Why didn't you tell me?'

'I was so young, Agape. I didn't know what to do.'

'You mean Sika…' His voice trails off as realisation descends. On both our heads. As my hands tremble at the handle of the door and my life dissolves before me.

I do not know how I move to find her. In the space between the indoor kitchen and the storeroom where they are ensconced. A private conclave for two. Or how I manage to stay upright. My legs not giving way. She raises her eyes to meet mine. Her make-up is ruined by her tears. Her pupils, lost in a pool of white. If I am breathing, I do not know how. My lungs have stopped. My heart has.

LONDON

JET LAG

There is no time difference between London and Accra, so there is no reason to feel jet-lagged. No reason for my body and mind to adapt to a new sense of night and day. The sun is where I last knew it to be. It rose in the east and set in the west. As sure as night follows day, the moon appeared thereafter. And yet I am exhausted to my core. I cannot concentrate on any single task. I feel sick in my body and in my mind. In every part of me. I feel sick.

Julian is waiting for me in the coffee shop around the corner from work. I have not found sleep since I arrived, but that has not stopped me from running late. I have lost time turning around in my hand the single photograph I have of Dad. The only photograph that survived the fire which engulfed the first flat we ever lived in. An electrical fault in the flat above. The fire where she – we – lost everything but the clothes on our backs. The fire that destroyed every last thing she had of Dad's. His records, his watch, his handkerchief. It turned to ash photographs of Mum and Dad at Aburi Botanical Gardens, where they went on their first date. At Accra Sports Stadium before kick-off in a football game between Ghana and Nigeria, Mum finding enthusiasm for the match only once they'd arrived. The two of them at Kokrobite beach, the day after they found out she was pregnant, Dad's hand cradling her belly, his face beaming with joy. The fire that explained why there were only ever photographs of the two of us and nothing of Mum and Dad before me. The fire I could not remember because I had only been eight months old. The photograph that had only survived because it lived in Mum's purse.

There was nothing of them because there had been no them.

Me: *Sorry running 15 behind*

Julian: *NO STRESS. Let me know when 5 mins away and I will order your coffee x*

I have lost time examining the lie that is my life. There is no end and no beginning. The lie that was the love they shared and the home they built together. Dad's joy in knowing that she was pregnant with me. The idea that I was wanted when that couldn't be further from the truth. The accident on the Tema to Accra motorway that had claimed Dad's life so violently. The lie that was her grief. The wake and the funeral and Dad's body in the fucking morgue! The lie that she was ostracised by Dad's family to explain why they are not a part of our lives. And why she would not start to look for them in Ghana twenty-seven years after they had rejected her – and me. The lie that explained why we would not start combing the cemetery for him. It is not the 'done thing'. It was all a fucking lie!

Outside the train station, there are dark clouds and heavy rain. I don't have an umbrella. And I don't even care. I am lost among a horde of commuters in a race to get to their corporate desks at their corporate jobs and do mindless corporate things. I know where the coffee shop is because it is where we meet, Julian and I. And yet I pause to recalibrate before I leave the shelter of the station and subject myself to the cold and wet. What if I walk there, along the main road and right down the side road I've walked a hundred times, and the coffee shop isn't there? What if it's gone? And what if Julian didn't say, when I called him crying hysterically, my words swallowed by grief, that he would meet me there first thing? Everything that was, is no more. Everything is nothing.

But Julian is waiting for me as he said he would be. In the place he always sits, with his arms outstretched.

'Come here, honey.'

He holds me while I wet his dry clothes with rain from outside and tears from within. His warmth and familiarity open the floodgates. I cry and cry and cry as he holds me in the coffee shop while my coffee goes cold and people stop and stare. I cry because I am in too much pain to talk. I shake with the weight of the past forty-eight hours, and Julian stands to absorb the aftershock.

'Breathe, Sika. Breathe. In through your nose and out through your mouth. You're okay. I'm here. I'm not going anywhere. Oh, honey! In through your nose and out through your mouth, that's it.'

'She has lied to me my entire life. What type of person does that?! What type of mother?!' My tears resurface as I try to give words to this nightmare. 'Everything she allowed me to believe about myself was just some bullshit story she invented. What the actual fuck!'

'Oh, honey.' He holds me as my pain peaks. Kisses my forehead. Squeezes my hand. 'I can't even imagine. I—'

'She didn't want me, Julian! Why would she?!'

'There is so much to take in, Sika.'

'Who would want a constant reminder of the fact that they were raped?! I know I wouldn't!'

'This is such a complex and delicate situation. Breathe, honey. Breathe—'

'I mean, who even am I? What does it make you when half of you is a rapist and the other half a liar? Like, how fucked is my DNA?!'

'Listen to me. Listen.' Julian shakes me by my shoulders so my tear-soaked pupils rattle upwards to look into his. 'That is not what you are or who you are. Do you hear me? Are you listening?'

The thought makes me heave and bring my hand to my mouth. Julian reaches for a handful of napkins and positions himself at a tactical distance. Wailing escapes in place of vomit.

'Have you spoken to her since you got back?'

'I don't want to see her or speak to her ever again.'

'Listen, this is a huge shock and you have been completely blindsided, I get that. But I don't think this is, or has been, easy for her either.'

'I don't know how she's kept on top of the web of lies she's spun over the years.'

'I think she's been trying to protect you, Sika. She'd never want to hurt you, not in a million years.'

'If I hadn't heard her, would she have let me go on believing the lie for the rest of my life? Would she have taken the truth to the grave with her?'

The waitress interrupts my grief with fresh cups of hot coffee and a sympathetic smile. 'On the house,' she says quietly, as if I have some dignity left to preserve.

'Thank you,' whispers Julian.

I look at the waitress intending to say the same, but the gesture of kindness shines a light on my pain and causes fresh tears to cascade down my face.

'I don't want to be in the house when she gets back.'

'It's all a bit too raw, isn't it? I'm sure she's desperate to speak to you. To explain—'

'There's nothing to explain.'

'Well, I'm sure she wants to tell you her side of the story. But you go at your own pace, Sika. You need time to process this.'

I open my compact mirror and see a casualty with swollen eyes and puffy lips.

'For God's sake, you're not coming in to work. Tell her you're not well. I'll tell her for you.'

'I'm fine. I'll be fine. I just need to do my face.'

'I think it will take a bit more than lipstick today, honey!'

I try to mirror his encouraging smile with a weak one of my own when my phone flashes. Our eyes go to the screen at the same time. It's Mum. I silence the call before I stand up.

'I'm so sorry you are going through this, Sika.' In his hug I find something close to comfort.

'Julian?'

'Yes, honey?'

'Do you think... Do you think Fred would mind if I stayed with you guys for a bit?'

'Of course not! Fred loves you. Let us take care of you. You can stay for as long you want.'

Outside, the rain shows no signs of stopping. Julian holds his umbrella over me as we walk to the office. His pace is slower than usual to accommodate the new challenge for me of putting one foot in front of the other.

At my desk, I zoom in on Danso's WhatsApp picture and understand the other thing I have lost.

Danso,
I'm so sorry I left without saying goodbye.
Please can we talk?

The blue tick tells me that the message has been delivered and that he has read it. He is online. I call. He goes offline. The call rings out.

The man in the photo of Dad, I don't even know who he is.

MELON MARKETING

I am in front of the marble desk in reception with a painted face and a broken heart. It is an ostentatious thing, the desk: Carrara marble. I have heard Caitlyn tell visitors it was imported from Italy. Porcelain-white marble with veins of grey running throughout its body. It is positioned opposite the double doors of the entrance, beneath gold-wire lettering that spells the words MELON MARKETING. It was installed by two men using a hydraulic suction device to move each piece into place and is the type of object that people who invest in things like art or jewellery would call a statement piece. It would look out of place in the reception of an office outside East or West London.

Joanna's petite proportions make the desk look larger than any reception desk ought to. She navigates the space around it with the delicacy of a fairy and the efficiency of a hummingbird. Caitlyn is happiest when the buttons on Joanna's phone are flashing red and she is fielding calls left, right and centre. 'It's a good way to assess the success of the business,' she says.

There are always fresh flowers in a vase on the desk. And the phone is always answered before the third ring.

'Good morning, Melon Marketing. How can I help?'

'Caitlyn, can you take a call from [insert name here]?'

'Sika, I have [insert name here] on the line for you – transferring now.'

Caitlyn's friends stop by the office throughout the week. They are not just from London. They come from Italy, France, Russia. All over the world. If I am in the middle of an urgent project and one of her friends comes by, I stop what I am doing, slide my feet into three-inch heels and get up from my desk. I pray that there is no lipstick on my teeth but understand that prayer alone is not enough. A compact mirror will be on my desk, or in my handbag, or both. I inspect my mouth and circle my tongue around my teeth to ensure that the only thing on show is my smile. Caitlyn says it's my USP and that I should use it to charm and disarm as required. Caitlyn says it is bad luck to put your handbag on the floor and something you should never do if you want to be successful. I sling my bag onto my desk. It falls on the ground because I do so recklessly. I step over it because I no longer care. I walk to reception to welcome the guest, and celebrate them as if they are an international dignitary on a state visit.

'[insert name here], so lovely to see you! Is Caitlyn expecting you? Let me just check if she's available. She'll be so happy you passed by! I'll let her know you're here.'

Superlatives are great. But the scenario I avoid at all costs is 'kiss chase', that awkward hesitation of heads as one person leans towards the cheek of another who is extending an open palm. Always let the client, guest, visitor lead.

The grey clouds of the morning have parted to reveal a brilliant sun against a clear blue sky. It is glorious although misleading. I press the button to release the door for Tristan. A gust of cold air blasts through reception as he steps inside with all the trappings of a confident alpha male in the business of luxury cigars: silk scarf, designer sunglasses, trendy manbag. Tristan straddles the position in the Venn diagram where the circles of friend and client intersect. It has its advantages.

'Sika, so good to see you!'

Tristan insists on stretching the first syllable of my name in a manner that must bring him joy, or at least a deep sense of satisfaction. I corrected him twice on our first meeting: equal distribution on both syllables and no need to exaggerate enunciation. I've given up the fight since, and left him to his own devices.

He holds me by my shoulders and gives me a kiss on both cheeks while I resist the coffee-induced nausea competing with heartbreak inside my chest. He smells of cigarette smoke infused with cologne.

'How are you, gorgeous?' His hands move from my shoulders to the small of my back. 'I haven't seen you in forever! What have you been up to?'

There is only one answer to the question 'How are you?' Because the reality is, nobody actually cares. No one is interested to hear that you've had your haemorrhoids surgically removed, or that your husband has low blood pressure, or that your grandmother is waiting for her hip replacement surgery. That was one of Caitlyn's first lessons. 'I've just learned that my mum was raped when she was younger and that I am the result!' said no one ever when a client asks 'How are you?'

'These details have no bearing on the client's life. The only information they want to hear is something positive, gushing or life-affirming as relates to them. Don't bore them with irrelevant details about yourself.'

I offer Tristan an update on my life since our last meeting, summarising my trip to Ghana with the right emphasis and omissions. He 'ooooos' and 'aaaahhhs' in all the right places like a cat purring after a bowl of milk. 'I've always wanted to go to Africa!' he says. 'A safari or something outdoorsy! Maybe Kenya or Cape Town!'

I am particularly skilled at making my recent activities sound like they are worthy of being featured on Instagram.

My workload is insane. I turn the word over in my head before inserting it into our conversation. Tristan says his is exactly the same. 'But your skin is glowing, Sika. I want whatever it is you're taking!'

I don't tell Tristan that I am not okay. I do not say that I went on the trip of a lifetime with my mum only to discover that she has spent the past twenty-seven years of my life lying to me about who she is and what I am. That, like the masqueraders who danced around the car at Christmastime in ghoulish costumes, she also wore a mask of deception. That she invented a man who was good, and kind, and loving, and gentle, and labelled him 'Dad' so I might believe I was born from a place of love. I do not say that she invented stories about him so at night-time I could close my eyes and see him in my dreams.

I saw his eyes so vividly because she allowed me to know him so well. The curve of his brows and shape of his chin. The veins in his hands and the shape of his feet. The cut on his forearm where he accidentally caught himself with the machete, slipping after rainfall. I saw him on the plantation handling cocoa: inspecting it, harvesting it, understanding it. The shirt and tie he wore to the office when he got promoted. I heard the joy of his laughter and the singing of his voice. I saw his gait in mine and felt him walk with me all the days of my life. Until now.

I do not say that this is the only thing I can think about. The only thing I have thought about since I overheard

Mum and Uncle Agape on the night of the party. Or that I was grateful to leave Ghana the next day, and to leave her behind. That Uncle Papa was the only person I would allow to drive me to the airport and that we drove there in silence. I do not say that I feel a double betrayal at the hands of Auntie Larjey, who was, after all, in on it. That I could not bring myself to look her in the eye as she stood at the gates of the house with tears streaming down her face. That on the drive to Kotoka Airport everything looked as it had before and yet nothing was the same. I do not say to Tristan that I left Ghana without saying goodbye to Danso, and that I don't know if I will ever see him again.

'I'm great, Tristan! It's so good to see you!'

I don't suggest that he swap his luxury face cream for a torrent of tears and trauma.

'Sunshine, Tristan. Vitamin D. There's nothing like it!'

AN AFRICAN SCULPTOR

Caitlyn believes that if you wear well-lined lipstick you will present as professional and poised. Irrespective of what else is going on with your face. Or worse, your body.

'It can distract from blemishes, dark circles and even something as garish as a cold sore!'

In dark plum with a perfectly matched lip liner, I ask Tristan questions about award ceremonies, product launches and new restaurants. I rely on it to distract from the fact that my tights are laddered at the ankle, at the site of the mosquito bite which weeps through the sheathing. I wonder if it will hold the ladder in the same way nail varnish would. I use the pointed toe of my shoe to scratch my ankle in between taking his bag, asking what he would like to drink and making small talk. It is the kind of itch that makes you feel like you have left your hair straighteners or iron switched on at home; the kind of itch you cannot forget. It distracts without pause, and it is not easy for the distracted to multitask. I wonder why Joanna would choose a moment like this to step away from her desk. I wonder how it is that this time last week I was bathing in the warmth of the sub-Saharan sun while today my tears are heavy like rainfall.

Caitlyn steps out of her office to walk the catwalk to reception. Deliberate strides to effect a gait that appears effortless. She is dressed in a hot pink and neon orange outfit with gold statement jewellery. To Tristan, she offers a greeting so effervescent it threatens to spill onto the floor.

Tristan gushes over the new office space with the type of enthusiasm usually reserved for puppies: 'Caitlyn, you have outdone yourself. It's absolutely stunning!'

'Do you love it?'

He is generous in his offer of compliments. The decor pushes the boundaries of corporate design in a sensorily stimulating way. The art is a metaphor for the renaissance Caitlyn is leading in the luxury marketing world. The attention to detail penetrates the skin in a subtle yet aesthetically satisfying way. It is music to Caitlyn's ears. She takes him on a personal tour of the space and explains the process by which she has curated Melon's new home. The deliberation and precision behind every feature is testament to the hard work she has put into creating the business that has earned Melon the title of 'PR and Marketing Powerhouse' two years in a row. The same effort has identified Caitlyn, its founder and director, as 'one to watch' in the world of luxury brand PR and marketing.

They return to reception to admire a bronze sculpture of a woman's pelvis and truncated thighs. Her legs are parted at the middle and her thumb rests on her right thigh, gently pressing on her skin. Her pinkie finger does the same on the left-hand side. In the centre, her third and fourth fingers bend at the knuckles and disappear inside her vagina. She wears a ring with the letters HER on her index finger.

'It's a custom piece by an African sculptor I've discovered, Keeka something or other. Her work is so culturally curious, Tristan. You've got to meet her!'

Tristan says it is thought-provoking as fuck before following a beaming Caitlyn into the boardroom. It is yet to be populated by an actual board: that's on the to-do list. Melon is a young business and the beginning of a whole movement: Rome wasn't built in a day. Caitlyn exchanges a discreet wink with me as Joanna returns with the morning's post, and thanks me for holding the fort. It is a well-choreographed dance we perform as we navigate our respective tasks. But it does not allow me to forget, as I struggle to stand still, that my ankle is desperate for relief. I take off my tights for direct access to the itch.

I return to my desk with a smile that disappears when I sit down. A wave of exhaustion sweeps over me and makes me wonder if I will ever be able to stand again. I look up to meet Julian's eye. He is looking at me over the top of his computer.

'I'm worried about you, Sika.'

Eighteen emails have populated my inbox in the fifteen minutes I have spent entertaining Tristan and removing my tights. My eyes feel raw, stinging when I blink and when I look at my computer screen. They sting with the effect of tears and lack of sleep. I examine them in my compact mirror. They are red now. But my lipstick is immaculate, my lip liner intact.

The marble desk, I hear Caitlyn say, cost ten thousand pounds. Excluding VAT.

AN EXPLANATION

The mosquito bite on my ankle itches like a demented thing. I scratch it incessantly. Scratching draws comfort and blood. The scab is long gone, and in its place is a small wound. It has grown from the size of a pinprick to the size of a five-pence piece. I press the pink skin that wants to blend with the surrounding area if only I could let it heal. The pressure releases a soothing sting and the blood offers a balm like chamomile. It cascades from the hair follicles on the top of my head downwards and almost reaches my feet. I cannot see the bite behind my ear, but I can feel the sting of impeded healing. I scratch it in the middle of the night. It gives me respite from my thoughts.

I am examining the bloodstain on my fingers when Mum's key turns in the lock. She has flown through the night to arrive at dawn and made her way home from Heathrow Airport to disturb the peace I am searching for. She is not supposed to be here; she must have changed her flight. She was supposed to come home to find my bed empty and my things gone. I have not responded to her messages. Not even to tell her to give me time. *I don't need you, I need to be by myself,* is what I should have said. I wish she had delayed her return. The messages have been incessant.

I am so sorry, Sika.
I love you so much it hurts.

Please let me know you are okay.
Please pick up the phone.
Please forgive me.
You are the joy of my life.
I love you.

Why couldn't she give me more time?

She knocks on my door and asks for permission to enter. She responds to my silence by pushing the door open, gingerly, like a timid child.

I do not recognise the woman standing in the door frame. Her face is bare and her eyes are red. I have never known her to travel that way. To leave her house looking dishevelled. To be seen by others looking anything but her best. She is always immaculate. She has always been immaculate. But I do not know this woman masquerading as Mum. The one who has built my life on a bed of lies. I try to look her in the eye but I cannot meet her gaze. I cannot.

'Sika...'

She walks slowly towards my bed, uncertain of this new terrain. She does not know where it leads or what she will find there. She sits down without invitation. Her new-found uncertainty is unbecoming. I can tell without looking at her that tears are falling down her face. Her hand reaches for my shoulder and tries to settle there. Her touch is rigid and unfamiliar. It makes me shudder. In a voice I don't recognise, she calls my name again.

'Sika...'

It is sickly sweet. Pleading. Desperate. When she says it for the third time, I know I have to leave. I cannot stay here with her. Not now. I stand up to go. But I am caught by something. My ankle is painful, the skin taut with swelling and hot to the touch. It does not allow me to move as quickly as I need to. She takes advantage of this by throwing herself in front of me, where she kneels like a person begging for food. She forces me to look down at her hungry eyes.

'Sika. Please. Please let me explain.'

She speaks to the rug on my bedroom floor. Her voice is quiet and hoarse.

'Please. Sika. I'm sorry. I will explain everything to you. Please. Sika.

'I...I met Agape when I was seven years old. At – at primary school. His family moved to the neighbourhood and he joined my class. He was – he was so quiet on the first day, we wondered if he knew how to talk at all. By day two, he wouldn't stop! He was...he was such a sweet boy. Playful. Kind. Silly but smart. At the back of the classroom he was talkative, so the teacher moved him to the front of the class, where he sat next to me. That's when a little rivalry developed between us. We fought for the teacher's attention because we both liked praise. When we weren't competing against each other, we would problem-solve together. In science, maths and geography. He was good at arithmetic; I was good at conjugating French verbs.

'At break time, we used to play games. It was me who taught him how to play oware. He was a fast learner, but he could never beat me at that game. When he started bringing me mangos from his tree, people teased us that we were in love, you know what children are like. It was me who became shy when they said that. The suggestion made him smile. He would walk tall with his shoulders back. He never denied it. He was never embarrassed by it. He said that when he was older, he would marry me. That was after he almost drowned. We were nine years old. I didn't know at the time that he didn't like mangos. I discovered that much later.'

She looks at me with a weak smile when she points to this detail rooted in truth. It is a needle lost in a haystack of lies.

'He would call for me at weekends to play. In our final year at junior school, we spent the entire summer outside. Playing board games, climbing trees for fruit, trying to catch geckos! We bathed at the stream, troubled the stall lady for bofrot. We even tried to train a goat. Oh, we had fun! The only time we went home was to eat and sleep. We knew that after we sat the eleven-plus we would go our separate ways to different boarding schools, and that we would not see each other for weeks at a time.

'When he returned from his first term at his new school, Agape sported dark hair above his lip and spoke with a squeaky voice. He was almost unrecognisable. But he still invested his time and energy into making me smile and laugh and swat him away like a troublesome fly. He still brought me mangos and challenged me to games of oware, even though he knew he could never win.'

She examines her hands, turning them over as if searching for the truth. She squeezes them, wringing out of herself a life concealed which she can finally expose to the light. Her eyes find comfort once more in the carpet at my feet.

'By the age of fifteen, I had conceded. We knew we liked each other, and we looked forward to school holidays so we could spend time together. Agape learned to distract himself at school with track and field. That's where he discovered his talent as a sprinter. By term two of his first year, he had broken the school's hundred-metre record. He had befriended the two-hundred-metre-sprint champion, a boy called Papa. They trained together and became close friends. Where you saw one, the other soon followed. That is how Uncle Papa and Auntie Larjey met. Through Agape and me. Papa was always mild-mannered and quietly spoken. Agape, you could hear him before you saw him. It took time for Papa to find the courage to ask Larjey out. But once he did, they became inseparable. Papa invited Larjey to senior prom and Agape invited me. Eiii, the preparations involved! You know Auntie Larjey already!'

Do I? Auntie Larjey, who said she would help me find my aunties and uncles and cousins on my dad's side? Who said she would intercede with Mum on my behalf to do so? Auntie Larjey, who I trusted instinctively and found no reason to doubt? She has been in on it with Mum this entire time. Withholding the truth. Allowing me to believe I am someone I am not. I'm not sure I do know her. I don't think I know her at all.

'It was as if we were preparing for a wedding – shoes, dresses, hair, nails. You can imagine the styles in those days. But in our minds we were the height of fashion. If you had seen us with our big sleeves and big wigs! The days before prom, did we even sleep? I doubt it. On the day of the prom itself, we were so excited! That day, Agape gave me a sculpture of two birds that he had carved out of wood from his father's workshop. He'd inscribed it with the letters *S&A* on the branch. They were joined at the breast, the birds. That's how we believed we would be, forever. I cherished that sculpture. And I cherish the memories of prom. That night we danced and danced and danced! Two young people, destined to be together. The sculpture, I still have it. I kept it. All these years.'

The idea that she treasured artefacts of theirs while inventing lies about things that belonged to a make-believe dad of mine is more than I can handle. Rage simmers in me.

'When he attempted the moonwalk underneath the glitter ball at Auntie Larjey's party, he made me laugh in the way he always had. Swatting him on the shoulder, in the way

I used to, was like muscle memory. I knew that he smiled because I laughed, caught once more in my happiness and his agency in it. He was always happy when I was laughing. That night, he found himself lost in something from which he had never been free. So did I, Sika. So did I.

'It was there on the dance floor that we started a walk down memory lane. He told me that he had always believed he would marry me. That he knew this the day I rescued him from the sea and patted his back to rid him of the salty water he had ingested. That he had made a promise to himself as I soothed him and scolded him at the same time. He had promised himself that we would grow old together and raise a family. He looked at me as he held me on the dance floor. And I felt that thing that had always been there. Between us. Everything felt the same, and yet nothing was. Because so much had happened. And so much time had passed. But underneath that glitter ball, it was as if we were back where we had always been, twenty-five, thirty, forty years ago. I went inside to shake myself back to reality. And he followed me, Sika. He followed me.'

The simmering thing is close to boiling.

As they walked into Auntie Larjey's house, Mum saw the path her life had taken, in stark contrast to the life she could have lived with the man she'd always loved. She had stayed away from Ghana for so long, for too long. She had stayed away from him. She knew she owed him an explanation and that he deserved one. She knew also that fear and guilt and shame had no place in her truth. She knew that now. She wishes she had known it then. She wanted him to know he had done nothing wrong. That she had always loved him. That she still did. So she hovered. Between the indoor kitchen and the storeroom. On the border of an invisible threshold that separated Mum from the woman who had destroyed the foundation of my world. She wore ruby red on her lips with a perfectly matched liner.

'I can't listen to this.'

It is all I can say, all I can offer. Those words, and a view of my back.

She understands, at the very least, that I don't want to talk to her. Or listen to her excuses.

Not now. Not ever.

NETWORKING

Caitlyn has done something extraordinary to her eyes for Julian's event. They are set: pupils in a pool of blue against a bed of lilac, and eyelashes that defy the beauty standards of mortals. I know from their length and fullness that they are fake and that they have been applied one by one by somebody who specialises in this field. Her eye colour, similar to that of a husky, is striking.

She has used one of those curling wands to run gentle curls through her silky hair. Or perhaps paid someone to do it for her. Sometimes, she will ask Joanna to book her an appointment at a fancy hair salon on the afternoon of an important evening event, then turn up looking like heaven on legs. It's the prerogative of a silky-haired siren answerable only to herself.

Three of the lift's four walls are made of glass. It will be somebody's job to clean them so they remain free of fingerprints. We reach for the fifth-floor button at the same time, but it is her finger that finds it first and determines the direction of travel. As we ascend, we are treated to a floral display of pinks and fuchsias, lilacs and purples, an indoor botanical offering created by skilled hands and creative minds. I wonder if she has had her lips done.

I have forgotten to floss. I always forget to floss. The last time I went to the dentist, I lied about it. Floss? I don't have time to eat sitting down some days, let alone floss. Flossing feels like a luxury for the time-rich, I wanted to explain. But instead I made a promise to myself to start. And I will start. I will. I want to breathe into a cupped hand to check whether I need a mint. But the lift is too small, and the space too intimate to do that.

Caitlyn's eyes penetrate me, even though her gaze is fixed ahead. She is quintessentially beautiful. Her beauty makes you want to stare.

'Is that a new perfume you're wearing, Sika?'

She doesn't wait for a response.

'It reminds me of a fragrance I used to wear years ago. Quite...floral, isn't it?'

I grabbed something from my desk before we left and sprayed it on my neck and the insides of my elbows instead of my wrist, which has only recently stopped bleeding. She is wearing statement earrings with a green velvet dress that fits her like a glove. I am wearing high heels with a swollen ankle that burns. I don't know if she is emphasising the floral scent because she likes it or dislikes it. Perhaps she used to like it but doesn't any more. The familiar scent of her perfume plays havoc with my mind and confuses my memories. Perhaps mine takes her back to another place and space in time? Perhaps I should never wear it again.

The lift is slow but smooth to rise. A masterpiece in engineering with no emergency button. The absence of a red button with the word EMERGENCY visible in white letters introduces a claustrophobia to the enclosed space and makes me anxious for breath. When we arrive on the fifth floor, my feet carry me out of the lift before the doors have fully opened, my mouth gasping for air.

I step into a reception area full of attractive people and staged lighting. It highlights the cheekbones of the beautiful women and makes the men look chiselled and handsome. An attendant waits to take my coat. Another offers me a choice of champagne, red wine or white.

I am relieved to see Julian's silhouette in my sight line. He is in front of a bar made of mottled bronze. A waiter behind it is shaking a mixer at the same rate as my heartbeat. Before I can reach him, I hear her voice.

'Sika!'

It carries above the sound of glasses clinking, people talking and laughter rising; it guides me towards her.

Caitlyn's gravitational pull has attracted an audience, and she is holding court. The group is starstruck or spellbound, caught in her web. I inhale, exhale, as I walk in her direction, grateful for the waitress who appears wielding a tray of inebriants in my direction. I take a glass of champagne and drink it quickly before swapping the empty glass for another. I catch the eye of the attendant and we exchange a knowing smile. I screen mine, blink open my eyes and continue my journey towards the bright light.

Caitlyn's eyes are back on her audience. She is giving them all of her: mind, vision and energy. In a few strides, I am there. The eyes of her new fans move in tandem with the movement of her hand as it wraps itself around my waist.

'This is Sika, she's my right hand at Melon.'

To watch her navigate a room of strangers is to watch a transformational force at work. She dazzles with her stature and her piercing blue eyes. Her brown hair, styled to perfection leaves in its place the fragrance of expensive shampoo which complements but never obscures, the smell of her expensive perfume. The aroma makes people ask questions like 'What fragrance are you wearing?' In response, she will pretend to let them in on a secret: 'Do you know what, I just grab whatever is closest to me and spray!'

But Caitlyn is too self-conscious, too deliberate and too precise to be casual about a detail like that. Not only does she know the name of the shampoo and fragrance she is wearing, she chose it with her audience in mind. Something mildly floral for a female audience: middle notes of bergamot, lily of the valley and ylang-ylang. The seductive top notes of Amalfi lemon, truffle and jasmine to captivate a group of men. She does not shy away from her five foot ten inches but extends her legs with the heels of red-soled shoes. She peacocks around strangers who will soon become clients after leaving her company, believing she has a service they cannot do without. She leaves nothing to accident or chance. Caitlyn is too calculated, too exacting to do that.

Caitlyn uses the introduction of canapes to alter the dynamics and tempo of the group like a conductor in charge of an orchestra. She takes me by the hand, interlaces her fingers in mine the way lovers do, and guides me a few feet away from the captivated group.

'Sika, let me introduce you to Oscar.'

'Hi Oscar, great to meet you.' I extract my hand from hers and offer it to Oscar, who transfers his glass from his right hand to his left to take it.

'Sika, Oscar owns a luxury female fashion brand and he is very interested in using our services to promote it on a European stage.'

Oscar holds my palm in his while Caitlyn explains his business. His soft palm is moist with condensation from the glass, or sweat, I don't know which. The stroke of his finger against my palm distracts me from making the right noises at the right time; the 'ooooohs' and 'aaaahhhhs' I am supposed to utter are instead trapped in my throat.

'Oscar would love to take you out to dinner to hear more about Melon and discuss opportunities for us to work together!'

Caitlyn smiles the smile of a lion who has secured food for her prey and, because the kill is so big, knows they will not go hungry for some time. This makes her eyes widen and encourages her to comment on future possibilities and projections, some of which extend beyond the limits of human capability.

'Oscar, Sika is the best of the best. I'm so excited for you to get to know each other!'

I know that many marketing hopefuls dream of working with someone like Caitlyn. And what they would give to work somewhere like Melon. To get their foot through the gilded door. But they have not crossed the threshold, so the view they enjoy is that of the grass on the other side. It looks so green, so inviting.

I remove my hand from Oscar's palm and he returns his drink from his left hand to his right. On his finger he wears a gold signet ring engraved with his initials.

'At Melon Marketing, we bash our heads together so you don't have to!'

Caitlyn ends the conversation with her familiar catchphrase and a smile that promises the moon, the stars, and the sun for good measure.

The waitress wielding the tray of drinks has got the measure of me. When she appears, I make a beeline for her; when I don't, she appears out of nowhere like a fairy. Her hand removes an empty glass from mine and replaces it with a full one.

The bubbles are so...bubbly! They distract me from the throbbing in my ankle and the pain in my head. They bring Danso to the forefront of my thoughts and make me long for his smell. His kiss. For everything about him.

I drink so much champagne that I run to the toilet, shut the cubicle door behind me and throw up a cocktail of

Bollinger and bile. When I have finished retching, I sit on the lid of the toilet seat and reach for my phone.

Danso,
Please can we talk?
Please let me explain.
Please pick up my call.

The blue tick tells me that the messages are delivered and that he has read them. He is online when I call. He goes offline. Again.

ASHAWO

My hangover struggles to accommodate the volume of the woman on the bus telling her five-year-old daughter to get off the bloody stairs, her seven-year-old to stop messing about before he makes her really angry, or her crying toddler. I am nauseated by the smell of the Doritos they are eating for breakfast, and irritated by her failure to answer the toddler's calls of 'Mum, Mum, Muuuuum'. The brightness of the morning stings my eyes, which have not seen enough sleep for multiple nights.

'If I have to tell you one more time, Bronx, I swear to God!'

She doesn't finish the sentence. Bronx, who is clearly battling an affliction of early-morning ants in his pants, is dragged from the second step of the bus by his right arm and relocated on an empty seat beside his sister. The mum is petite, but that does not impede her strength. She strong-arms him into the chair. Bronx does not react. He is, I understand, a child made of steel or a child immune.

'Sit down and shut up!'

Bronx bounces on his seat instead, maintaining his mother's unblinking gaze. She must swear to God regularly. Up down up down up down. He bends briefly to retrieve a drink from the bottom of the toddler's pram: a can of Dr Pepper.

'If you pour that down yourself, I swear to God...'

The sister has started to cry for Dr Pepper, and the agitated toddler, restricted in the pram, cries for freedom. The little girl swings her legs in rhythm with the excavation of the near-empty packet of Doritos. Crumbs on the floor. Crumbs on her uniform. Crumbs in her hair. Her fingers are coated in orange dust, which she wipes on her tights and the bus seat when all the crumbs are gone. Only they are not gone, they are everywhere. The mum scrolls through her phone and subjects the bus to the TikTok audio that holds her attention. Underneath her seat, a banana peel, aged with brown spots, brings on another wave of nausea that I struggle to suppress.

She is around the same age as Loli, the little girl. The same age and yet worlds apart. I scroll through the pictures on my phone and land on the one of Loli in Auntie Larjey's wig. She is smiling like a deranged unicorn who has reached the end of the rainbow. I feel a smile spread across my face. It triggers an ache for her in every muscle of my body, most of all my heart. I miss every part of her. Her big eyes, her sweet smile, the lullaby of her voice. I miss talking to her, playing with her, and learning about her favourite things. I wish I could hold her baby Sika and back her with Loli's help. I wish I could hold her hand and walk with her. Or watch her skip beside me, filled with glee because I am hers. I wish she was here or that I was there. I wish so badly that I had said goodbye.

When my phone flashes with a +233 number, I answer it before the second ring. 'Danso?'

It is not Danso. It is not a man's voice. It is a rushed voice, a panicked voice. It is a voice spoken through the lips of a mouth that belongs to someone I no longer trust.

'Sika, it's Auntie Larjey. Please don't hang up!'

I do not speak. Nor do I hang up. Because Auntie Larjey is not the type of person you hang up on.

I get off the bus and sit on a bench outside a coffee shop. In front of me are two pigeons fighting over a slice of tomato displaced from its sandwich. They attack it with their beaks until the fast-approaching footfall scares them away. My heartbeat competes against the sound of Auntie Larjey's voice and the hustle of corporate London. My eyes lose themselves in the cloud-filled sky above.

'Sika, thank you. I'm so glad you picked up. Sika, listen to me, please. I know that you are in a lot of pain right now. I know you are hurting. You feel betrayed. You feel lied to. You are feeling so many things. And you must have so many questions. Please, just listen to me, okay? When I have finished you can hang up. I just want you to hear me out, okay?'

She talks with the urgency of someone who has a lot to say and little time to say it.

'Hello? Are you there? Hello?'

'I'm here.' My voice is a stranger even to me.

'Sika, my own mother called me ashawo before I had any idea what the word meant. Edem said it described those girls who were motherless or had no home training. The ones whose fathers were too lazy or too drunk to farm properly and who didn't know how to share the food they had: "They leave their homes late at night wearing tight, tight dresses made of stretching fabric. And their favourite colours to wear are red and purple." We were just children. "Ashawo!" Because of the way she said it, her mouth twisting like she had eaten something bitter, and moving like it wanted to touch her nose, I knew that I couldn't ask my mum what it meant or why it sounded like something that only adults should say. She spat the word on the floor with saliva and disdain. "Ashawo!"

'I was lucky that Selom had an older sister in senior

school. It meant she understood things that adults spoke about before most children our age. I asked her the next day if she knew the meaning of the word. It was just after morning break. Selom's hands were already on her head as we walked, single file, out of the classroom to the playground. She ran, singing "Che Che Kule!" Everyone in earshot put their hands on their heads and called back, "Che Che Kule!" Selom's fingers touched the curls of her hair, and of course I mirrored her. My own mum did not have time to braid my hair, let alone put beads in it, so she had cut it. At the time, I wished more than anything that she would let me use straightening cream to make it silky like Edem's. I longed for it to move in the breeze or when I shook my head 'no'. But I knew there was no way she would let me do that and I knew better than to ask. Edem said the cream made her head burn but she would rather feel fire any day of the week than wear her hair in thread to look like Anansi the Spider. "Sometimes after it burns, scabs form on your scalp, but you can pick them off," she told us. After it was cut, I wondered how long it would take my hair to become the same length as Selom's, which was always braided neatly in cornrows or single plaits.

"Che Che Kofi sa!" Selom called out, moving her hands from her head to her shoulders. "Che Che Kofi sa!" we sang back, everyone's hands touching their shoulders through the yellow shirt of their school uniforms. "Kofi sa langa!" I knew that when Selom moved her hands to her waist, they would touch the colourful beads that were hidden by her brown skirt. "Kofi sa langa!" I remembered, when I held my own waist, how my mum had reacted when she saw the beads your grandmother had fixed for me just below my hips. "You want to draw attention to yourself, eh? What kind of decoration is that?"

"Kaka shi langa!" Selom's big smile showed how much

she loved to be the leader in Che Che Kule. Everyone did. "Kaka shi langa!"

'When I moved my hands to my knees, I realised that I hadn't moisturised them well at all. At lunchtime, I planned to use plantain oil on the areas of dry skin before I got home and my mum found another reason to shout.

'"Kum Aden Nde! Kum Aden Nde!" Selom moved her hands from her knees to her ankles twice to finish. "Kum Aden Nde! Kum Aden Nde!" We followed her lead before everyone ran off in different directions to look for more fun. That's when I asked your mum, that's when I said, "Selom, have you heard the word 'ashawo' before?" Together we asked Edem after school. Ashawo means prostitute, slut, whore. I didn't tell your mum that my own mum had called me by that name.

'By the time I started to develop breasts, and they started to show underneath my vest, I had become scared of my own body. One day, a friend of my dad's came to the house with his big voice and big stomach and said, "Eiii Larjey! You are becoming a big girl!" He twisted my nipples, one at a time. "Mosquito bites" is what he called them. "Bring me Guinness," he said when he let go. He spoke with a smile. I couldn't move at first. I felt like my body was on fire. Like when you are running and your chale wote bends at the front so you accidentally scrape your big toe on concrete. But I couldn't scream in the courtyard like I would if I had injured myself. He gave me five cedis before he sat down, and I went off in search of Guinness. My mum was in the kitchen when I went to fetch it. "What are you doing with that?" she asked. "'Mr Miezah is here to see Daddy," I said. "He wants Guinness." "Does he think because he does not work that nobody else works? How could Ima be home at this time?!" My mum took the cold bottle of Guinness from my hands and put it on a green plastic tray with a glass and a small plate of achomo for me to take to him. I did not ask her why she didn't take out the silver tray that we usually used to serve my dad's guests. At least if I dropped it by accident, it wouldn't make that crashing sound that takes such a long time to settle and stop.

'I removed my chale wote before stepping into the living room. That's when Mr Miezah moved his eyes from the TV to the bottle on the tray. I knew he wasn't blinking, even though I was looking at the tray and not his eyes. I could feel it. I felt as if I had something written on my forehead in red paint. Something that made him stare. It reminded me of the time I heard my mum argue with my dad about whether you could tell if a person had AIDS – "Ima, even if you can't tell, I can tell!" she said. "How can you tell? They don't have it written on their foreheads," he replied. My mum said that AIDS was not something she would take chances on. If they were now saying you could catch it by sharing water with an infected person, it was not something she would do to find out if they were telling the truth or not. Why should she touch a person who was infected? For what reason? My dad told her that science had come a long way. But it was not something my mum wanted to discuss.

'I had to take small steps to make sure that the achomo didn't spill. It made the Guinness move like the waves of a sea that wouldn't settle until I placed it on the side table. I didn't know why Mr Miezah chose to sit in that faraway seat, of all places. My dad's friends knew that on weekday evenings he didn't entertain visitors for a long time, so it was better to sit at the dining table, which was closer to the door. Mr Miezah had passed the dining table, crossed the carpet and walked to the other side of the room before sitting at the chair with the footrest, closest to the television. That made me wonder if he really knew my dad at all. "Are my arms long like a gorilla? How can I reach a drink that is so far away from me?" he asked.

'Instead of breathing though his nose, Mr Miezah breathed through his mouth like someone who hadn't dried himself properly after getting caught in the rain and was sick with cold. His loud breathing made me shiver. And his eyes burned the part of my skin that was exposed by the neck of my T-shirt. "Fine girl," he whispered when I set the tray down. I don't know whether it was my walking that had caused the Guinness to move like the waves of the sea, or my hands, or both.

'Before I left the room, I heard the whoosh of the bottle being opened and Mr Miezah belch loudly after taking a large sip. "Fine girl."'

PERIOD

'Sika, are you there? Can you hear me?'

'Yes, I'm here. I'm listening.'

Auntie Larjey exhales deeply before she speaks again. I sense her relief at my presence on the other end of the line. And perhaps something else. Perhaps the pain of revisiting her childhood and the memories it forces her to unearth.

'Okay.'

I have abandoned the concern that I will be late for work and redirected my focus. If my eyes were lost in the sky above, they are now shedding silent tears. Auntie Larjey speaks dispassionately, as if the details she is sharing are some minor thing and not the type of experiences that can leave a person maimed, transformed and traumatised. I have lost track of the passage of time. I am lost in Auntie Larjey's story.

'When I told my mum that there was blood in my pants and on my bed sheets, she said that my period had started early – too early. "Larjey, you are only eleven years old, for God's sake. What is wrong with you?" Her voice got higher and higher until I thought she was going to start speaking with the birds nesting in the trees. She said it as if I had prayed for blood to appear between my legs during the night or rejoiced at the fear that I would die before sunrise. "So you think you're a big woman, eh?" she scorned. "You want to grow fast fast?" The truth was that I wanted my body to stop changing in all the ways that I could feel and see. The bumps on my chest that invited Mr Miezah to hurt me. The curls of hair that appeared between my legs and under my armpits. The comments my mum had started to make. The comments. The never-ending comments.

"'Larjey, you have a scent! Can't you use a deodorant? Kai!" When she said "kai", she twisted her face like she was standing next to someone who smelled of sewage and moved away from me as quickly as she could. When I was alone, I stretched my neck to see if I could smell the thing that made her look like she was going to draw phlegm from her mouth and spit. I knew that bad smells could make nostrils sting and eyes water, but I couldn't smell sewage – not the sewage that me and Selom would be scared to fall into when we jumped over open gutters as children. But I didn't smell like myself either. Pimples appeared on my face overnight. My mum said my pimples made her feel too sick to eat. At the dining table, she scrunched up her nose as if I had brought the smell of waste to the table where we were eating. When our eyes met, she didn't blink. "Please, may I be excused?" I would ask, still hungry but unable to eat. "Please, excuse yourself!" she would reply.

'When he came back from work, my dad would ask me about my day at school until he knew which subjects I had studied, what I had learned in each one, and which teachers had given me homework. My dad was the opposite of my mum. His love was a thing you could touch and feel and see. He wouldn't let me leave the table until he was satisfied I had eaten enough. It was hard for me to chew and swallow my food in front of a mother who wouldn't blink. Sometimes I thought it would get stuck in my throat. If I coughed too many times to clear it, it was my mum who would excuse herself from the table with a look of disgust on her face.'

'At first, I thought I had misheard when she stood on the steps of the tro tro and said, "Hoh! You've soiled yourself!" The tro tro was full of people, packed tight like sardines. If she had whispered it, the way she did when she dressed to go out and said "Ima, do I look fine?" no one would have heard. But she didn't whisper at all. She used the voice she used in Makola market to shout it. The voice that carried over sellers announcing their goods for buyers to hear above the noise of the market. Fruit, vegetables, fish, meat and every other thing. Buyers haggling for the best price. Butchers bringing steel axes down hard on wooden boards to separate animal flesh from animal bone. Women unravelling colourful wraps of fabric and beating their folds against the air to display the fullness of their beauty. Others setting down from heads to hot tarmac large steel bowls or wooden crates balanced on mounds of fabric, filled with items too heavy for hands to hold. Men hauling goods on makeshift carts to various destinations, squeaky wheels testament to their makeshift design. That was the voice my mum used.

'The eyes around me shifted from the back of my jeans to the place I had been sitting and back again. Even though the tro tro was packed, nobody took my seat. Because the seat was empty, everyone could see the red mess that had seeped from my pants, through my jeans and into the soft yellow sponge coming out of the tired and torn grey leather. I wondered if this was the way a goat felt before it was slaughtered, while the farmer sharpened his knife. "'So you could feel you were soiling yourself and you just sat there like a fool?" my mum asked. People were still boarding the tro tro, so the doors stayed open while my mum spat out her words.

'The suggestion that I would sit in my own blood like a child in its dirty nappy confused me. I knew that it was better for me to stare at the floor than try to answer the impossible question. Perhaps it was the heat of the day, intensified in the confined space of the tro tro, where there was little space to move and no fresh air to breathe. Or the distracting rhythm of the potholed route which had caused my mind to drift from the pain of stomach cramps. Perhaps the tiredness that accompanied the betrayal of my body made me a stranger to it. I didn't know that I had bled through my jeans and onto the seat. I hadn't felt it. And I didn't know how to clean the mess that my mum forced me to look at in front of so many people. I watched as passengers leant further into each other and away from the bloody seat, until the doors of the bus finally closed. Their stares burned my skin, and words, spoken under their breath, pierced my ears.

'I tested the craftsmanship of my sandals, trying to keep up with my mum, who marched away from me as if running from a mosquito. A shooting pain had established itself in the base of my spine and travelled down to my calves. My legs felt as heavy as lead. Outside the salon, she paused to look at me. "I dare you to sit down on one of these chairs and disgrace me in this place today," she said. By then, I had learned to read her eyes very well.'

'In the salon, I avoided the gaze of the other customers and stood quietly in the corner while the hairdresser washed, set and styled Mum's hair. In front of me was a girl trading gossip with her client while braiding her hair. Her hands moved so rhythmically, so mechanically, so consistently, that it made the lids of my eyes heavy with sleep. She surprised me when she did not reach for the pointed tail comb to part the next section of hair as the sequence directed she should.

She reached, instead, inside her bag and walked towards me. "Do you need a pad?" she asked quietly, sliding a purple-wrapped sanitary towel into my hands without waiting for an answer. "The bathroom is that way." Everything about her was discreet. "Thank you," I said, with my eyes and my hands. My mouth made no sound.'

'At home, it was Edem who showed me how to line the Kotex towel in my knickers properly and change it before it became full. "If your stomach is paining you, use a hot-water bottle and hold it like this. Do you have one?"

'"Yes."

'Sometimes the pain was so bad it made me feel like I was going to faint.

'"You can take two aspirins to help with the pain. Whatever you do, don't wear a white dress until you have stopped bleeding for two continuous days. Do you hear?"

'"Yes."

'When Selom started her period, your grandmother fried onions in palm oil, boiled and mashed yam, and mixed the two together. She served them with eggs for breakfast to celebrate that Selom had come into womanhood.

'"Ayekoo. You are now a woman!" your grandmother told her. "You can no longer play with boys!"'

UNCONDITIONAL LOVE

Caitlyn storms into the office with a bouquet of pink peonies. She sets a gift bag on my desk and scoops me up in a hug. 'Happy International Women's Day!' she calls over her shoulder, disappearing as quickly as she came. My shoulders save the weight and impression of her hands.

The gift bag is white with black, block letters. Inside is a beautiful card, the message written in her unmistakable cursive hand.

'There is no limit to what we, as women, can accomplish.' Michelle Obama.

Happy International Women's Day! Love Caitlyn x

Alongside the card is a small box containing a gold bracelet. Julian holds it against his wrist and laments that, as a non-female member of staff, he does not qualify for this annual act of performative generosity. My stomach registers the smell of the flowers and causes my nausea to surge. Julian follows me to the bathroom and rubs my back.

'You don't look yourself, Sika. As in, you look really fucking awful. You need to go home. You need to rest.'

'She wants the pitch for Paris finalised by the end of the day—'

The rest of my words are lost to the toilet bowl as I retch.

'She's not going to look at it before next week. Seriously, go home.'

I go home because I cannot stay.

I call Auntie Larjey back from my bed, but not before throwing up again. I am shivering under my duvet from alcohol-induced sickness and I have only myself to blame. She picks up before the second ring.

'Sika?'

'Hi, Auntie Larjey.'

'Hello sweetheart. Thank you for calling back. I've been waiting by the phone. I didn't want to miss you.'

She wants to tell me one of the greatest life lessons she has learned.

'The greatest myth in life is that it is supposed to be easy. Life is not easy. It is full of challenges that we must learn to navigate. We can be hurt by people we love in unimaginable ways. But a mother is the one person who is supposed to love her child unconditionally. If you mistreat a child, they will still long to please you. They will still seek your love and affection, because that is how children are programmed. And if a child does something to offend her mother, if she causes her embarrassment or shame, anger or hurt, a mother should still love her child. She should love that child and expect nothing in return. That is unconditional love.'

She wants to tell me that, as a child, she did not know unconditional love.

'My mother did not love me unconditionally. I have asked myself if she ever loved me at all. Why else would she have mistreated me throughout my childhood? Why else would she have abused me the way she did? If I had not looked like her, I would not have believed that I was her biological child. No way. What mother would carry a child for nine months, only to loathe them when they are born?'

I don't know what to say, because I do not know the answer. I don't know why any parent would be so cruel, or how.

'Sika, do you know why I am sharing this with you?'

'Why?'

'Because I want you to know that I understand. I understand what it feels like to have your heart broken by the person who gave you life, the one person who is supposed to love you unconditionally. And not just love you unconditionally, but protect you from every type of harm. My mum broke my heart so many times, I lost count.

'It is not for me to speak for Selom, but I know that your mum has broken your heart. I know that is what you are feeling. I know you feel that your heart is broken into so many pieces you wonder if it will ever be whole again. I know that it hurts when you lie down at night and first thing in the morning when you wake up. And that is if you are able to find sleep. Everything hurts right now, but most of all your heart. I know. I understand.

'I know you feel hurt by me too. You feel that I have let you down. That I have kept the truth from you. That I have had a hand in breaking that beautiful heart of yours. That day when you asked me to help you find your father's people, I thought the ground beneath me would give way. I… Sika, listen to me. I cannot tell Selom's stories in my own words. I cannot tell you how it is that you were conceived. I cannot speak of her experience or her pain, or the decisions she has had to make in her life. I cannot tell you what it was like for her to leave Ghana under those circumstances. To go to a country she did not know, to create a new life there and call it "home". I will never understand what it was like for her to give birth to you or to raise you as a single mother in a foreign land. I cannot tell you any of those things and do them justice. I cannot tell you Selom's stories, in the same way she cannot tell you mine.

'Selom cannot tell you the extent to which I questioned motherhood. Or that at one stage, I decided I would not have children at all. How could I? When I did not know what it was that made my own mum hate me the way she did. What if I had a child and loathed them in the same way, what then? No. I was not prepared to do to my child what my mother had done to me. Your mum cannot tell you that Papa and I nearly divorced because of it. Because he wanted children and I did not. She cannot tell you that the tension between us was made worse by the constant questioning of others: *When are you people going to have children? Are you waiting for twins? Eiii, two years married and no pickin, what dey happen?* The prying eyes of people outside our marriage. The rumours and gossip. She cannot tell you those things, because they are my stories to tell. Do you understand?'

Somehow I do.

'Do you know that Papa was very poor as a child? He was. But he always had a generous spirit. Before he had money, you would see him thinking about how he could put a smile on someone's face. He was creative and imaginative in that way. It was one of the first things I noticed about him. The year we celebrated our fifth wedding anniversary, he came home with a Father Christmas costume in the middle of December. He wore it before we sat down for dinner. Sika, I couldn't eat because I couldn't stop laughing! What a sight! That year, we filled the car with presents for the children's orphanage. I had never been to an orphanage before, but it wasn't Papa's first time. When he was eleven, he won a scholarship for children whose parents could not afford the fees to send them to school. That's how Papa ended up in the same school as Agape. Giving back to disadvantaged children has always been important to him. If he had not been given such a chance, where would he be now? So, we went to the orphanage together. And Sika, when I got there, something happened to me.

'"Papa Bronya has come to visit you! Ho ho ho!" Papa announced when we arrived. He spoke in a voice I had never heard him use before. I didn't know Papa could speak like that! But the way the children's faces lit up, eh? Their faces filled with happiness in a way I can still remember. Sika, the joy of giving to those children was so profound. I couldn't stop thinking about them after we left.

'There were two little boys who stuck in my mind. They had been dropped at the orphanage a week or so before we visited. Newborn babies, less than three weeks old. They were left by an old man who said they had been born to his daughter. She was a single mother who had died of malaria. The grandfather was not able to care for the boys – he had lost his wife some years earlier and had no relatives nearby to help. The orphanage was his only hope. He knew that they would at least be fed and sheltered there, and that they would receive a basic education. That was the best chance he could give them. Panyin and Kakra is what they were called, the unisex names traditionally given to twins.

'Sika, after we left, I could not stop thinking about those beautiful boys. Their tiny hands and feet, so new that they were still wrinkled from the womb. Their little faces and scrunched-up foreheads. Their soft curly hair. The parts of their heads that were soft to the touch. The tiny whimpers they made from the cot they shared. They were so small that their babygrows hung loose around their limbs. They were so delicate, so fragile, so in need of protection. Papa and I had not expected to meet children so young at the orphanage, so we had nothing to give them.

'I was so sad that we had taken nothing for those babies. But you know what? As I lay in bed on Christmas Eve, I realised that we did have something for them. We had a home. We had resources. And we had so much love to give.

'On Christmas morning, I told Papa that we had to go back to get them. Straight away. I had not slept for thoughts of them and the life we could give them and the family we would be. We were not ready – we had nothing in the house to care for one baby, let alone two! Can you imagine? But I was ready to be their mum. We were ready to be their parents.

'Corey and Casey are not of my body, Sika, but they are of my heart. It is those boys who have healed my pain and mended the pieces of my broken heart. They have been my sunshine after the storm of my childhood, the double rainbow in my life. There is no Christmas or birthday or anniversary gift that could ever compare. They have taught me the gift of unconditional love.'

My tears no longer fall silently. They are loud with a pain I don't know how to stem.

'Sika, it is her story to tell. When she is ready to tell it and when you are ready to hear. But what I can tell you – what I know for a fact – is that your mother loves you unconditionally. It is you who has healed her broken heart. Do you hear? You are her rainbow.'

SURRENDER

I summon the strength from some faraway place to breathe in through my nose and out through my mouth. Breathing has become an act of hard labour, an act that requires thought. The cotton sheet on which my body lies has been soaked and dried and soaked and dried in the darkness of the night. The sickness inside me disturbs and distorts. It makes me weak and confines me to my bed. It forces me to surrender.

Mum wanders in and out of my room. She holds a cool compress to my forehead and a straw to my mouth. She wants me to take a sip. Just a tiny one so I can stay hydrated. She mops the space between my nose and my lips with a flannel, before touching my cheek. The back of her hand is cool against my forehead. She takes my hand. The one with the bites which I have scratched so hard I am certain scars will form. She rubs the aches and massages the pain from my fingertips to my wrist, my wrist to my elbow and my elbow to my shoulder. She lays my left hand on the bed and sets to work on the right. I am too weak to pull my hand away from her. To tell her to leave me alone. To close the door behind her. Everything hurts.

My head pounds with the force of a hammer and the power of a pneumatic drill. To look to the right is to invite the cascade of a thousand nails from the left side of my head to the right. They embed themselves in the back of my eyes and remain there until I move again. To dislodge tears is the only way I can express my pain. It is best to cooperate with the pain. And blink. It is better to blink and let the tears fall than to resist. I lie still and will the pain to pass.

My eyelids are better shut than open. To open them is to see her stare at me from the edge of my bed with wide eyes and quivering lips. She is slow to open her mouth, to offer some remedial something, and quick to close it again. Her lips are nude, unvarnished and bare. They part to reveal the gap between her two front teeth. It has lost its familiarity; she has.

Behind her in a double photo frame is a picture of Mum holding me as a newborn. She cradles me to her chest, her right hand supporting my entire spine, her left hand cupping my bottom. I am a mass of dark curls in foetal position. And I am hers. Her expression could be mistaken for one of joy. But where does joy end and grief begin? Grief for the life she had left behind and the one she was now burdened with? A life she had no desire to create. One that disturbed every hope and dream she had for herself and her future. She looks both shell shocked and starstruck. She looks so very young.

Since her return from Ghana, Mum has sought my affection like a puppy coveting the attention of its owner.

'Sika, please. Can we talk?'

She has not respected my need for space, my desire to be alone and away from her. The walls of the house have shrunk, and the result is claustrophobia. She is a labyrinth of false words and a fabricator of reality. What she says with her mouth and what she feels in her heart are two completely different things.

'My Chou Chou. My angel. My love.'

I do not know what it means to realise you are neither your mother nor your father as you understood them to be. To learn that your DNA is part poison, that half of you is a monstrous thing. So awful that you cannot bring yourself to imagine how it is that you came to be. But you know that by virtue of that word. The word you heard her say to the man she loved and wanted to create a family with. The word that describes the moment of your conception. You know you were conceived in violence. A spear tearing taut flesh whose only desire was to remain intact and untouched. You were not born of love. You were not wanted. And your life has been moulded around lies to conceal that fact.

Who am I, if my father is a rapist? What am I?

'It breaks my heart to see you sick.'

What does it mean to know that your mum wore her pregnancy like a cloak of shame? That she left Ghana in hurry and distress because she could not reconcile who she was before with who she became? Leaving behind family and friends, abandoning the love of her life. Because she could not undo what that man had done to her. She would have hated him for it. And the part of him that grew inside her. A nightmare in living form. A monster made flesh. Her last months in Ghana spent in shame and fear. Her first months in London in anguish and denial. She must have hoped that it would all go away. That I would.

'You'll be fine, okay?'

She bathes me like a baby as I sit listlessly in the bath and dries my limbs as I shiver outside it. I am too weak to move. My teeth chatter violently, narrating a nonsensical story even I do not understand. She washes my tangled hair and, like a newborn baby yet to discover the coordination of her limbs and strength of her muscles, I do not resist her. Nausea on an empty stomach prevents thoughts of protest. So I sit there as she dusts me in talcum powder, handling me like delicate porcelain. She dresses me in soft cotton before she takes a comb and manoeuvres her body around mine to part my hair in sections. From the ends to the roots, she combs, using her body to bear my weight. I succumb to the pull of sleep as she braids. Her hands. Her fingers. The rhythm. It is nostalgia. It is childhood. It is almost like love.

'Sika? Sika?'

She stares at me again with wide eyes and quivering lips. An eagle-eyed sentinel. She is slow to open her mouth, to offer some remedial something, and quick to close it again. Her lips are nude. Unvarnished. Bare. They part to reveal the gap between her two front teeth. It is almost familiar; she is.

'Sika, I need to take you to the hospital. I think you have malaria.'

HOSPITAL

I am not taken to the Hospital for Tropical Diseases, or even to intensive care. Instead I sit in A & E at our local hospital suffering an assault on the senses. The perforated steel chairs bolted to the floor of the reception area are too cold and too straight. But they are nothing compared to the artificial brightness of the clinical lighting from which there is nowhere to hide.

'Sika, sit down here. Let me speak to the nurse.'

Mum holds me like a rag doll, releasing her hand from my back only when she is confident I will not collapse at the lack of support. Floor-to-ceiling windows, designed by someone who has never experienced the violence of a migraine, add to a brightness that could blind. I wonder if I have been put here to atone for the sins of my father. To do penance on his behalf. My peripheral vision cannot ignore the yellow flickering of a bulb that needs to be replaced. The movement encourages bile to travel from my empty stomach and up, and up, and up. I heave.

'Sika! Are you going to be sick?'

A kidney-shaped dish made of recycled pulp is produced. Mum holds it underneath my chin until my torso succumbs to gravity. I rest my head on the chair next to me. The steel cools the fire on my skin before it starts to burn again.

'It's there if you need it, okay?'

I need silence, but it is impossible in this place. There are too many bodies, too much movement, too much sound. A cacophony of the sick and injured, their carers and dependants, makes it impossible to find quiet or peace. A drunk man on the other side of the room promises loudly that he will punch the receptionist's lights out; another seeks urgent care while carrying a forty-two-inch TV screen, its cable trailing behind him. A nurse has called for security. I am desperate for darkness and for quiet. I am desperate to leave this awful place.

I have never died before, but I imagine that if I had, this is what it would feel like just before the final curtain descends.

'Sika Akollor?'

My name is called as a man who has had no contact with soap or water for at least a fortnight takes a seat beside me. I heave, again, with the effort it takes to stand up. The nurse leads us away from the chaos and in the direction of a small cubicle behind a blue curtain. Mum queries whether it would be possible to source a wheelchair as I shuffle along the vinyl floor, which has been recently mopped but is already stained.

If you look at the needle as it pierces the skin, it hurts. I know it hurts less if you look away, and yet I find it impossible to do so. I want to see the colour of pain. I want to know if you can make it stop by will alone.

By the time the doctor sees me, I am on a bed in a dark cubicle with an ID tag around my wrist. It bears my name and vital statistics. But it omits the part about who I really am. The thing that is in my DNA. The fact from which I cannot escape. I am connected to a drip to stay hydrated. Because inside me, there is nothing left.

The doctor asks questions about my medical history which I open my mouth to answer, but I cannot find the words. Mum speaks on my behalf. She tells of our recent trip to Ghana, and highlights that we were very careful to take our antimalarial drugs. We stayed in places that had mosquito nets or air conditioning, and took the additional precaution of using repellents outside the house. We even wore citronella bracelets in the evening. She doesn't tell the doctor about her lies. Or her betrayal. Or even the truth.

'She was only bitten a handful of times.'

She holds my hand like an exhibit to show the wounds on my finger and wrist, which I have not allowed to heal. And because I am a rag doll, she sets my hand down on the bed gently, so it does not fall any way or anyhow. She peels back my ear to show the wound that is pink from disturbance because it has been scratched raw, and explains that I got back to London two weeks ago. I have been back to work since then. She shares that I have a demanding job and work long hours but that I am otherwise in good health. What she does not say is that I have recently learned that I am the product of rape. Or that I learned this fact by accident. She does not explain how I feel inside, because she does not know. She does not know that she has turned my world upside down and shattered the foundation on which my life has been built. She does not know that she has broken my heart. And that I don't think I will ever be able to forgive her for it.

'Well, the good news is that you don't have malaria.'

'Really? Oh thank God! Thank God!' Mum expresses relief in the form of slow tears.

'But your infection markers are high, and I'm pretty sure this is the reason why.'

The doctor shows compassion for my pounding head by using the overhead lamp to shine a light away from my face and onto my ankle, which she examines wearing latex gloves. What started as a mosquito bite has long since developed into a weeping sore. It has not been allowed to heal, or even to rest. I have not allowed it to. I have scratched it into a state of infection, and the skin around it has become painful, hot and swollen. It hurts to touch. My ankle bone and Achilles tendon are lost in the swelling that surrounds them. It is so infected that if my skin were white, it would not be white, it would be angry and red.

'This looks like cellulitis to me.'

'Okay—'

'Now, cellulitis is a bacterial skin infection that is easily treated. But left untreated, it can develop into sepsis, and we certainly don't want that. It's good you came in when you did, because it looks like you have just crossed that threshold.'

'Oh dear! I was so worried it was malaria, I hadn't thought it could be something else.'

'Thankfully not, but cellulitis can be serious, so we need to get on top of this infection sooner rather than later.'

'Okay, I understand. Thank you, doctor. Sika, you'll feel better soon, okay?'

I am admitted to hospital for a seventy-two-hour course of IV antibiotics before being discharged with oral antibiotics and strict instructions to finish the course.

'Remember, lots of fluid, lots of rest.'

In the darkness of the cubicle, the drugs trickle from a transparent pouch, suspended at height, into a vein at the crease of my elbow. Drip. Drip. Drip. Drip. The rhythm adds weight to my eyelids and makes the call of sleep impossible to resist. When I open my eyes, Mum is there. When I open them again, she is still there.

'Can you call Caitlyn from my phone. Please. Can you tell her I'm not well. And that I'm sorry.'

I am too sick to go to work.

THE PAST

A week on antibiotics has brought me back to myself. I washed my hair today. It felt good to massage my scalp, to use a deep conditioner under the cover of a steam cap and comb the strands from root to tip. It felt relaxing to sit in a hot bath, with bubbles and candles and music. But for the presence of a dark spot forming around the dried wound, my ankle has come a long way. It will probably leave a scar, but I'm okay with that. It's self-inflicted, after all.

'Sika, dinner is ready!'

I open my door to the smell of food which, after a week of reduced appetite, is welcome and inviting. Today I graduate from a diet of rice pudding, toast and orange juice to the food of the functioning. Today I decide to eat at the kitchen table.

'How are you feeling? You look so much better, Chou Chou.'

'I feel good, stronger than I did yesterday. I'm hungry.'

'I was hoping you'd say that. Guess what I've made you?'

'What?'

I open the lid of a pot on the stove to find the answer for myself.

'Red red.' The plantain is soft and caramelised to perfection.

'I made some tatale with the overripe plantain, I know how much you like that. Should I dish you?' She plates up my food before I can answer, serving at least a whole plantain with a mountain of beans and four plantain pancakes – tatale – on the side.

'That's too much, Mum!'

'Just eat what you can. There is more if you want it.'

We sit opposite each other at the kitchen table where so many of our weekends begin. The wind has stripped the leaves from the trees of Mum's carefully tended garden, leaving the branches bare. The bulbs in the flower beds are a secret until spring. I study the rose bush she has trained along the back fence. And the red robin tree that is taking on a life of its own.

'I need to cut that tree,' she says, following my gaze to examine it.

Mum eats only when I return my focus to the food in front of me, taking one mouthful for every four of mine. I glance up from my plate to see her smiling at me. She is making reparations through feeding.

'Can you believe I'm full?' she says.

Vicariously. She has been satiated by my eating and puts her fork down next to a barely touched plate. She turns her attention from her food to the dishes in the sink.

I am not full because I am empty. The not-knowing sits between us like a parasitic thing, feasting on the absence of truth. The more we try to avoid it, the more space it takes up, until the distance between us is so wide that we can barely reach each other. I am scared to ask. But I need to know.

'Mum. I need to know. About my...About my biological father. I need to know the truth. Please.'

I am startled by the words as they exit my mouth. They cause Mum's rubber-gloved hands to pause at the sink and her shoulders to flinch. I do not know the road I am asking her to take. I do not know where it will lead her. Or me. Or us. My heart beats hard and fast in my chest during the silence that follows and fills the kitchen. It is a silence that makes my pores prickle. It makes of me a conductor of electricity and exposes me to bolts of lightning. I place my palms flat against the wooden table to ground myself before looking up.

She does not look at me. She looks at the dishes. Her eyes are fixed on the contents of the sink when she starts to speak.

'I didn't know him. Not really.'

Her mouth is slow to move. Slow to draw breath. Slow to give life to her words.

'I know you referred to him as your father. I cannot think of him like that. To me, he is…a donor. Nothing more. I'm sorry. I don't want to hurt your feelings, I…'

Her shoulders rise and fall with a deep intake of breath. With the back of her hand she wipes her face.

'Before I moved to London, I was a qualified teacher in Ghana. I retrained when I came here so that I could teach the British curriculum. But I had always planned to teach in Ghana, at secondary school level.

'It was the summer before my first placement. Auntie Larjey and I had finished our training. We were going to spend the summer holidays in the States with her auntie in Maryland. It was going to be my first time abroad. We were so excited. Not just about the vacation but about what the future had in store for us. We had both got our first choice of schools in Accra. We were young teachers, soon to have our own classes and salaries! We were on the cusp of realising our dreams. But it wasn't to be. It wasn't to be.'

She stares into the garden, seeing something I cannot, before returning her attention to the sink. Her back faces me. Her crestfallen shoulders. Her still hands.

'There was an administrative error at the British High Commission and I didn't get my visa in time. We held out hope until the day before we were due to fly. We were devastated when it didn't arrive. Larjey didn't want to go without me, and I didn't want her to miss out. In the end she went, but only because I insisted. We made a promise to each other that we would go again the following year. I missed her terribly when she left.'

I stopped chewing when she started to speak, too scared that she would stop. I fight the dryness of my throat to swallow the plantain and beans in my mouth. I need to free my mouth so I am able to breathe.

'Larjey had always been around for my birthday, but of course this year was different. And Agape – he was recovering from malaria. He had been very sick and was too weak to go out. My birthday fell on a Saturday. I didn't have a plan to celebrate like I had done ever since I had known Larjey. And Edem could see that I was at a loose end. There was a new spot in town that she was going to go to with a few of her friends, so she invited me along. Going out with Edem sounded much better than staying at home on my own, so I agreed. Edem was very different in those days. She liked things that were bright and shiny and loud. She always knew where the parties were, you know. She was always at the parties.'

I try to imagine Auntie Edem sitting in the passenger seat of her boyfriend's car wearing a minidress, cigarette in one hand, the other stroking the back of his head. Auntie Edem who didn't want me to show my shoulders in church. Auntie Edem who removed pink nail varnish from her daughter's fingers and toes.

'It was his father's car. I didn't know cars by make and model back then. I never really have, but I could tell it was a big man's car. A 4x4 with shiny wheels and expensive-looking features. The car was so high off the ground that it was hard to get into without exposing your upper thigh. It was a good thing I had worn shorts. Edem had done my make-up. I even wore lipstick, which I never really did back then. But if you can't wear lipstick on your birthday, when can you? When I got in the car, the guys wished me happy birthday. There were even…what are those things called, the party things you blow into and it makes the "woo woo!" sound? Edem had bought me a badge with the number twenty-six on it. The night started well.'

I try to imagine Auntie Edem blowing smoke rings out of the car window, music pumping so loudly from the speakers that you had to shout to be heard. Auntie Edem who never wears make-up and frowned at my multiple piercings and earrings. Auntie Edem who wakes up at dawn to pray.

'I didn't know that Edem's boyfriend – Ekow, his name was Ekow – I didn't know that he had been drinking until he started driving. He was not driving like a sober person, instead throwing the car round sharp corners and speeding over potholes. At the traffic lights, he passed a bottle of brandy to his friend in the back seat next to me. That's when I smelled the alcohol on his breath. The others took turns drinking from the bottle, Ekow, Edem and Ato, and invited me to do the same. But I was too scared by Ekow's driving to drink. Our dad had always warned us against such things – drinking and driving. So it was not a journey on which I could relax and have fun like that. I reached for the door handle to steady myself and prayed that we would arrive at the club in one piece.

'Ato was not as loud or as drunk as Ekow. He was the one telling him to slow down. To take it easy. He even offered to drive. Edem did not seem bothered by the drink-driving.

Perhaps she was used to him driving that way. But it was not something I was used to, not at all. The air conditioning circulated cigarette smoke throughout the car. I was relieved when we finally got to the spot. Before I got out of the car, I knew that I would put my money together with Edem at the end of the night so that we could go home in a taxi. However drunk Ekow had been on the drive to the club, it would only get worse as the night went on.'

I struggle to imagine Auntie Edem drinking alcohol and getting drunk. Auntie Edem, whose only reason for purchasing alcohol is for the Prophet's consumption? Auntie Edem who buys the consecrated blood of Christ from the Church of Incredible Miracles at a price that makes light of inflation. Auntie Edem, who considers her daughter's stammer a weapon of spiritual warfare.

'Outside the club, we parked behind a guy whose car had broken down. Three men were pushing it from the back while the motor failed. It was funny to see them transform from partygoers to mechanics in party clothes. But we are a resourceful people, so I wasn't surprised when they got it to start again.

'Ekow took his time to enjoy the envy of the crowd outside as they gazed at his car. The music coming from the club was the type that made you dance before you had even seen the dance floor. It was a nice spot, a courtyard where partygoers gathered. There were places you could sit outside to hang out and chat, people in corners selling snacks like plantain chips, peanuts, bofrot, that kind of thing. There were motorbikes lined up next to each other on one side, big shiny things brought by people who had come to show off. The right girl would be wooed by a boy sitting on a stationary motorbike that didn't even belong to him, revving the engine and sending fumes into the night. Me? I just wanted to dance. Now that we were out of harm's way, I could finally enjoy myself. We walked into the club laughing and joking, the four of us together. Let the celebrations begin, I thought.'

The plantain on my plate lies cold in the bean stew next to the neglected tatale.

A GREAT NIGHT

'Ato was a good dancer. He wasn't one of those guys who got to the club and spent his time sat in its dark corners buying expensive bottles of champagne while others stood around him growing thirsty. The DJ was playing hit after hit, all the best songs. We danced until we needed the coolness of the courtyard more than the music inside, our limbs exhausted and our bodies sweating. Outside, we enjoyed a view of young people having fun and soaked up the excitement caused by the arrival of a well-known Afrobeat artist as he was making his way to the club for a live performance.

'It was rare for him to go out like this, Ato explained. He was careful to blow his cigarette smoke away from me as he spoke. He was based in Cape Coast, where he was doing his second naval officer placement. It turned out that Ekow wasn't Ato's friend but his first cousin – their fathers were brothers. Learning that allowed me to see a similarity between them. Their height, for example. They shared the same hairline and walk. Ato described Ekow as "fun-loving", in contrast to his calm and quiet nature. He loved the discipline and sense of purpose that being in the navy gave him. He didn't think Ekow would last ten minutes in that environment, he enjoyed freedom and fun too much. Ato was easy to talk to and effortlessly funny. Before we knew it, the evening breeze had cooled us and the dance floor was calling again. He finished his cigarette before we went back inside.

'I spotted Edem and Ekow under the purple and white lighting of the club, and went over to check that Edem was okay. It was hard to tell where Edem began and Ekow ended, or vice versa. She didn't want to dance because she was having a good time where she was. They were all over each other. So in lust, or in love, or whatever you want to call it. Ato bought a bottle of champagne on our way back to the dance floor and said that it was his responsibility to make sure I had the "best birthday ever". And I was. I was having a great night.

'I didn't notice when Edem left the club with Ekow – she didn't say goodbye, and I didn't see them leave. It was only at the end of the night, after the DJ had played his last track twice and the main lights were turned on, that I started to look for her. By that time, people had gathered in the courtyard, their faces shiny with a hedonistic glow. No one was in a hurry to go home, or for the night to end. I looked among them for Edem, but she wasn't there. I looked in the ladies' toilet with no luck. I searched the line of people queuing for food. Nothing. Outside the gates, Ekow's car was not where he had parked it. The car was gone, and so were they.

'Ato must have seen the panic on my face, because he told me not to worry. He knew that Ekow was a little tipsy, but he had the instincts of a Formula One driver. He had no doubt that they would be fine. No doubt at all. And he would ensure that I also got home safely. He even offered to accompany me home in a taxi before heading back in the direction of Accra Central, where he was staying with his father while he was home.

'"Accra Central School of Christ? That's where my placement is!"

"'You're a teacher?"

"'Newly qualified; I will be teaching there from September!"

"'My father is the headteacher at Accra Central!"

'Sika, what were the chances?!

'Knowing that my future was meeting my present in this unforeseen way made me even more excited to begin the next chapter of my life. I was so excited to tell Larjey!

"'I'll be moving into my new accommodation next weekend."

"'Next weekend? I will still be here. If you want, I can help you move your things?"

"'Oh, that would be wonderful, thank you!"

'I knew that Agape would understand. It would be a great opportunity for me to meet the headmaster before the start of term. He wasn't the jealous type. We trusted each other. And Ato knew I had a boyfriend. I had heard that the headmaster was a kind man, stern but fair with the children. His kindness was reflected in his son's gestures. I was annoyed at Edem for leaving me like that, but in a way I was also grateful to her for connecting me with Ato.'

She stops pretending to do the dishes and removes her washing-up gloves to take a seat opposite me at the table. I study the tiny rainbows in the soap suds that glimmer on the surface of her gloves and around the sink as she reaches for a glass of water. When the glass touches her lips, I notice a tremble in her hands that causes the water to ripple, like waves on the surface of the sea.

'At that time of night, you would only find a taxi on the main road, and even then you could be waiting for some time. So we turned left at the end of the road and walked from one dimly lit street to another in search of a ride. It's funny how your feet start to hurt only once you stop dancing, isn't it? The gravelled path didn't help. In loafers, Ato had no problem. But he slowed his stride to keep pace with me, and we walked side by side.

'He was explaining the rankings of the navy to me. Sublieutenant to lieutenant to lieutenant commander, commander, captain and so on. He recited them in a way that suggested they were easy to commit to memory. But I think I would have struggled. When he got to vice admiral, something changed. At first, I thought he had reached the end of the list, and that vice admiral was the highest rank for a naval officer…

'He turned to face me and…There was something different. Was it the light of the street lamp, or…I didn't recognise the look in his eyes. The way he looked at me, I…It all happened so quickly. In a single stride, he stepped forward to close the space between us. He grabbed me by my waist. His tongue…I remember the cigarette smell of his breath. It was so stale. It was the type of smell that you wouldn't want to breathe in. But he was so close to me…It was overwhelming, the smell. Before I could do anything – step back, reclaim my space, breathe…his tongue was…It was against my lips. I closed them tightly. But he was so forceful…I was in shock. And then his hands…His hands became a vice around my waist. Maybe I froze, I…His grip was so tight. He scratched at my breasts. My thighs.' She is cradling herself like a child. Her left hand around her stomach, her right hand at her neck. She blinks a heavy tear when she says, 'It was when he grabbed me by the throat and pushed me against the wall of the gated house that I knew I was in trouble.'

My hand reaches for hers at the same time hers does for mine. And we hold onto each other as if holding onto life itself.

'It was a moment of paralysis for me. Full-body paralysis, both physical and mental. I felt as if I was hovering above my body looking down at it. I was looking at that poor girl squashed against a whitewashed wall as she lost her autonomy and her agency. In that moment, she lost it all.

'When he finished, he leant against the wall and took out a cigarette from his pocket. He lit it as I struggled to find my footing. And sent smoke into the air as I fought the zip of my shorts with shaking hands. He walked in the direction of the main road as I tried to control my limbs. My body had stopped cooperating. My head couldn't connect with my legs, my heart with my lungs. He carried on talking, as if…as if nothing had happened. I questioned myself as I placed one foot in front of the other. Was I losing my mind? Daydreaming? Sleepwalking? The closer we got to the main road, the higher the sun rose in the east of the sky, and the more my hands shook.

'I sat in silence with him in the back of the taxi as he made small talk with the driver. I tried to place my palms against the seat to steady the trembling. Everything inside and outside my body was trembling. But the seat was leather. And my hands were sweaty, so I…I tried to look out of the window. But everything was blurry. Because my eyes…The only thing he said to me…as he got out of the taxi…the only thing he said was, "Fun times. Let's do it again!" I sat in silence as the driver took me back to Tema. Silent but for the pounding of my heart. And the pain between my legs.'

'I was sat on the step of the courtyard when Edem opened the steel gate, making as little noise as possible so she didn't wake our parents. She looked drunk in the way babies do when they have taken all their mother's milk. With her heels in her hands, she walked across the tarmac in bare feet and uneven steps. "Selom, are you home already? I haven't slept all night!" she attempted but failed to whisper as she rubbed at her groin area before heading inside. By then I had showered and scrubbed myself with hot water and Dettol. But I felt like I had fallen into open sewage and that I would never be clean again.

'I sat in the courtyard with the crickets and the chickens and the grasshoppers as they greeted the rising sun. It was the first day of the rest of my life.'

SIKA

Mum lays her tears at the foot of my altar. In her hands she gathers them. Tears for a secret unshared for twenty-seven years. Tears of shame and pain and trauma. Tears for the relief the truth unburdens from her.

'I knew I'd be a mother one day. I say "knew", I assumed I would. That's how girls are raised, isn't it? You grow up, you get married, you have children. You assume that you will meet someone and fall in love. You assume that you will both want children. You assume that you will conceive without difficulty. You don't assume that you will…you don't assume that you will be raped. You don't assume that you will get pregnant as a result.

'I was in denial for the first three months. I told myself that the trauma of the night had interfered with my cycle and that was why my period was late. I knew that stress could do things like that. In the second month, I was spotting lightly, so I told myself I was having a light period. My body started to change – still, I denied it. I was bloated because I wasn't exercising. My breasts were getting bigger because I was comfort eating. Both were true, but I was also pregnant.

'The hardest thing I had to do was tell Mama and Dada. It was not just my hopes and dreams for the future that had disappeared in the course of one night, one moment. It was the hopes and dreams they held for me, too. It was their faith in me and their trust, their expectations. Disappointing them in that way was incredibly painful for me, and very difficult to navigate.'

'Did you tell them what happened? What he…did to you?'

'No. No. I could just about tell them that I had missed my monthlies for four months and allow them to draw the conclusion. I will never forget the look of disappointment on Dada's face. The way his brows furrowed and his lips curled downward. His hard-working, intelligent and ambitious daughter had gone to lie somewhere for a man to impregnate her. Just before she was about to begin her career as a teacher at one of the top schools in Ghana. Before she had married? He just couldn't understand it. It didn't make sense to him. Mama was so ashamed she could barely look at me. What Ato did to me became my secret; and I became theirs. Mama and Dada used me as a cautionary tale for Edem, an example of what not to do – "Look at your sister! Do you want to end up like her? Do you want to throw your life away like Selom?"'

The memory causes her a pain so physical that she doubles over at the waist and cries, tears I do not know how to stem. I stand up from my seat and wrap my body around hers.

'I am so sorry, Mum.' I do not know what else to say, what comfort I can offer, or how. 'I am so sorry. I am so sorry. I am so so sorry.' I cannot breathe for how sorry I am. For how guilty I feel. And for how much I hate him.

It takes a long time for calm to take its seat at the kitchen table amongst us. A long time, after which my body and mind ache in a way that takes me back to the sickness from which I have just recovered.

'Why didn't you report him to the police, Mum?'

'Hmmm. Honestly, I didn't consider it an option, Sika. His father was the head of Accra Central. It was one of the top international schools in Ghana at the time. He was a man of power and influence. Forget the fact that I could not take up my teaching post in September, what was I going to say to the police? That I had sat in a car with my sister, her boyfriend and his cousin and allowed myself to be taken by a drunk driver to a club? That my sister had left me there with a man I barely knew, to go and have sex with her boyfriend? That I had shared champagne with my attacker before I followed him in the dark and allowed him to push me against a wall? I didn't know how I could speak those words. I didn't know how to explain what had happened to anybody, let alone the police.

'Auntie Larjey came back from Maryland and went on to teach after I left Ghana. Before the end of my second trimester, I was living with Papa's sister in north London. Our lives took two very different paths after that. I wasn't even able to be at her wedding. And with Uncle Agape, I didn't even know where to begin.

'The things I told you about your "dad" are the things I wished for you, Sika. I wanted you to have a father who loved your mother as much as the man I told you about. A father who had adored and protected me and taken care of me during my pregnancy. A father whose heart soared when he felt your kick, and who dreamt of the first time he would hold you in his arms. A father who was proud of you before you were even born. I wanted you to be born of the love that your parents had for each other. I wanted those things for you so badly.'

I lay my tears at the foot of Mum's altar. In my hands I gather them. Tears for a lie lived for twenty-seven years. Tears of shame and pain and trauma. Tears for the weight the truth now burdens me with.

'I was traumatised by what had happened – by what he did to me. So unimaginably traumatised. Of course I was. And as much as I had not wanted to be pregnant, as much as it terrified me to bring you into the world, the moment I laid eyes on you, something happened to me. I fell in love with you. And I have loved you since that moment in a way that is difficult for me to explain. I am so sorry that you had to hear what you heard in the way you did. Please forgive me, Sika. I'm so sorry. I love you so much.'

She chokes on a deluge of tears and I drown under a tsunami of my own.

'I called you Sika because you were my treasure. That's the meaning of Sika. You know that, don't you? You were my treasure then and you are my treasure now. You healed my broken heart.'

She smiles at me through her pain. And a surge of love pours out of my heart and radiates through my body.

'Mum, the man in the photo…'

She looks down at the table and wrings her hands. 'It's a picture of a man I met here in London. Everyone called him Danny the Friendly Rasta. He hadn't started growing locks when that photo was taken. But it was knowing Danny that inspired me to get sister locks. I went on two dates with him when you were about three years old, but my heart – it was always with Agape. And I was happy with it being the two of us, me and you, so nothing developed with Danny. But he was a good man, a kind and thoughtful man. And I thought that my daughter, my beautiful little daughter…I thought you deserved a father like…I'm so sorry.'

'It's okay, Mum. It's okay.'

I rest my cheek against hers in a hug from which neither of us hurries to let go. Skin-to-skin contact. It calms us both. Restores us. Reattaches the fibres of the bond on which we both depend.

THE RED DRAGON

When I return to work, the skin around my ankle no longer feels like the embers of a dying fire. The wound has dried and the skin has started its miraculous healing process: a dark circle around the bite is the X which marks the spot. The swelling and the pain have both disappeared.

'Sika! You're back!' Joanna jumps up from her seat when she sees me and offers a warm welcome in the form of a hug. 'How are you feeling?'

'So much better now, thank you.'

'Oh my God, your hair! You've cut it! It looks so good!'

'Do you like it? I wasn't sure at first, but it's growing on me.'

'I love it! It really suits you.'

Something has changed in her, and it takes me a few seconds to understand what.

'Have you grown taller, Joanna? How is that possible?'

'I wish! You're in your trainers, that's all!'

'Oh my God!'

I never wear trainers from the train station to the office.

'You can tell a lot about a person by looking at their shoes,' Caitlyn says. She encroaches on the prospective client like a predator orbiting its prey, discreetly eavesdropping on their conversation, preparing to launch a charm offensive. Before she approaches, she knows at least three things about them: their business, their passion, their style.

Is she in trendy, environmentally conscious and sustainable trainers? Caitlyn will bring her Shoreditch Self to bear. She will greet the prospective client with a hug; overfamiliar but warmly received and reciprocated. She will suggest a chat over an iced matcha latte or similar 'somewhere local?' She is prepared to travel to the client from her home in North London and, unless asked, will pretend to be from East London. She will turn up on a bike which she will claim is her preferred mode of transport, and express concern for the environment 'and what humankind is doing to it'. She doesn't want to contribute to air pollution if she can help it. She will deploy statistics about Melon's carbon footprint that I have never heard her mention before. 'We're reducing year-on-year,' she will claim. She will emphasise a commitment to working with clients who hold similar interests and values. She will be silent about the fact that she eats salad for lunch every day and tosses the plastic container in the bin next to her desk when she has finished. She will not mention her near-daily use of Amazon Prime, or her reliance on retail services offering free returns. Or that she gets Joanna to run these errands for her. She will suggest seeing each other again sometime soon – 'yoga, Pilates, a sound bath?' She will see the connection made and give the prospective client the attention of a first-time mother to her newborn child.

Is she in black patent-leather court shoes? Caitlyn will wear hers to match. She will walk towards her, confidently, and shake her hand, firmly. Firmly enough for her to extend an umbilical cord of sisterhood. To communicate silently that she knows what it is to be a successful woman. To be the only woman in the boardroom. To be asked, without words, to quieten her voice and suppress her femininity so she doesn't 'distract' her male colleagues; to help them 'maintain focus', only to be asked – expected – to use the same beauty and femininity to strategic advantage when required. To be vulnerable, but only if it benefits the business. To suffer mansplaining with a smile. To dumb herself down when required. She will mirror her prospective client's presentation: manicured nails, contoured face, perfectly coiffed hair. Because with each other, they can be who they are. It is not her fault she is 'hot'. It is not something she should be punished for in a corporate environment. She will wear an expensive designer handbag at the crook of her elbow, her palm facing upwards. She will suggest they see each other soon, 'for cocktails, or a glass of wine?'

Is he wearing Chelsea boots and a rugged smile? Does he have facial hair and a strong profile? A deep voice and a contagious laugh? A chest of hair visible from the opening of his shirt – top two buttons undone, confirming his status as an alpha male? Do the muscles of his arms and back suggest that he played rugby in his youth? Flanker, scrum half, full back? Or that he is committed to CrossFit, minimum three times a week? Perhaps these days he alternates with golf. What is his handicap? What is his...weakness? Is he wearing a wedding ring? Yes? It doesn't matter. No? Even better.

He won't see her coming. That is Caitlyn's way. She will emerge out of the blue. An apparition. A beautiful rainbow calling attention after the passing of rain. Her handshake is different this time. Not assertive, but gentle. She allows her soft palm to sit in his for one second longer than custom dictates. She will fan him with her eyelashes and cause him to lose himself in the study of her blue eyes. The movement of his lips will at some point become involuntary. They will curve upwards into a smile. She will mirror it, and in doing so reveal her perfectly straight white teeth. When he speaks, she will lean in closer to 'hear' him. 'Sorry, can you say that again? It's so noisy in here.' When it's her turn to speak, she does so in a quiet voice. He has to move closer – to hear what she is saying.

The contact is negligible at first. Her tousled hair brushes his shoulder, his cheek, his ear. And from there, deliberate. A gentle pat on his forearm, a soft touch on his wrist. His hand on the small of her back. Boldness allows her to pull him towards her by his shoulder and speak directly into his ear. This time, her lips graze his earlobe. Neither of them acknowledge the contact. But both revel in it. They are now entering an intimate space.

'Do you fancy another drink?' he will ask.

Of course she does. At the point of inebriation, she is whipping her hair back and forth seductively in his stratosphere. She has cast her spell. The evening will seep into the night like watercolour bleeding. And because there is now a magnetic field between them, they cannot pull away from each other just like that.

'We should grab dinner sometime.'

'I would love that!'

'What about now, do you have to head straight home?'

'No, I don't…'

They will agree a plan to extend their evening, knowing full well that nobody eats dinner past 11 p.m.

She is the sun around which orbits a solar system of contacts and associates and potential clients. She has the confidence of someone who has never had to question who she is, why she is or what she is. It is a type of self-belief you cannot buy or imitate; you either have it or you don't. It separates the extraordinary from the ordinary, the haves from the have-nots. When he leaves her company, he does so knowing that she has something he not only wants but needs. She brings clients, money and business to Melon. Caitlyn, the rainmaker.

It is in Converse trainers that I meet Caitlyn in front of the Carrara marble desk from Italy.

'Hi, Caitlyn!'

'Sika, you're back! Do you have five minutes?'

'Sure!'

I follow her into her office before I am able to change my shoes. She is wearing towering heels with pastel-pink palazzo trousers.

'How are you?'

'So much better, thank you—'

'So, I met up with Oscar while you were off.' She doesn't invite me to take a seat, and talks without looking up from her screen – at first. 'He said your dinner didn't go so well?'

'I actually wanted to talk to you about that, Caitlyn, but the timing…It was just before I got sick and—'

'He said you didn't represent Melon in the way I'd led him to believe you would.'

'What?!'

'That he struggled to understand why I would describe you as my right hand. That you seemed distracted and uninterested. As if there was somewhere else you would rather be.'

'No, that's not what happened at all. He—'

'You know our business is all about the soft skills, right?'

'Yes, of course—'

'Tell me I haven't wasted the past five years training you. Tell me you know that much?'

'Yes, of course. It's just that—'

'Do you have any idea what kind of opportunity Oscar's business presents? Luxury female fashion. The European market. You do get how major that is? How major *he* is?'

'On paper it sounds incredible—'

'Do you know that he flew in from Amsterdam to have dinner with you? That his assistant moved meetings in his diary – for you?! Do you have any idea what that means? Or how long the waiting list for the Red Dragon is? That it's only because he knows the owner personally that he was able to get a reservation at such short notice?'

'Caitlyn, I don't know how well you know him, but he behaved really inappropriately—'

'You got up and walked out of the restaurant?! A restaurant of that calibre?! While he was still seated?'

'Yes, but only because he kept—'

'It's a direct insult to the chef and to your host. What on earth were you thinking?!'

'He put his hand on my thigh—'

'He expressed a personal interest in you, Sika. That's why I assigned the prospect to you and not Julian.'

'He kept trying to—'

'You could have sealed the deal for Melon!'

'I asked him to stop—'

'Do you know how lucrative that would have been?'

'Yes, but—'

'Your behaviour has made me question if I can rely on you, Sika.'

'Three times.'

'Could you not have given me a heads-up so I could have attempted some form of mitigation?!'

'I asked him to stop three times.'

'That's not how I've trained you, Sika. The business is growing, you know. It's growing because we are the best. To be the best I need the best team. And I don't know if that includes you right now. I don't think I can risk you leading on the pitch for Paris this week.'

I feel my tongue writhe in my mouth as I try to explain how uncomfortable Oscar made me feel. How he invaded my personal space as I tried to eat soft-shell crab. And grazed my cheek with his lips when he spoke. How I felt his hot breath travel down my ear canal and inside my body. And that it made me feel sick. I want to tell her that, as I positioned my chop sticks to try the sea scallop and mui choi dumplings, he rested his hand on the silk tights of my thigh. And that it started to wander northwards before the grilled black cod was served. I want her to understand that by the time the Cantonese-style lobster and egg noodles arrived, he had torn the fibre of my 15-dernier tights with his fingernails and told me that I made him 'hard'. I want to explain that he touched me in a way that was more than inappropriate. Over and over again. And that I did not consent to any of it. That he ignored me when I asked him to stop not once, not twice but three times. I want to say that I exercised control over my body because that is my right. And that I got up and left because I was not going to have some man do to me – what that man did to my mum. But I do not say any of those things because Caitlyn is not listening. She does not want to hear. I feel my mouth open and close like a fish.

It is over. She will never trust me again. She won't just stop giving me quality work, she'll stop giving me any work. It will be uncomfortable for everyone else to watch: me telling her that I have capacity to take on a new project and her replying: 'Thanks for letting me know, but there's nothing going right now.' She will freeze me out subtly, gradually, slowly. I've seen it happen to others. Over and over again. I will become a shadow of my former self, a bird whose wings have been clipped. I will become a spare part, surplus to requirements. A drain on resources. I will no longer function or exist on a level Caitlyn acknowledges or respects. She will no longer see me. And I will no longer be her right hand.

Before she dismisses me, excluding me from her office and universe, she stares at my trainers with her husky-blue eyes, unblinking. She stares for longer than comfort directs. And for long enough that I am forced to look down and stare at them too. My focus falls on my choice of footwear as she returns hers to the screen in front of her.

'Close the door on your way out, Sika.'

DECEMBER

It is early December when I tiptoe into Mum's room with a hot-water bottle under my dressing gown.

'Morning, Chou Chou.' Her eyes are closed when she calls my name and invites me into her bed with an outstretched arm.

'Morning, Mum.'

'Has the heating come on? Are you cold?'

'I'm not cold, I just have cramps.'

'Oh! Have you taken painkillers? Are you hungry?'

'I've taken painkillers, they'll kick in soon.'

'Okay, good.'

'What do you think about going to the café for breakfast?'

'I like the sound of that.'

We are forced out of bed by the incessant screaming of foxes: London's alarm clock. It is a reminder that we are a million miles away from the sub-Saharan call of crickets and crowing of cockerels.

'They're at it again!'

Mum opens the curtains to reveal a dark winter sky. The moon is reluctant to set and the sun slow to rise. Frost coats the grass under which foxes mate loudly, leaving little to the imagination. They are a bold species, these urban foxes, and have long since abandoned their nocturnal roots. Ice coats the windscreens of cars parked under yellow street lights, waiting to be removed with an ice scraper or warm water. An unprepared driver will be taken by surprise by this overnight development. It will add minutes to a journey for which they are already running late. A promise to invest in a windscreen frost protector will be made in earnest and forgotten by spring. Alternatively, the ice will thaw under the warmth of a bright sun in a clear blue sky on an otherwise cold day. Black wheelie bins await refuse collection, their lids sparkling with the night's frost. Their overspill, interrogated by foxes overnight, leaves household waste scattered on the street.

'They say it's going to snow,' Mum says, returning with a cup of tea for herself and a coffee for me.

'Really? I'm not sure if I trust Google's weather forecasts these days.'

'I hope I didn't use too much milk.'

'No, it's perfect, thank you.'

'Do you remember when you were little and you refused to sleep in your own bed?'

'That's because I was scared of the dark – and you had better pillows.'

She laughs a gentle laugh and takes a sip of tea.

'Do you remember when I was little and you used to tell me to draw you sleeping so you could get twenty minutes of rest?'

'I do! That's how I knew you were an artistic soul.'

'Mum, I'm thinking about leaving Melon.' I offer it as a casual thought, knowing the decision has already been made for me but also by me. I just need her to tell me that it's okay.

'Sika, you must do whatever is right for you. Whatever decision you make, I will support you. But honestly, I am happy to hear this. You are young. You do not have dependants. You must make the most of your situation and your life. That boss of yours, I worry that she takes advantage of you. You can't relax when you are on holiday because you have to check your emails. You must be able to switch off, Sika. I want you not only to live but to enjoy your life. I want you to…I want you to do things I didn't get the chance to do.'

'Mum?'
'Yes?'
'Thank you.'

We let in a blast of cold air as we open the door to the Garden Café. Despite the heating inside, Mum says she needs time to acclimatise and sits in her hat, scarf and gloves until she defrosts. The café is beautifully decorated, and it is hard not to appreciate the festive effort. A Christmas tree decorated with wooden figurines features Father Christmas, reindeer, snowflakes and stars alongside glittering baubles of gold and cream. Warm-white fairy lights hang generously around the tree and on the walls. And through the speakers festive songs play, one after the other. A blackboard decorated with candy canes details the highlights of a special Christmas menu.

'I like that song by Elton John and Ed Sheeran. What's it called again?' Mum offers an instrumental rendition in need of fine-tuning.

'"Merry Christmas". It's called "Merry Christmas", Mum.'
'That's it!'

The irony prompts joint laughter, which subsides as Claudio arrives wielding hot drinks and warm food.

'Morning ladies, I've got an English breakfast tea with regular milk, a cappuccino with oat milk, one eggs royale and an eggs Benedict, voila.'

'Thank you, Claudio!' we chime.

'Can I get you anything else?'

'No thank you. That's perfect.'

Minutes later, he returns with complimentary mince pies and a generous smile.

'You are so sweet,' Mum says. 'Thanks, Claudio!'

Mum is rehearsing the nativity play with the children at her school and has started to have doubts about her choice for the part of Mary. The seven-year-old girl has no time for, or interest in, Joseph or baby Jesus at all.

'The way she handles that doll! As if baby Jesus has kept her up all night and denied her sleep!'

'That is so funny.'

'If you are not working this year, you should come and see it!'

'Yeah, that would be nice.'

'What else have you planned for Christmas, Sika?'

'I don't know. I haven't thought that far ahead, to be honest.'

'You know Auntie Larjey has been calling? She is asking if you will come for Christmas. You know she would love to see you. She mentioned Danso...'

I feel the pain of ruining things with Danso. And sadness that he thinks I am the type of person who could leave without saying goodbye and without good reason. I wish he would give me a chance to explain.

'I left without saying goodbye to him, Mum.'

'I know. It's okay. Nothing has been done that can't be undone. He seems like a nice boy, Sika. He seems respectful and gentle and caring. He has Auntie Larjey's approval, which counts for a lot.'

'Yeah, I like him. We had a really nice time together. He's smart and kind and funny.'

'Those are important qualities.'

I look down at my phone and scroll through our WhatsApp chat. Danso hasn't replied to my messages or returned my calls. He doesn't want anything more to do with me, he has made that much clear.

'How did you leave things with Uncle Agape?'

Mum looks down wistfully before offering an answer.

'I was so devastated by what happened with you and the way it happened that we didn't talk much after you saw us. He comforted me. He was comforting. And he told me that he would always be there for me. I know he means it. But Agape and I have had our chance. Our time has been and gone. That doesn't mean I don't care about him. Or that I don't want to see him again, or spend time with him. I do and I will. But so much has happened. And so much has been done that can't be undone, you know. We are at a different stage in our lives now. But maybe when I retire, I can spend some more time in Ghana. And with him. I would like that.'

'I think I'd like to spend more time in Ghana too.'

'You know, Danso reminds me a lot of Agape when he was younger.'

'Does he?'

'Yes. He is a good soul, Sika. Don't throw him away. Don't leave him like I left Agape all those years ago. My life took a different path, but that doesn't mean I ever stopped believing in love. Talk to him. I've seen how you speak to your clients. You could convince the kenkey woman to give you everything for free. Talk to him. He will understand.'

'I really want to see him again. I really want to see Loli, too. I miss her so much. I don't want her to think I abandoned her.'

'I know.'

'I worry about her, Mum.'

'Me too, Sika. Me too. I don't know how, or who, Edem is raising her to be. That church of hers. That Prophet…'

It causes me physical pain to think of Loli wondering where Mum and I disappeared to. Or to imagine any explanation for our leaving that could satisfy her confusion. I wonder what, if anything, Mum has told Auntie Edem. I wonder what Auntie Edem has told Loli in turn.

'Mum, what happened to Auntie Edem? Why did she change so much from the person she used to be?'

'Edem? I think that Edem's lifestyle caught up with her. Hedonism caught up with her. Being footloose and fancy-free caught up with her in a way she struggled to manage.'

'Does she know what happened to you? Did you tell her?'

'Edem knows. Edem knows because I went to her for help. She had a friend who worked at a pharmacy. It was from her that Edem got the pregnancy test that confirmed what she suspected when I told her that I'd missed my period for three months. I was stunned at first when the test returned a positive result. And then I started to cry. Tears that would not stop. "Don't cry," Edem said. "It's not a big deal." It had even happened to her, she told me. There was somewhere I could go. Somewhere they would end the pregnancy before the baby started to grow. She had done it herself, the December before you were born. That was the year Edem spent Christmas Day in her room. The year she couldn't get up to open her presents. When we thought she was sick with food poisoning…Ekow paid for it.

"'Mama and Dada won't find out, don't worry."

'She said that Ato was a foolish boy. That he was probably not used to seeing beautiful girls since joining the navy, and that I shouldn't mind him. When she "officially" learned about my pregnancy at the dining table in front of Mama and Dada, she feigned a shock so persuasive it had me convinced that she was hearing the news for the first time. We never spoke about Ato or that night again. But Edem knows what happened to me. She knows.

'Our relationship never recovered from those words, or from her pretence that she was the virtuous child and I was the one who risked leading her astray. There was no way back after her feigned disappointment at my "life choices" as my belly swelled with pregnancy. As she pretended to pursue a sewing career with vigour while my career came to an end before it had started. The hypocrisy of it all. I had expected more from Edem. She was my older sister, after all. How could she have left me with Ato in the first place? How could she continue to be friends with him after what he had done to me? How could she care more about Ekow than she did about me?

'I didn't speak to Edem for years after I left Ghana. Not until Loli was born and something in me started to thaw. I have never asked her why – why did you leave me? Why did you go without saying goodbye? Why did you allow this to happen to me? I have never asked her those questions. The truth is, I thought I could move on. I thought I had moved on, but the Edem I have come to find all these years later... it's complicated, Sika. I really struggle to find peace with her. I don't know if I ever will.'

I ask out loud the question I internalised after I saw him sitting at Auntie Edem's dining table like the man of the house. Drinking spirits served to him as if she was his wife or he a king. Since I saw him without the distraction of his fingers pressing into my forehead under the spotlight of the congregation at the Church of Incredible Miracles.

'Mum...is the Prophet...do you think he might be...do you think there's a chance he's Loli's father?'

'Hmmm. It is something I have also wondered. The truth is, I don't know. I have never asked about Loli's father. And

Edem has never told me. I'm sure she would have me believe that Loli was born by immaculate conception. But I suspect he is. I think her eye shape is exactly like his. And the shape of her nose. That distinct hairline they both have. But only Edem knows the answer to that question. I hear that some years after I left for London, she started spending time with him and attending that church of his.'

DECISIONS

I meet Julian at the coffee shop. He is waiting for me in the same place he always sits, his hands outstretched to hug me. We are around the corner from work. Only I no longer work at Melon. I have resigned and I am officially unemployed.

'I'm not far behind you,' he says when I tell him I have handed in my notice.

Julian knows it is no coincidence that he has now become Caitlyn's 'right-hand man', her 'go-to guy'. He knows the role is not one to be coveted, that it can never end well.

'As soon as the sale goes through on the flat, I'm out. Fred earns enough to tide us over for a bit until I find something else. He's seen how unhappy it makes me. Working there – working with her. Working without you. It would be one thing if I could switch off, but I can't. I bring it home, every day, even on weekends. It's not fair on me and it's not fair on him. It's not what I want for my life.'

'What stage are you at with the flat?'

'We've just had the survey done and everything looks good, so not long now, fingers crossed.'

'I think we owe it to ourselves to try and live our best lives, Jules. We spend so much time at work. It's too important an environment to be unhappy.'

'Preach, honey.'

'I'm really going to enjoy not seeing her name flash up on my phone or in my inbox. God, I can't wait!'

The smell of caffeine charges our confidence and fuels our drive to do, to go and to be.

'What will you do when you leave?' I ask.

'I have no idea, Sika. It feels like I'm starting from scratch. I don't even know if I want to stay in the industry. Maybe I'll become a house husband!'

'OMG, do it!'

'Can you imagine, me cleaning up after Fred?'

'Not really, but you would look good in an apron.'

When it hits our veins, the caffeine accelerates our heart rate and makes us question whether we are doing the right thing. Making the right decisions. Moving in the right direction.

'I really want to be in the garden. You know I'm out there every chance I get. I've been thinking about a course in landscape design. Combine passion and career. What do you think?'

'That sounds amazing! You always say how much peace gardening gives you. It's so you. Do it!'

'What about you? What's next for Sika?'

'Oh, I don't know. I'm still trying to figure it out. I'll probably still be living at home with Mum when I'm thirty.'

'Free board and lodging? Can I move in too?'

'She says you should come over for dinner, by the way. You and Fred.'

'Oh yes please! Can she make those plantain fritter things? What are they called again?'

'Tatale. They're good, aren't they?'

'So good!.'

We are on the brink of something new. Another hit of caffeine. Another shot. A chance to curate the lives we want to live.

'Don't be a stranger, Sika.'

'Don't *you* be a stranger!'

'I can't. I won't. I'm going to miss you so much. I don't know how I'd have survived without you.'

'Nor me you, Jules.' I'm only crying because he is.

'That's such an ugly cry,' he says, blowing his nose.

'Oh, because yours is so attractive?! I think I just want to be still for a while. Just breathe, you know. Maybe go to Ghana for a bit…'

'Sounds like heaven. I can't wait to get to where you are, Sika.'

'You'll get there. I'm excited for you!'

'I'm excited for us!'

'Is Joanna sorting out your things?'

'Oh yeah, I meant to ask. Can you liaise with her to send me my bits, please?'

'What, the tens of pairs of shoes under your desk?'

'Yes, please!'

'Sure thing. You know she's already started interviewing for your replacement.'

'Poor thing. I hope they know what they're letting themselves in for.'

'Meek as a mouse. I give her two weeks.'

THE TRUTH

He agrees to meet face to face when I message to say that I will be at Auntie Larjey's in the evening, if he is free to pass by. I am going to spend Christmas in Ghana. And I am just about to board my flight.

Danso: *Cool*

He gives me monosyllabic. Monosyllabic gives me hope.

I am surrounded by the hibiscus, lilies, bougainvillea, and other floral companions that form a border around the courtyard of Auntie Larjey's garden. Mosquito-repellent coils burn their distinct orange glow, protecting the space around me.

My stomach somersaults when Danso's engine quietens to a stop. He walks opposite the coconut tree on the other side of the garden, one hand in his pocket, the other holding his phone. The mango tree has lost the fruit it bore when I was last here.

He passes the large terracotta pots with aloe vera, orchids and other plants whose names I don't know. He looks down and around but not at me as he walks past the barbeque, extended seating area and towards me. He glances at the rock pool from which the fountain flows and meets me at the outdoor bar. The stillness of the wind chime confirms the silence that hovers between us.

I stand to hug him and meet his fragrance. The smell activates all the memories that have brought me here.

'Hey.'

'Hi.'

'Thank you for coming.'

'Sure.' He is slow to reply.

I search his eyes for something familiar. I am looking for a place to start. 'Can I get you something to drink?' I offer.

'No thanks, I'm good.'

He opts for fleeting eye contact to convey his feelings towards me. It is hard to connect, and yet I try.

'I'm so sorry about how I left, Danso.'

His expression is neutral. His body language unresponsive. I take a deep breath and a sip of water to help my dry throat and mouth.

I tell him what happened the night of the party. The conversation I overheard between Mum and Uncle Agape. The truth I heard her reveal. I tell him that it altered the foundation of my world and changed everything forever.

I explain why it felt that my whole life had been a lie. That everything I believed about myself was wrong. That in that moment, I lost my identity, and became orphaned. How everything that was, is no more.

I struggle to give words to the truth I am still learning to understand. To accept. And to speak.

'My dad… The stories I told you about…my dad. None of it is…It was all lies. She lied to me. Everything. My whole life… none of it was true. She didn't know him. She didn't even know him. It was all…Everything I knew about him. Everything I believed. It was all a lie. He forced himself on her. It was her birthday. There was nothing she could do. It all happened so quickly. She was…Mum. She was…she was raped. Mum was raped. By him. He raped her. And she fell pregnant. As a result.'

THE TRUTH

I cannot look him in the eye when I say the thing I am.

'She fell pregnant with me because she was raped. That is how I was conceived. That is what I am. That is why I was born.'

I cannot say the thing I am without breaking from the pain it brings.

'I was born from rape.'

He holds me as I fold at the waist.

'It was so much for me to process, Danso.'

Broken by the weight of the truth.

'It's so much to process.'

And held there by the weight of my tears.

'Too much.'

By the violence of the new identity I have been forced to assume.

'I'm so sorry I left without saying goodbye.'

I collapse into his arms as he holds me.

He holds me until I find my breath. Until I stop shaking from sadness. Until I can bear my own weight.

He holds me.

He holds me.

He holds me.

A RAINBOW

The sun rises in the morning, as it does after the most solemn of sunsets. We are going to a special place.

He dodges potholes with care as we drive through an Accra that is just beginning to stir. There is no need to fill the silence in the car. It is not a silence that occupies space. The window showcases bursts of early-morning activity frame by frame. Commuters on their way to work by car, by tro tro, on foot. Sellers offering goods to passers-by at the traffic lights and along the roadside.

We drive along remote and scenic roads of red earth, punctuated by verdant green. Through foothills and valleys to leave the city. We leave the sound of car horns and hawkers in our wake, and eventually find quieter parts.

A small herd of cows meanders slowly but determinedly along the path, unperturbed by the heat of the rising sun. A chicken pecks at the ground for something imperceptible. Her mate emerges from the bush to join her. Danso navigates around and past them. His gaze oscillating between me and the road ahead. When his right hand is not on the wheel it is on mine. The further we drive, the higher we climb. We are going to a peaceful place.

'Your mum arrives on the twenty-first, right?'

'Yeah, just in time for Christmas.'

It feels strange, but not lonely, to be in Ghana without her.

A RAINBOW

I am not lonely.

'She said she could help me find him if I want to.'

Despite him. Despite what he did to her. Regardless of her own pain. Out of love for me, she offered.

'Your biological dad?'

'Yes.'

'Okay... I mean, how do you feel about that? Is it something you want to do?'

'When I thought of him as someone who had died, someone who had been taken from me before I was even born, I used to say if only I could see his face, just for a minute, I would never ask for anything else for the rest of my life. I wanted to stand next to him and see how tall I was compared to him. I always thought my head would sit just under his shoulders if I stood without slouching. I used to imagine what it would be like to look up at him and into his eyes. To touch his face, his eyebrows and his beard. I wanted to see if he had wrinkles on his forehead. And trace the shape of his ears and nose. I wanted to examine his hairline and see if it held secrets for the future of mine. I wanted to feel both sides of his hands. And for them to hold me the way I've seen fathers hug their daughters, you know?'

I look into the distance while I consider the present and the past.

'But that was before.'

Danso has switched off the music in the car and slowed his speed to reduce the sound of the engine. He listens to me intently. I feel safe to speak and comforted to be heard.

'But now I know the truth, what he did to Mum and who he is...I don't want to have anything to do with him. I have no desire to meet him. I mean, what would I even say? "Hi, you raped my mum, you psychotic piece of shit monster?" There's nothing he can say to change what he did or to make it better. And there's nothing he can give me. I don't want anything from him anyway. In a weird way, I almost don't want to know that he is real – to give life to the idea of him. Does that make sense?'

'Yeah, it makes perfect sense. I think it's like your mum said – he donated his sperm to her, in horrific circumstances, and she did the rest. Your greatness, your heart, your beauty, that's all your mum. He had no hand in raising you. And he can't take credit for who you are, and how you are, twenty-seven years later. But most importantly, Sika, he is not you. He is not you and you are not him.'

His words resurrect my tears.

'Danso?'

'Sika?'

'Thank you. I told her that I don't want to see him or to meet him. I told her that she is everything I need. She has always been enough. So much more than enough.'

The sky is dark and cloudy. It threatens rain.

'Even if it rains, it will pass quickly. Don't worry.'

Danso smiles at me before we take a left turn. A warm smile. A smile filled with kindness and care and encouragement. A smile filled with protection, promise and hope. I am not worried. Not about the weather. I am not worried, because I am with him.

A call from Auntie Larjey connects to the car's loudspeaker, although her voice projection doesn't need it.

'Have you people arrived yet?'

'Not yet, Auntie. But we are not far.'

'Okay. Danso, please drive carefully.'

'Yes, Auntie, I will.'

'Good. Good. Sika, are you there?'

'Yes, Auntie. Good morning.'

'Good morning, sweetheart. Have you had your breakfast yet?'

'Not yet, but I will do soon. I'm just building up my appetite.'

I realise that I am shouting by some instinct to match her volume. The result causes Danso to suppress laughter and me to resist it.

'Okay, and what will you people eat for dinner?'

'Oh, Auntie—'

'Don't worry, Sika. I know you are a pesca— what is it again? So you don't want chicken with—'

The increasing altitude interferes with the signal at just the right time.

The moment requires Danso to slow down so we can purge ourselves of laughter. It is the kind of laughter that makes our eyes tear up and our shoulders shake. It is the kind of laughter that subsides only to start again moments later.

We find a place to park.

It is nice to stand and stretch. And to breathe the air here. It offers a different type of experience. Clean air. Unpolluted. Free from the smoke of the city. Free from its sounds. It is quiet here, calm and peaceful. I hear the call of birds and the rustle of leaves. The hum of insects between and among them. From the car, we walk along a winding footpath. It is clearly marked in some places and less obvious in others. Where it narrows, Danso extends his hand to take mine, and we navigate the path together. We pass tracks left by nocturnal wildlife taking their rest during the day. He points them out along the way, identifying species and their habits. We are in the midst of pangolins, chimpanzees and elephants, antelope, hyena and baboons. We are unlikely to see them beyond the thistle and the foliage. 'Don't be scared,' he says, 'they won't disturb us.' I study the colours, sights and sounds beside him with a steady heartbeat. They culminate in a spectacular apex, a waterfall of dreams.

There are small children playing in a stream nearby. Small children in their underwear, with closely shaved hair. There is one girl among nine or ten boys. She is formidable, the boss of them all. They are quiet when she talks and follow where she leads. They are the same age as Loli and older, their laughter innocent and free. I want Loli to laugh that way for the rest of her life; I want her to be happy. I smile at them and wave before we climb along the rocks that line the water's bed.

A flock of migratory birds fly overhead in a westerly direction and towards the drifting clouds. The sun has broken through the canopy of green in front of us and a rainbow arcs proudly in the sky. The spectrum of colour is beautiful. A gift from nature; an offering of hope.

The waterfall pounds the rocks below and offers a sacred sound bath which washes over and through me. A vibration with soothing properties. There is no beginning and no end. It pounds the rocks and cascades into the pool where we stand. Where he holds my hand in his and I reacquaint myself with the warmth of his eyes. The waterfall calms me. As I breathe in, and out. As he holds me. As I am.

ACKNOWLEDGEMENTS

Thank you to everyone who has supported me through stillness, silence and solitude to write *Sister of Mine*.

To Ruth Pinkney, Ama Sogbodjor, Elizabeth Smaller, Helena Chow Eleanor Ashby, Oniz Suleyman, Kika Sroka-Miller, Sarah-Kate McIntyre Rule, Michelle Dobson, Steph Wilkinson, Katie Hernon, Eugenia Asafo-Boakye, John Keal, Craig Beevers, Victoria Hutton, Charlotte Solanet, Esther Underwood, Caro Gates, Ruki Ware and the Keenans. Your support has been varied and significant. Thank you Sally El-Bogdhadly for leaving the door open and Natasha Reddy for lighting up the room. Thank you Barbara Yankah and Jada-Rose Yankah.

To my essential writing community: Orlaine McDonald, Peace Adzo Medie and Jeffrey Boakye, you are incredibly important to me and my process, thank you.

Thank you to my editors, Juliet Mabey and Polly Hatfield, to Paul Nash and to everyone at Oneworld Publications for bringing this book to life.

To my agent, Juliet Mushens: your understanding, encouragement and patience has sustained me as a writer. I am so very grateful to you for everything you have done and everything you do.

To my nephews Musa, Eesa and Ibraheem, I love you so much and I'm so proud of you. To my godsons Zachy,

Freddy and Basta. To River and Penny and all the children in my life whose beauty surrounds me, I adore you.

Finally, to my dog Blue. You are everything, thank you.

Marie-Claire Amuah is a British Ghanaian author. *One for Sorrow, Two for Joy* (Oneworld, 2022) was her debut novel. In 2021, she was awarded the John C. Laurence Award by the Society of Authors in support of her writing. In 2023, Marie-Claire was named winner of the Diverse Book Awards for adult fiction.

She combines her work as an author with her legal career as a barrister. In her spare time, Marie-Claire enjoys long walks with her French bulldog, Blue, and time spent with cherished friends.